Highlander Oath of the Beast

by

Donna Fletcher

Donna Fletcher

No part of this publication may be used or reproduced in any manner whatsoever, including but not limited to being stored in a retrieval system or transmitted in any form or by any means, electronic, mechanical, photocopying, recording or otherwise without permission of the author.

This is a book of fiction. Names, characters, places, and incidents are either the product of the author's imagination or are used fictitiously, and any resemblance to actual persons, living or dead, business establishments, events or locales is entirely coincidental.

Highlander Oath of the Beast

All rights reserved.

Copyright January 2021 by Donna Fletcher

Cover art
Kim Killion Group

Chapter One

"How long does he stand out there each day waiting?" Arran asked.

Royden didn't have to follow his brother's glance to know who he asked about, but he did anyway. Their father stood on the top of the keep's steps staring out beyond the village. Parlan was a sturdy built man for his four ten and six years. No gray touched his dark hair and the few lines and wrinkles age had graced him with hadn't hampered his fine features. Yet he had chosen to pass the reins of the Clan MacKinnon to Royden, his eldest son. He had been reluctant to accept his da's decree but had done so with pride and was now Chieftain of the Clan MacKinnon.

"A month now, I believe," —Royden turned back to Arran— "ever since Brother Noble, informed your wife that he discovered our sister, Raven, was on her way home."

"The leper could be wrong. It could be nothing more than useless gossip," Arran said. "Brother Noble's contagious illness doesn't exactly win him friends nor does it make him a welcome guest anywhere but his home at Stitchill Monastery."

"True enough, but one would think that living in such isolation, even when traveling, he hears and learns much. And you must admit all our efforts to find Raven have proven fruitless. Brother Noble's news brought back the hope Da had lost of ever finding her." He gave a quick nod at his da. "He doesn't speak of it, but I know it weighs heavily on him that she, a young lass of ten and four years, saved his life. He should have been the one to keep her safe."

"It was a task meant for the three of us," Arran argued. "We all failed to keep the oath we swore and Raven suffered for it. And let's not forget the suffering the brutal attack left on others." Arran looked at the stump where his brother's left hand had once been. "You lost your hand."

Royden rubbed the leather-covered stump, needing no reminder. "We all lost, Arran, in one way or another. Fortunately, we've been reunited and you and I are happy, wed to women we love. We have even more to be grateful for with my wife due to give birth in the spring and your wife, following a few months later. Even Da has found love with Wren after being alone for too long. Life is good for all of us—except Raven."

Arran looked away for a moment and Royden understood his brother fought to contain his anger. He did as well. It gnawed at him just as it did Arran and their da, that none of them had been able to protect Raven the day the clan had been attacked and now there was no way of knowing what she had gone through, what she might have suffered. And what she would be like when she returned home.

Arran drew in a deep breath as he turned his head to face his brother. "I fear for what the last five years on her own, hiding from our enemy, may have brought her."

"I fear the same, but she will be well-loved and cared for here between the attention Oria and Wren will give her. And your wife will visit with her often."

Arran nodded. "Purity and Raven had become fast friends all those years ago and had formed a strong bond. She will do all she can to make sure Raven does well."

A strong gust of wind hit the two men and they turned their backs to it.

"Winter's arrival is two weeks away, yet the biting cold in the air and overcast sky warns of possible snow. I fear the winter will be a cold one," Royden said.

"I grew to hate the cold while with the mercenaries in the far north and beyond the North Sea," Arran said, then smiled. "But I look forward to this winter, for I intend to hibernate in the keep with my wife and enjoy her warmth."

"We should start that today with it being so bitter cold out."

The two men turned and Arran's smile grew when his wife, Purity, hurried to his side as he spread his cloak wide to welcome her in his arms. Her arms circled his waist and he tucked her snug against him and wrapped his cloak around them both.

Royden greeted his wife, Oria, in a similar manner. His one arm went around her waist while the other brought his hand to rest gently on her rounded stomach. She rested eagerly against him, but her worried expression had him asking, "What's wrong? Aren't you feeling well? Shall I get Wren?"

"I do well. It is your da who has me worried," Oria said, looking to the keep steps where his da stood, his eyes scanning the distance while paying them no heed. "He waits day after day, and Wren says he hasn't been sleeping."

"Brother Noble was adamant about the news of Raven's return," Purity said. "He insisted that he had learned it from a trustworthy source."

The two couples watched as Wren walked toward their da. She turned her face away from a sudden gust of wind, it tearing red strands from her braid to whip at her lovely face.

"She's a healer. She'll know what to do for him," Arran said with more hope than confidence.

"If only she could see when Raven will return," Oria said. "It would ease Da's worry, since many of her predictions have proven true thus far."

They watched as Parlan reached out to Wren when she got close and took hold of her hand with an anxiousness that warned of his worry. Her soft smile and words, that couldn't be heard, appeared to offer some comfort, and they weren't surprised when she remained by his side and stared off into the distance along with him.

"All we need is Raven home and our family will be complete," Oria said.

Another gust of wind brought a sprinkle of snow with it.

"We should go," Arran said to his wife. "Though home is not far, I don't want to chance getting caught in an unexpected snowstorm." He gave a quick look to his brother. "You'll let me know—"

"Immediately," Royden said, knowing his brother referred to Raven.

The bell alerting the village to approaching riders tolled, startling them all.

"Riders!" Parlan called out and both couples hurried to join their da to get a glimpse in the distance of who approached the village.

"Six riders and they take their time," Arran said.

"A long journey can slow one down," Parlan said.

Arran and Royden shared a glance, both knowing their da searched for any excuse that one of the riders could be Raven.

"Angus rushes to us. He must have some news," Parlan said, spotting and pointing to the seasoned MacKinnon warrior racing toward them and, keeping hold of Wren's hand, he hurried her down the steps.

Royden and Arran followed suit, first sending stern glances to their wives to remain where they were.

Purity shook her head and held her arm out to Oria. "I don't know about you, but I'm not waiting."

Oria smiled in agreement and took Purity's arm to make their way down the stairs.

The few snow flurries had increased and though yet to leave a trace on the ground, the stone steps were growing damp and Purity wanted to make sure Oria kept a firm footing.

Parlan hadn't reached the last step when he called out, "Tell me, Angus, is it my daughter? Has she finally come home?"

"It looks like a ragtag crew in need of shelter and food from what we can see so far," Angus said almost apologetically, the whole clan knowing what Parlan waited to hear and praying Raven would return soon.

Parlan bent his head, discouraged by the news.

"Have them escorted here," Royden ordered. "Perhaps they have some news of Raven."

That perked his da up. "Aye. Aye. They may know something. Bring them here, and we'll give them food and shelter."

"They could be thieves," Angus warned.

"See that a watch is kept on them wherever they go once settled, since this snow might grow heavy and keep them here for the night at least," Royden said.

"Aye, sir." Angus bobbed his head respectfully and went off to do as ordered.

"Thieves hear things, know things. They could very well know of Raven," Parlan said to Wren as if expecting her to confirm something.

Wren laid a gentle hand on his arm. Her eyes suddenly went blank and she stared as if not seeing him at all. After a couple of moments, she shook her head but failed to speak.

"You saw something. Tell me," Parlan demanded.

Royden and Arran stepped closer to Wren.

"Tell us," Royden said. "We need to know before the group reaches us."

Wren nodded but directed her words to Parlan. "I only know that you will get answers but some will distress you."

Parlan's hand went to his chest. "She's dead? Raven is dead?"

Arran grabbed his da's arm, to keep him on his feet, seeing his legs tremble. "Wren didn't say that, Da."

"Tell me, Wren," Parlan demanded.

"I didn't see that, Parlan. I only know what I strongly sensed but I can't say what it actually relates to," Wren explained. "And if you recall, I saw you all reunited so please hold on to that vision I had years ago and don't assume the worst."

Parlan nodded vigorously. "That's right, you did see my family together once again."

Arran released his da's arm and went to his wife. He hadn't expected her to stay put and he was glad she hadn't. His arm went around her once again to pull her close. His heart ached for his da. He understood now more than ever how he must feel not knowing what happened to Raven, what she'd been through, how she'd survived. His hand went to his wife's stomach that was yet to round with their child. The thought that he would fail to protect his bairn or his wife was a thought he couldn't bear to even conceive. He didn't know how his da had lived with it these past five years.

"Raven is strong," Purity whispered, knowing her husband's thoughts by the worrisome frown on his handsome face. Unfortunately, it didn't ease his worry.

Royden reached for his wife to draw her close. "You will stay near."

Oria felt his worry, his muscles tightening as she rested against him. The failure to protect his sister had resulted in his constant worry of keeping her safe and more so since she had gotten with child. She understood and she prayed that Raven's eventual return home would ease much of that worry.

Six riders approached the keep, Angus walking in the lead with several clansmen following alongside the small group and behind them. All the riders wore cloaks. Three wore their hoods pulled down over part of their faces while the other three didn't seem to mind the snow and cold that stung their cheeks red.

Arran took note of the one fellow who was rail-thin and had droopy eyes, as if he was unconcerned with his surroundings. He moved to stand beside his brother, keeping his wife to his other side and whispered, "The thin one watches without watching."

Royden kept his voice low and his eyes on the approaching group. "The dark-eyed one with the fine features has two knives at his waist and two in each boot."

"And the red-haired, bearded man's dark eyes are more cunning than curious," Arran said.

Royden's hand went to the dagger tucked in the sheath at his waist at the same time Arran's hand went to the hilt of his sword that hung at his side. There might be only six, but six skilled men could cause pain and suffering before they could be subdued.

Royden saw that his da was oblivious to any possible danger. His only concern was to learn from the group of misfits what he could about his daughter. And Royden wanted to make sure his da could do that without incident.

Royden signaled Angus to bring the group to a stop a safe distance from them and he did, forcing the riders to come to a halt behind him.

Two of the three whose hoods covered a good portion of their faces pushed their hoods back.

"Clive!" Oria called out, happy to see the man who had posed as a merchant to bring word of Raven to her through the years.

Purity followed, smiling, pleased to see the soft-spoken man who had delivered messages to her in the woods where she had spent the last five years. "George!"

"You joined a group of thieves, George?" Arran challenged.

"Leave it to the likes of you to belittle my men," came the female voice.

Arran's brow narrowed, trying to place the voice that sounded familiar.

"Good God, have you grown that lazy in thought that you don't know my voice?" the female challenged.

Royden broke out in a huge grin.

"OH MY, GOD, you haven't changed a bit, Raven!" Arran called out, a big smile breaking out across his face.

"Raven?" Parlan asked as if not sure he'd heard right as tears sprang to his eyes, and he hurried forward.

The woman dismounted with speed and agility and she pushed her hood back as she rushed to her da.

Parlan stopped in his tracks, his hand going to cover his mouth as tears ran down his cheeks. His hand fell away to spread his arms wide. "My God, Raven, you're even more beautiful than your mother."

Royden stared at their sister. Raven had barely been entering womanhood when the attack on the clan occurred. She'd been full of mischief and curiosity, and a good amount of stubbornness. And her features then gave evidence to the beauty she might become, but she had surpassed what Royden expected. Raven's beauty was breathtaking. Her long, black hair shined like the wings of a raven, which had earned her her name. One look at the thatch of shiny black hair when Raven was born had her mum naming her after the beautiful bird. Her stunning blue eyes captivated, adding to her overall beauty. She'd also grown, standing taller than most women and from what he could see, she was slender. She showed no signs of physical suffering. Quite the opposite, she appeared fit. And his heart swelled with relief when he watched his sister fall into their da's arms.

Overwhelming joy filled Raven, feeling her da's arms wrap tight around her. She had hoped, dreamed, and planned for this day, the bittersweet thought of it always tearing at her heart. This time it was real. Her da's arms were actually around her. It wasn't a dream. He was hugging her tight as he had done countless times when she was a young lass.

"You're home. You're finally home," Parlan said, keeping his daughter snug in his arms, fearful of letting her go, fearful of losing her again.

Raven lingered in her da's embrace, it having been far too long since she'd felt his warmth and love. She had hungered for it over the past five years and she wanted to linger in it as long as she could since time was short.

"Give her over, Da," Royden said and her da reluctantly let her go to share her with the family.

Raven found herself wrapped in her oldest brother's large, muscled arms and she fought back tears, refusing to cry. She also fought against the memory of that day of the attack. The day that was meant to be joyous. The day meant to unite Royden and Oria in marriage, but never got the chance. The day she had watched her brother lose his hand.

"You are good, Raven?" Royden asked, easing her at arm's length to look her over and see for himself.

"Aye, Royden. I'm good," she confirmed, but saw doubt in his eyes and she knew that he wondered how much truth there was to her words.

She was suddenly grabbed out of Royden's grasp and wrapped in her brother Arran's arms. He was lean and more muscular than she recalled, but still the handsome devil he'd always been.

"This motley crew of yours better not have done you harm in any way or they will not live to see another day," he whispered in her ear.

Raven struggled to free herself enough from her brother's tight grasp to look him in the eye. "I will not see them harmed. They were, and continue to be, the family I missed and longed for these last five years."

It was answer enough for now, though Arran didn't like that she had avoided confirming that no one had harmed her. In time, he'd learn the truth and make anyone who caused her pain suffer.

"My turn," Oria said and hurried her arms around Raven. "I am so happy you are finally home. I have missed you."

Raven forced a smile. She'd let them be happy for this short time. They would learn soon enough.

"I have missed you as well," Raven said and patted Oria's protruding stomach. "You and my brother have been busy."

Oria blushed. "The first of many."

"It's good to know the MacKinnon Clan will grow and flourish," Raven said and looked to Wren. "And that you will have a wise healer here to see that you deliver safely."

Wren stepped forward with a smile that faded when Raven hugged her.

"I can see you know. Say nothing," Raven warned with a whisper.

Wren nodded to confirm as she said, "It is so good to have you home."

Raven turned to Purity, standing off on her own and the two young women hurried to each other, their arms reaching out and grabbing hold to hug tight.

"You remained a good friend, Purity," Raven whispered.

"Always," Purity said, not able to stop her tears from falling. "And somehow I got the man I loved. Your brother Arran and I are wed."

Raven stepped away from Purity and turned a wicked grin on Arran. "You know you don't deserve her."

"Aye, but she took pity on my poor soul and wed me anyway," Arran said with a chuckle.

"Lucky you," Raven said.

Arran's warm and loving glance went to his wife. "Something I tell myself every day."

"Praise the Lord, you're home!"

Raven turned her attention to the top of the keep steps and ran up them to give and receive another loving hug, this time from Bethany. She might be the keep cook, but she was more than that to Raven. She was the closest thing to the mother she never got to know, her mum living only long enough after giving birth to bestow a name on her.

"You are beautiful just like your mum," Bethany said through tears. "She would have been as proud of you as I am. I knew you'd survive and return home. You're too stubborn not to."

Raven walked down the steps with Bethany in tow. She glanced around to all of them as questions fell rapidly from their lips and she answered vaguely, at least for now. The years had changed them just as they had changed her. Her da looked good, though he was thinner than she remembered and he had aged enough for her to notice. Arran's tongue wasn't as charming and witty as it had once been. More serious thought had left permanent lines on his brow, a reminder of the pain he had suffered. Royden was bigger, more muscular than he'd once been and his dark eyes more attuned to all that went on around him. He would not be caught unaware again. Oria's face bore the scar she had seen her get during the attack on the clan and her bravery still astonished Raven, as did Purity's. If it hadn't been for Purity's courage, Raven's da would have died.

"Enough! Enough!" Parlan announced. "We go inside and celebrate Raven's return home."

"There's food aplenty," Bethany said and rushed up the steps and into the keep to see it served.

"My crew will join us. I want you to meet them," Raven said with a nod to the men who dismounted at her signal.

The sudden clang of the bell had everyone jumping, except Raven's crew. The five men stepped forward and circled behind her.

Someone came yelling through the village. "The Beast! The Beast rides on the village with a large troop of warriors."

Parlan couldn't hide his fear when he looked to Royden. "The clan isn't strong enough to defend against him."

"He's not here to attack, Da. He wouldn't dare do that to Oria, his sister," Royden said, looking to his wife.

"Royden's right, Da," Raven said.

"How would you know that?" Arran asked, his hand gripping the hilt of his sword.

"Because I know why he's here," Raven said.

Royden's gut stirred wondering how his sister would know such a thing and why she hadn't looked surprised when he mentioned Oria was the Beast's sister, and he asked, "Why is he here?"

"For me," she whispered, not intending for anyone to hear her.

"Did you say something, Raven?" Arran asked.

"Aye, I did." She lifted her chin with courage as she had done so many times when she'd been young and was about to admit to something her father wouldn't like. "The Beast is here to collect me… I'm his wife."

Chapter Two

"NO! NO! NO!" Royden's words echoed his brother's.

Raven let her two brothers protest and argue that there was no way she was the wife of the man who had brought such pain and suffering to the Clan MacKinnon.

"You'll not be wife to our enemy," Royden yelled, shaking his leather-clad stump at her.

"Royden's right. I'll gut him before I let him lay a hand on you," Arran argued.

Raven remained silent through their tirade as did her crew. They kept their vigil around her without uttering a word.

Tears pooled in Oria's eyes and Purity had turned pale and, strangely enough, Raven felt the two women—her friends—understood.

"Enough!" Her da's strong command silenced his sons and he went to his daughter. "You paid a high price."

Her da realized what she had done. "I listened outside the solar door that day when you and my brothers made a promise to see us all safe. I made that promise along with you, though you never heard it, and I, like you, honor my word." She tilted her chin not in defiance but with pride.

"You didn't," Arran said, shaking his head as he realized what she meant.

Royden shut his eyes tight for a brief moment, it dawning on him as well.

"You secured mine and Royden's freedom from the mercenaries by agreeing to wed Wolf," Arran said and waited for her to confirm what was painfully obvious.

"It was a small price to pay," Raven said.

"No, it wasn't," Royden said. "You may have freed us, but you've condemned yourself to a life with a beast of a man."

"We can't let you do that," Arran said and saw that Royden agreed with a nod.

"It's already done and do you really want to leave your wives and return to the mercenaries never to know your bairns? Because that is what will happen if you attempt to defy what has been agreed upon," Raven said, looking from Royden to Arran.

Oria took hold of Royden's arm, letting him know she wouldn't let him go, and Purity was quick to do the same to Arran.

"Your wives have no intentions of letting either of you go. They are the wise ones," Raven said. "Besides, it is done, the marriage documents confirmed."

"But not the consummation," Arran argued.

Raven squared her shoulders. "This is done, Arran. There is no changing it and I would advise you to keep

Purity and your unborn bairn in mind before you do something foolish."

"It wouldn't be any more foolish than what you've done," Arran accused.

Raven forced a smile. "Is that the thanks I get for freeing you to return home?"

"It's no excuse I give," Purity said, speaking up before her husband could and keeping hold of his arm. "But he's angry that you saved him and Royden when it should have been them who saved you."

"I don't need you to speak for me, wife," Arran snapped.

"Then admit it yourself, since it's the truth," Purity scolded.

"You as well," Oria urged, tugging at her husband's arm.

Arran and Royden exchanged scowls.

"There is nothing that can be done to change this?" her da asked.

Raven shook her head. "No, Da. If I don't keep this agreement, Royden and Arran will be returned to the mercenaries to live out their lives." Gasps were heard from Oria and Purity and Raven wasn't surprised to see them tighten their hold on their husbands.

"And how is that any different from you being condemned to spend your life with the Beast, if you live that long. What's to keep him from doing away with you?" Arran asked, rumbling anger sounding along with his words.

"You think I'm foolish enough to agree to such a union without taking precautions? I have more sense than that," Raven said and shook her head. "This is done. There is no changing it and at least I will be close, living at Learmonth."

"We can visit often," Oria said, her smile, though forced, a welcome relief to the scowls of Raven's brothers.

"Not with winter approaching," Royden argued. "The first good snow will make travel difficult."

"You both," —Purity looked from her husband to Royden— "need to see this more clearly. You worry about Raven being wife to the Beast, perhaps you should worry for the Beast being wed to your sister."

Raven smiled at her friend for having such confidence in her.

There was no more time to talk, the Beast and his men were not far from the keep.

Parlan took hold of Raven's hand. "Please tell me I have at least a few days to talk with you before you're gone from me again."

"You have today and more days to come since I will visit here often," Raven assured him.

"I will hold you to that, daughter," Parlan said, squeezing her hand.

"And I will make sure of it," Raven said, finding it difficult to believe it had been five years since she'd last seen her da. She promised herself she'd never let that happen again.

Silence surrounded them when the Beast and six of his warriors drew close, the remainder of his troop waiting on the outskirts of the village.

All of the men were large, the Beast being the largest of them all, though not as one would expect. Some warriors were thicker and broader in the chest, not so the Beast. He was leaner and harder with muscles. His skin was fair, his long hair dark and his eyes were as dark as Raven's hair. His features were more than fine. They rivaled even Arran's, and her brother Arran was a man of extra fine features. Though, unlike Arran, the Beast wore a beard that was cropped short. He wore the furs and leather garments of the tribes across the North Sea. He was a Northman and enemy of the Clan MacKinnon. And from what her inquires about him had taught her, like the Northmen, his name was an indication of his nature, hence the name—Wolf the Mighty Beast—and the reason many referred to him as the Beast.

Raven had learned all she could about him even before the chance had risen to free her brothers and she wondered if she knew more about him than he did himself. She had prepared herself well and she was ready to take on the Beast.

The warriors waited until Wolf dismounted, then they followed and remained standing by their horses, their large size and their empty stares causing the villagers who had followed them to keep their distance.

Raven wasn't surprised that when she stepped forward, her brothers did the same.

Raven offered no greeting. "You weren't to arrive until tomorrow."

"It matters not. We leave now," Wolf ordered.

"Not likely," she said and catching, out of the corner of her eye, Arran's slight smile.

"You're my wife and you'll obey my command," Wolf demanded.

"I may be your wife, but as far as me obeying your command—that's never going to happen," Raven said and turned her back on him. "Tomorrow was when you were to arrive here and I was to go with you, and I will leave here no sooner than that. Stay if you wish, camp outside the village. I care not what you do. I will see you tomorrow." She heard her men chuckle as she took her da's arm. "Come, Da, we'll talk, drink, eat, and celebrate my return home."

Raven nodded to her men as she walked up the steps to the keep and they followed behind her. She smiled when she heard Arran's hardy laughter and the words that tumbled out with it.

"You might just have gotten what you deserve for foolishly marrying my sister."

***

Raven sat at a table by the hearth with her da and Wren, who had followed along with them into the Great Hall. Her men settled at the table to her right, the reason she ignored the dais. She wanted her crew close by.

"They go with you tomorrow?" her da asked, turning to the five men.

"We go where she goes," the man with good features said.

Raven smiled with pride as she introduced the man. "That's Fyn, Da, a good friend and skilled warrior."

"I'm relieved and grateful to hear that," her da said.

Raven continued to introduce her men. "The red-haired fellow is Iver, an exceptional tracker and archer. The wiry fellow at the far end of the table is Brod. I believe you know Clive, the merchant who stopped here often, and George is the scholar among us. They are all good men and they are all like family to me."

It wasn't lost on her father that she hadn't mentioned Brod's skill and he wondered if it had been on purpose.

Royden and Arran had entered the Great Hall with their wives and joined them at the table, listening to the introductions.

Royden looked directly at his sister, still startled by the beauty she'd become. He went to speak and felt his wife squeeze his thigh under the table. He bit back the words he was about to say and instead said, "It's good to finally have you home, Raven, and it's good to have your friends join us."

Raven smiled, her rigid shoulders easing some. "I'm so happy to be here with all of you again, and happy for you to meet my men."

"To your safe return," Arran said, raising his tankard and everyone raised their tankards with a cheer.

"I'm thrilled you're home and that we'll be able to visit often," Purity said when the cheering died.

"*My wife* will visit when I allow her to."

Everyone turned to see Wolf standing just inside the Great Hall, his men fanning out to his sides.

"You should know now I don't take well to orders," Raven said.

"And you should know I don't take well to being disobeyed," Wolf countered.

Arran stood. "And you should know that I'll cut your heart out if you hurt my sister."

"Enough!" Oria said, jumping to her feet, to her husband's surprise. She looked to Wolf. "You and your men are welcome to join us if you can be civil."

Wolf recounted with a stern scowl and a sharp tone. "I expected my sister to at least show me respect."

Royden noticed that Raven didn't appear surprised now or previously when it was made mentioned that Oria and Wolf were siblings. He shouldn't be surprised that she was already aware of it. Raven always had a way of finding things out.

"And I expect my brother to show respect in his sister's home," Oria retaliated.

"Remember that when it comes to my home," Wolf said.

Oria pointed to a table to the right of her. "Join us or not."

Wolf went to the table, his men following, and he whipped off his fur cloak and dropped it on the bench, then to everyone's surprise he sat next to Raven, while his men made themselves comfortable at the other table.

Raven almost moved closer to her da when Wolf sat close enough to her for their arms to rest against each other, but she stopped herself. She wouldn't show this man an ounce of fear even if he did send tingles of dread racing through her. She could feel his taut arm muscles through the sleeve of his dark wool shirt and could see the soft, leathery covering he wore over it fit his chest snugly as did the wool shirt. She feared his scent might be offensive but he smelled mostly of pine and campfire smoke.

"I can't wait any longer, daughter, I must know what happened to you all these years," Parlan pleaded.

Fear was something that had been a constant when Raven had first been on her own, but time had taught her how to face it rather than run from it. She turned to Wolf with a smile. "You must be curious to know as well, since you searched for me and failed to find me these last five years."

She fought to keep the lump of fear that rose in her throat from enlarging when he turned his eyes on her. Never had she seen such intense dark eyes. They weren't black, but one would think they were, they were such a deep brown color. They were eyes that lacked fear and were filled with self-assuredness. This man was confident in his worth, his skills, and his power.

"I am most curious," Wolf said and held her eyes with his until she turned away.

"It's a short tale. I dressed like a lad and joined a band of," —-she paused and looked to her crew— "misfits. They taught me how to survive."

"I'm grateful to all of you," Parlan said with a nod to her men.

"How did you become their leader?" Wolf asked, since fighting and strength were ways of retaining leadership within his tribe. He also doubted that her tale was a short one. There was more to it and he intended to find out.

"When she proved herself wiser than us," Clive said with a jovial laugh.

"Much wiser," George agreed.

Wolf remained silent as talk went on around him, listening while he carefully kept watch on his surroundings. He had taken note when he first arrived at the way her crew of motley men stood ready to defend her. They were a loyal lot and he'd have to keep that in mind. They also obeyed her well and he wondered why. She had to have done something to win their loyalty, another mystery about his wife he intended to solve.

What had surprised him the most, though, was to see that she was far more beautiful than he had expected. One glance at her captivated the eye and held it, her features were that striking. It wasn't a soft beauty she possessed but more of sharp angles and curves melded to perfection. Her pale skin was in direct contrast to her long dark hair that shined with a silky softness and had him wanting to reach out and touch it, a surprising thought. She was also taller than he expected, the top of her head reaching past his chin. It was difficult to tell much about her body, the shirt beneath her plaid a bit big for her. Her plaid was cinched tight at her narrow waist and from what he could make of her legs, they did suggest a slender build.

It would not be a chore to bed her—when necessary. But first there were things he needed to know.

Wolf reached for his tankard and swallowed the entire contents, easing the thirst that had plagued him. It was quickly refilled and he drank half the contents this time. He ate from the food offered, the flavor far better than he expected.

He caught his sister, Oria's eye. She was a beauty, though opposite in coloring to Raven, her hair a honey blonde, her features soft, and she was shorter in height. It pained him to think of all the years they'd missed together, she having been abducted from their home when a mere baby and taken to Scotland and sold to William and Clare of the Clan MacGlennen. The couple hadn't known she belonged to the Northmen and it had been a shock to him when he had discovered her here. Even though he had helped Royden save her life when she'd been taken captive by a man once loyal to him, she still didn't seem to trust him or show any signs of truly accepting him as her brother.

"You feel well, Oria?" he asked, though she looked well enough.

"I do," she said with a soft smile. "I am well and I am happy." She turned a broader smile on Royden. "That is all due to the love I have for my wonderful husband." She turned back to her brother, her smile fading. "That would not be so if he was to be taken from me."

"Royden isn't going anywhere," Raven assured her and turned to face Wolf. "Your brother gave his word to honor the agreement. And I was told he is a man of his word."

Wolf brought his face close to hers. "Unfortunately, your word couldn't be proven as honorable, since you and your crew are nothing more than a band of thieves."

Raven's men shot to their feet before Royden and Arran could, and Wolf's men did the same.

"Disparage her again and she'll gladly make herself a widow, while we see to your men," Clive warned and grinned at Wolf's men, a little more than an arm's length from their leader. "You'd never reach him in time. The knife she holds to his side will see to that."

Wolf looked down, shocked to see the point of the blade nearly pressed to his side. He hadn't even seen her move. "You better know how to use that, wife."

"Trust me, I do," she warned.

That her hand was steady and her startling blue eyes showed not an ounce of fear, told Wolf she'd use the weapon without pause. It annoyed him that he'd been caught off guard, and by his wife, and that she was skillful enough to see it done. He'd have to keep that in mind.

She raised her hand, signaling her men without taking her eyes off Wolf, and they sat. "I gave my word and I will honor it. Now you have proof of my word, since I could have easily killed you and between my men and my brothers your men wouldn't have stood a chance."

"My warriors are far more skilled then your men," Wolf said.

"Then how is it that one of my men holds a knife to one of your warriors?" Raven asked with a smug grin.

All eyes turned to see Wolf's warriors glancing around, except one. He stood stock still, anger flaming in his eyes.

"He's under the table, holding a knife between my legs," the warrior said.

Arran laughed, though it did nothing to ease the tension. "I think your warriors have met their match."

"Brod," Raven called out and by the time she turned her head, Brod was back at the table, slugging down a tankard of ale.

Her men laughed and sat, refilling Brod's tankard when he was done and returning to enjoy their food.

With grime faces, Wolf's men sat and quickly reached for their tankards.

"It is good your men show me their skills," Wolf said, his words measured so as not to show his anger. "They will make me fine warriors."

That got Raven's men's attention, though they held their tongues.

"My men will be no warriors of yours," Raven warned. "My men stay my men. Or did you forget?"

"Forget?" Wolf's brow scrunched, then went wide.

"He remembers," she said with glee that sounded far too victorious.

Wolf nodded. "You had protection for them put into the agreement with the proposal you offered. They remain free of my dictate and free to stay with you."

"That's right," Raven grinned and reminded. "And you are a man of your word, so you say."

Wolf stood and his men stood with him.

"Taking your leave so soon?" Raven asked, her smile remaining victorious.

"I'll return," Wolf said and stepped around the table and grabbed his cloak.

"See you tomorrow," Raven called out.

Wolf stopped and turned to glare at her. "You'll see me tonight. I'm your husband and it's your duty to share my bed—and that starts tonight. And since you are a woman of your word, I expect you will honor it."

Chapter Three

Raven sat in Royden's solar, once her da's domain, joining him, Arran, and their da at the round table that sat six. Her da had conducted meetings here where battles had been plotted, victories and defeats discussed, and problems solved as best they could be. She hadn't been welcome here when young, of course, but age wouldn't have mattered anyway since she was a female and not privy to such conversations. It made no difference to her since she'd sneak, hiding herself in the shadows outside the door, and listen to all the talk, learning about men and battle, and the lies often told. The ensuing years had taught her even more and made her realize there were few she could trust, her family and her crew being the exception.

"Have your say, for I will not linger long here," she said once they were all seated. "I wish to have time with Oria and Purity before Wolf returns."

Arran didn't waste a minute. He rested his arms on the table and leaned in, glaring at her. "Whatever possessed you to agree to such a horrendous bargain?"

She mimicked him, placing her arms on the table and leaning toward him with a glare of her own. "You scold me for rescuing you?"

"You've grown even more strong-headed," Arran accused.

"How do you think I survived?"

Parlan laid a gentle hand on his daughter's arm. "And I'm grateful that you did, but I worry how you will survive a marriage where only hatred and no love exists."

"Da is right, Raven. As grateful as I am, and I know Arran is as well, you freed us by imprisoning yourself. Unless—is there possibly an eventual way out of the marriage?" Royden asked with a shred of hope.

"Only through death," she said.

Arran looked to Royden. "That could be arranged."

"Wolf's death would only bring retaliation and it would be a never-ending battle with both sides losing," Raven warned. "This is done. I am his wife and he my husband, and I will make the most of my situation just as I learned to do five years ago."

"How bad was it?" Arran asked, concern arching his brow.

"At first more frightening than anything, realizing that Da might die and Royden as well after seeing his hand severed. I wasn't even sure if Oria would survive after seeing her attacked and her face slashed. And I worried if Purity would be strong enough to do what she needed to do. In the end, I feared there might be only you and me left, Arran." She grinned wide. "And that really terrified me."

Arran returned the grin, but said, "I would have never stopped searching for you. But you didn't answer my question. How bad was it for you?"

Raven sat back in her chair, her glance appearing to drift off for a few moments. When her glance returned to Arran, she spoke without an ounce of emotion. "It was my worst nightmare come true and it took me time to wake from it and forge ahead." When she saw Arran ready to ask her more, she stopped him. "Don't ask me anymore, Arran. It's in the past and that's where I want it to stay. Now, if we're done, I would like to speak with Da alone before I go talk with Oria and Purity."

"We're not done talking," Arran said as he stood. "But it can wait for another time since we expect you to visit often and we will be visiting you frequently."

Royden joined in, agreeing. "Arran's right. We will see you often to make sure you stay well and that Wolf is treating you good. We will keep you safe this time, Raven."

"I have no doubt you will," Raven said, though she wouldn't need them to do so. She had learned to keep herself safe.

Parlan took his daughter's hand as the door closed behind his sons. "You would tell me if there was anything I needed to know?"

"There is far more to this agreement than anyone knows and it goes far beyond Wolf and me," she said, hoping her da understood without her saying more.

"You are bound by silence," he whispered.

Raven nodded and hoped again he would see the plea in her eyes.

"I will ask no more of you and keep my lips tight to others about this, Raven, but I know you. You grow even more relentless and tenacious when…" Her da searched for words and Raven provided them.

"Kept ignorant."

"Some people prefer ignorance," her da argued.

"Then they are fools and I am not a fool, Da."

"No, you certainly aren't, Raven. I admire and respect the strong, courageous woman you've become in spite of what you have had to endure."

"It is what I endured that made me that woman, Da."

"I only wish…" He shook his head, unable to finish, tears clouding his eyes.

No tears filled Raven's eyes. She hadn't allowed herself to cry in a long time. "I know, Da, I wished once too, until I realized if I wanted that wish to come true I needed to do something about it. That wish finally came true. I'm here now with you and my family."

Parlan hugged her and she held tight to him, happy to know this was the first of many hugs to come.

"What say we meet early tomorrow and share some time together before you must take your leave?" he asked, wiping away his tears.

"I'd love that, Da," Raven said, wishing she had far more time with her da before she had to leave.

"Good, I will wait for you in the Great Hall and perhaps we'll be able to catch the dawn of a new day together, a new start."

"Aye, Da, a new start for us all."

***

Raven sat wrapped in a blanket, her knees drawn up to her chin, in front of the hearth.

"Let me have another chair brought for you," Oria said, leaning forward in her chair, ready to stand.

Raven shook her head. "No. I am good where I am, warm and content, and with friends I have sorely missed."

Purity smiled, hugging the wool shawl draped over her shoulders tighter around her. "I am so thrilled that you have returned home." Her smile withered. "Though I am disheartened at your plight, yet ever so grateful for what you've done for your brothers."

"I feel as Purity does, forever grateful, yet upset with your situation," Oria said.

"See the joy in it, for I do. I will be close, a short ride from both of you," Raven said, trying to reassure them and possibly herself.

Purity's smile grew again. "We'll raise our bairns together." She cringed, her smile quickly dying. "That was foolish of me. I didn't think."

Oria reached out and patted Purity's arm. "You are not foolish and we will raise our bairns together." She turned a gentle smile on Raven. "And we will be here for Raven if she has any questions or concerns about intimacy with her husband."

"Forgive me, I can't help but ask for I am concerned for you," Purity said. "Do you fear coupling with the Beast?"

Raven chuckled. "It is he who should fear coupling with me. I'll do my duty and get with child and then we are done. He can have whatever woman he wants to please his beastly ways."

"It is such a shame that you will never know the joy of coupling with a man you love," Purity said. "I yearn being with Arran, holding his hand, having his arms wrap around me, his every kiss tingles me senseless, and the pure joy of coupling with him leaves me breathless."

"You really do love my brother," Raven said, happy for Purity and Arran and a tad envious, never realizing how powerful love could be between a husband and wife.

"I feel the same," Oria admitted. "Your brother was a changed man when he returned home, but what hadn't changed and never will was his love for me and my love for him. Not a day goes by that I'm not grateful he's home and we are wed. And like Purity, I yearn for the touch of his hand, his arm snug around me, his lips on mine, and the way we sleep wrapped around each other."

Raven felt a catch in her chest. So that was love, a craving and a fulfilling of simple things, the touch of a hand, a comforting arm, the need of a kiss, and the desire to share intimacy. She had never known that and now never would and surprisingly, it saddened her.

"Perhaps Wolf will be a good husband and you will grow to at least like him," Purity said, offering some encouragement.

Raven nodded toward Oria. "Have you grown to like your brother?"

"You knew that Wolf is my brother?" Oria asked.

"I learned all I could about him long before the proposition presented itself. But news that he was your brother came later and I wondered and worried how you would take the news and how my brother would feel about it."

"It was a shock to learn that I was born a Northwoman and taken from my family. And even more of a shock to learn the man responsible for taking Royden from me and the one who brought such misery and heartache to this area was my brother. I don't know what I feel for him. I haven't spent much time with him, though I can say I do favor my sister, Demelza."

"Her husband Trevor was Wolf's right-hand man before Wolf laid claim to, what was once your clan, the Clan MacGlennen and made him chieftain. They were also best friends, growing into mighty warriors together," Raven added.

"You do know a lot about him," Oria said, impressed.

More than anyone knew, but Raven didn't let Oria know that. "I learned what I could. I also learned what great and trustworthy friends I have in both of you. You kept secrets for me even from your husbands and that I truly appreciate."

"The secrets were necessary to protect you," Purity said with a nod at Raven. "And I understand now it also protected your brothers from finding out what you were up to."

"They could have ruined your plans and our husbands would have been lost to us," Oria said with a shiver.

"But thankfully all went well with both your help and we are all reunited again," Raven said, the joy of being home and talking with her friends filled her with warmth and, if only for a short while, contentment. "With Learmonth about to become my new home and with you knowing it well from being wed to the old lord for a short time, I thought you could tell me about the place. By the way, your da was wise in seeing you wed to Lord Burnell right after the attack to keep you safe until Royden returned."

A tear slipped from the corner of Oria's eye. "I didn't realize that at first, but I did after a while. He knew Lord Learmonth didn't have much time to live and being wed to him kept me safe. When he died I worried, but Royden came home not long after and though we had a bit of a rough start, our love managed to save us." She wiped away another tear. "You wanted to know about Learmonth. It's not a big keep. The rooms are small and drafty, the hearths always lit or you will shiver down to the bone. Detta is an old woman who oversees the keep. She probably can tell you more about the keep than I can. She is a quiet woman and keeps much to herself, but she is pleasant and was kind to me. They lacked a healer when I last was there, the old one that had served them well having died. There was also much building going on when I last saw the place, though what it was about I couldn't say."

"That helps much," Raven said, though she already knew most of what Oria told her. She was hoping that Oria could provide something about Learmonth she didn't know.

"You should also be aware that the walk, though it feels more like a climb the path is so steep, to the keep can be taxing," Oria said, memories bringing a smile to her face. "At first, I dreaded leaving the keep, knowing the return home would exhaust me, but I proudly conquered that climb."

Raven had no worry of the climb. She was more than fit and knew it wouldn't rob her breath.

"You should also know that Wolf has settled many of his warriors there," Purity said. "Your brothers had worried he planned another attack. But that was soon dismissed when it was learned the land now belonged to him as did the title, and he would soon make it his home. Though they didn't know it would be with his wife—their sister."

Raven learned a few missing pieces from her friends, but nothing that would change any of what she thought. She continued to talk with them, cherishing the moments of laughter they shared, recalling the past and even thinking that perhaps the future wouldn't be as dismal as she had believed. She was among family now and that surely would help with the ordeal of being the wife of Wolf the Mighty Beast.

***

Supper filled her heart with joy. It was as if the troubling years had melted away, forgotten, and time hadn't separated them. They were family once again, teasing, laughing, sharing happy stories of the past and promises of a bright future. Arran and Purity had remained, even though the snow had continued to fall lightly. They wanted to share in the rcunion and so they sent word home to let their clan know they would return on the morrow.

Wolf arrived in the middle of supper along with his warriors. He took a seat next to Raven at the table by the hearth as he had done earlier. She once again had avoided the dais, preferring the warmth of the fire on her back. She'd been too cold far too many days and nights and she feared she'd never get warm again, so she kept close to a hearth when possible. She had confided that to her da when she had entered the Great Hall to find only him there at the dais. He had quickly moved to the table closest to the hearth and made it clear to all that was where they would have their meal.

She loved her da and had missed him terribly. It hurt her heart to know she would have to leave him so soon after only returning home, and make a home with a man that was more foe than husband.

Raven did notice that Wolf kept careful watch to all going on around him and his attention drifted to anything his sister had to say. He was learning about her, hearing how happy her childhood had been and the loving parents she'd had, and how she loved Royden from when she was just a wee lass.

Purity and Arran had everyone laughing with the antics of their animals. King was a cat that she'd had since he was a kitten. Princess was a large, one-eyed dog whose back King rode on and helped guide her with a tap of his paw to her head. Then there was Hope, Arran's mare who he had bought in poor shape and helped heal her.

Raven was glad to see how happy her family was and how it would grow with the birth of Oria's and Purity's bairns. She also saw that while her brothers smiled, teased—mostly Arran—and joked, they cast her glances of concern. They weren't happy with her situation and no doubt felt guilty over it. After all, it was her brothers who were to save her, not for their sister to save them.

The night grew late and though Purity and Oria yawned often, neither remarked about retiring for the night. Raven knew what everyone was doing. They were delaying seeking their own beds so she wouldn't have to seek her bed with the Beast.

Raven decided to settle it for them. "It grows late and I grow tired. It is time to seek my bed." She cast a glance to Bethany.

The woman answered without Raven saying a word. "Your bedchamber is ready and awaits you."

Raven stood, Wolf slipping off the bench as she did to stand as well. She turned to her men. "You'll bed down here in the Great Hall."

"As will my men," Wolf said with a nod to them.

Raven looked to Bethany again.

"I will see them settled," Bethany said.

Raven hugged her da and whispered, "Meet you here in the morning."

He nodded and hugged her tight before releasing her.

Raven bid her brothers and their wives good-night.

"My bedchamber is not far from yours if you should need me," Arran said, though it wasn't his sister he looked at.

"Raven has a husband now. She has no need of her brothers' protection," Wolf reminded.

Raven was quick to speak up. "Husband or not, my brothers will always be there to protect me."

Arran and Royden both smiled.

"Come, husband," Raven said with a wave and led the way to the stairs.

Royden stood beside Arran watching her and whispered to him, "You may be right. The Beast may be getting what he deserves."

Chapter Four

"Let's get this over with," Raven said, sitting on the bench near the hearth to remove her boots.

Wolf flung his cloak to land on a chest next to the door. "You have much to learn, *kona*,"

Wife or woman, equal in his language, though she wondered which he meant it to be. When she learned Brod was versed in several languages, a natural skill to him, she had him begin to teach her. She was especially interested in the language of the Northmen. She wasn't fluent in it but she could understand a good portion. Not that she would make her husband aware of that. That would remain her secret and one, she was sure, that would serve her well. She had been surprised to find out that he spoke skillfully in her tongue as did his warriors. He was not an ignorant man nor a fool and she'd be wise to remember that.

"I could say the same of you," Raven said and placed the boot, she had slipped off, near the hearth to keep warm.

"I intend to learn everything I can about you," he acknowledged, remaining where he stood near the closed door.

"You mean you've learned nothing about me before agreeing to this arrangement or do you mislead me to believe that?" Her other boot joined the one already by the hearth.

She had a quick mind and she had proved she was skilled with a weapon when earlier she had drawn her knife on him, two attributes he'd be sure to keep in mind. He hadn't expected that of her. He actually hadn't known what to expect, since she'd been right about his failure to find her these last five years. At least now he knew why the task had proven difficult. She had disguised, and well, herself as a lad and joined a band of thieves. He had been so intent on dealing with her father and brothers, he had failed to learn about her. He had assumed she was a weak woman, pampered by her family and would easily follow his command. He was wrong.

"I'd say your lack of response tells me it's the latter, but since you couldn't find me, it means you don't know anything about me. And I doubt Oria confided anything to you about me, since she's like a sister to me and feels no kinship to you." The slight tic at the corner of his eye told her that her words, like an arrow, had hit its mark.

"You reveal much about yourself to me already, *kona*," he said annoyed he had allowed her barb to sting him. Oria was a sore spot with him. He wanted, at least, a friendship to grow between them, but he feared his sister would never forgive him for what had happened to her husband.

She grinned. "See that, I'm pleasing you already."

"You will please me often, wife," he said without a hint of a smile.

Raven had learned well to mask her feelings.

Let the mask slip and you become vulnerable.

She let the old man's, who'd once led their band of misfits, words linger in her head. She missed him every day and wished she had had more time with him, but he had taught her more about life and how to survive it in the few years she had spent with him than anyone else, including her family.

She stood and began to remove her garments. "But will you please me, husband?"

She had to turn her head when she caught the tic appear once again at the corner of his eye, another of her barb's striking its mark. She didn't want him to see her gloat. She was actually relieved with the banter they shared. It allowed her to focus on anything but what she was about to do—couple with the Beast.

Her stomach churned and she had to focus hard so that her hands wouldn't tremble as she unwrapped her plaid. She had to keep her mask in place, not let him see how anxious she was about coupling with him. She certainly wasn't ignorant of the act, though she had no experience herself. After catching a man trying to force himself on her, and seeing the culprit meet his maker, the old man had ordered his band of thieves to teach her everything.

His words rang again in her head. *You'll know how to defend and kill like a man.*

He had kept his word and then some. She silently admonished herself for not keeping her mind clear, especially when she turned and saw that her husband was nearly naked. But her mask was firmly in place and she displayed not a trace of surprise.

She turned to let her plaid fall away and stood only in her shirt, the coarse linen falling to the middle of her thigh. That was as far as she would go. There was no need to stand completely naked in front of him or even do so to couple. She turned back and saw that he thought differently, since he stood naked, not a stitch of clothing on him.

His eyes not only intimidated, his honed body did as well. There wasn't an ounce of flab on him. He was pure muscle. He was lean yet not thin, but not huge like her brother Royden. It was as if a master craftsman had chiseled him to perfection and the way he stood, commanding and confident, only added to his appeal. She was, however, surprised and somewhat relieved, to see that his shaft lay flaccid against him. And even though limp, it was sizeable.

Thanks to her crew, though more to the old man since he'd insisted she listen when the men laughed, boasted, or poked fun of their conquest of women, she knew more than she would have preferred to know about coupling. But the old man had told her that she'd be wise to know the true nature of men and, like always, he'd been right.

That her husband wasn't aroused meant he didn't find her appealing, though she was aware that a man didn't have to find a woman appealing to poke her. It was more a need, an ache and evidently he didn't have either.

A shiver of relief ran through her and she took a closer step to the hearth to warm herself. His dark eyes followed her every moment with such chilling intensity that the heat from the flames did little to warm her. She wanted to turn away from him, not look at him and certainly not feel as if he was laying claim to her with his eyes alone. And if his eyes could shiver her senseless, how would his hands feel upon her or his shaft feel inside her?

The only way to get through coupling with him was to get it done and over. Her stomach churned at the thought and to delay any longer just might see her losing her supper, an embarrassing thought.

"Let's get this done," she said and his strong command stopped her before she took one step.

"NO! I will not touch you until I know you have had your monthly bleed."

His words not only shocked her, but relieved her, her stomach instantly calming. Then his reasoning dawned on her. "You want to make sure I don't carry another man's bairn."

"You shelter with thieves, live the life of a thief, behave like a thief," he accused.

"So you assume I've spread my legs willingly for any man," she said what he had implied.

"The life you have lived tells me this."

"And how many women have you poked willingly and unwillingly?" she demanded.

"I have no need or want of an unwilling woman."

While she was glad to hear that, she wasn't certain if she should believe it. She had heard stories of the Northmen that would chill a person to the bone. "I am glad to hear you will never force me to couple with you."

"I will not force you but I expect you to do your duty as a wife."

She spread her arms invitingly, knowing full well he'd refuse her. "I'm willing."

The quick tic at the corner of his eye was clearly visible this time and what was even more telling was the arousal of his shaft. It popped to life and he quickly turned away from her and went to the bed, slipping beneath the blankets.

So he did have a need, yet he would deny himself to make sure another man's seed didn't grow within her. That suited her, since she'd only recently had her monthly time. At least now, she had time to, somewhat, grow accustomed to him. Hopefully, that would make it easier to couple with him. Or would it make it worse?

"Come to bed. We leave at dawn," he ordered.

"No!" she snapped. "We leave later. I have plans with my da early in the morning."

He rested his arms beneath his head, the muscles growing tighter in each. "You had today."

She slapped her hands on her hips and scowled. "And I'll have the morn with him as well or you'll have to drag me away and I promise that will not be easy."

He turned an equal scowl on her. "Don't tempt me."

And damn if she wasn't tempting him, something he hadn't expected. But he couldn't deny that he didn't imagine how her long, slender legs would feel wrapped around him and how her taut nipples that poked at her shirt would taste against his tongue. And her shirt covering her intimate parts only made him more eager to explore what lay hidden beneath.

His lustful thoughts only worsened his arousal and he silently cursed himself. He may be straddled with her—he silently cursed himself for that word popping into his thoughts and painting an image of her doing just that. He might be stuck with her but he'd make certain that the first child she gave him came from his seed. With her thieving ways, who knew how many men had touched her and the thought sparked anger in him.

"I'll sleep elsewhere, since you have no need for me," she said, taking only one step when he bolted up in bed, halting her.

"Where I sleep, you sleep. Now get in bed!" he ordered and pulled the blanket back on the empty side.

Something in his dark eyes warned her not to argue. Besides, if she made a fuss it would draw not only her brothers but her men as well, and she didn't want that kind of confrontation. She walked over to the bed and slipped in, keeping to the edge and turned on her side so her back faced him.

She felt him turn, grateful it was away from her. She'd survived much, she could survive this night. She closed her eyes, willing herself to sleep, needing strength for tomorrow and all the days to come.

Raven stared at the flames in the hearth, letting their fiery dance soothe her as had campfires done many nights through the years. Her thoughts calmed as did her worries and that's when something he had said came back to gnaw at her.

The proposal you offered.

She hadn't initiated the proposal to wed him. She'd been told he had.

Chapter Five

Raven didn't glance back, if she did she was afraid she'd burst into tears. She'd only returned home and she had to leave her family again. She wasn't going far this time and she'd be able to visit often, but still, she'd barely gotten to speak with her family, visit with them, before having to leave once again.

She'd been grateful for the time she had gotten with her da this morning. She had quietly left her husband sleeping soundly in bed and met her da in the Great Hall. The day was barely dawning and so as not to disturb or be disturbed they had left the keep and walked through the village that was beginning to stir to life.

They had spoken of many things as their footfalls left tracks in the light snow that covered the ground. She had clung tightly to his arm as she had done as a child when she needed his attention, only now she didn't speak of what troubled her. She had gotten him to talk about what had happened to him after the attack five years ago and near the end of their walk, when close to the keep, he had reminded her that she had yet to confide to him all that had truly happened to her in the years they'd been separated.

She had promised him that in time she would tell him and he had graciously accepted her excuse. But truthfully, she didn't know if she ever wanted to share it with him.

Oria and Purity had promised they would see her soon and she hadn't needed her brothers to tell her the same, she had seen it on their scowling faces.

"You are hurting."

Raven turned to Clive riding alongside her. "I won't deny it. I am hurting. I miss my family, though I am grateful you and the others, my other family, remain with me."

"We'll never leave you. We gave our word and we'll keep it no matter what others think. Most don't understand it, but there is honor among thieves."

"I know and I am grateful that all of you gave your word," she said, recalling the day the five men stood around the dying old man and swore to keep their word to always protect her just as her brothers and da had done those many years ago. Not one of her men had expressed any desire to leave her when they had learned she would wed Wolf. Fyn had said it best. *We're family and we stay together.*

She would see them kept just as safe as they would her.

Clive cleared his throat, an indication he wanted to ask her something that he was having trouble asking.

"Get it over with, Clive, or you'll make your throat raw," she said with a chuckle.

Clive hurriedly spit it out. "Was he kind to you last night?"

She didn't have to blush at the question, Clive did it for her. And he more than blushed when she said, "He won't touch me until he knows I don't carry another man's bairn."

Clive's face burst red with anger. "He thinks you a whore?"

"He thinks me a thief and all that supposedly goes with it."

"Those who have never known hunger or cold know nothing about thieves. A bit of stolen food and a blanket can help one survive."

"I know that all too well." Raven shook her head. "Though, I never thought I would learn it through experience."

Fyn came up from behind her to ride along her other side. "We've all been there. It's often what forms a thief—the need to survive. Some are lucky and can begin life anew. Many, however, are stuck in the life they never meant to enter. Then there are others, the lazy lot, who choose such a life. But none of that matters now. As I've said many times and will repeat as often as necessary. We're family and we stay together."

Raven was eternally grateful for having met up with the band of thieves and to have a second family and one that would always remain with her.

It wasn't a far ride to Learmonth and while she recalled being there once when she was very young, it didn't mean she hadn't returned. Unknowing to those at Learmonth, she had visited a few times, and Clive and

George had visited when they posed as traveling merchants. So she had some knowledge of the place.

What Oria had confirmed for her was that there had been more building going on there. Of what nature, she didn't know, though was curious to find out. She didn't care that Wolf had ignored her since leaving her family. He rode with his men and paid her no heed.

It made her realize that he thought her unimportant, a mistake on his part. If he thought she was going to be a docile wife who minded his every word, he was in for a huge surprise. Though she was also aware that the Beast should not be taken for granted nor should she assume he thought in a particular way. She had learned he had a cunning mind for strategy, which made him victorious more often than not when it came to battles. He was not a warrior to underestimate.

Raven was shocked when they entered the village occupying the area at the bottom of the hill of the keep. It had changed tremendously from her last visit. More land had been cleared, doubling the number of cottages and the size of the village. The people seemed content enough, though she surmised those who called out greetings to Wolf and his men were his people and those that turned their heads in uncertainty were those original to the Clan Learmonth.

Her attention was quickly drawn to just beyond the new portion of the village, where a large, long structure appeared taking up a good portion of the area.

Her men fell back when Wolf approached and brought his stallion up beside her horse as they ambled toward the structure.

"That's your new home," Wolf said.

Her brow wrinkled as she said, "I thought we were to live in the keep"

"It is not to my liking. I prefer the longhouse of my people, though I have added some of what your people are accustomed to," he admitted.

She shrugged as if indifferent, though she had been looking forward to making her home in a keep once again. "As long as it provides shelter and will keep me warm when cold, I care little about it. Where will my men make their home?"

"I may have forgotten about your men remaining with you, but I can assure you Gorm hasn't," Wolf said.

"Gorm?" she asked, though knew full well who he was and intended to learn even more about him.

"The man who oversees things when I am not here and continues to do so even when I am here. And a man who has been a longtime friend. He is the one who made sure our home was built to my specifications."

When they stopped in front of the longhouse, Wolf summoned, with a wave, a man standing just outside the door.

Raven's eyes caught on the older woman standing next to him, small in size, her white hair drawn back in a tight braid and pinned near the top of her head. Her age was marked by her many wrinkles, but her eyes were alert and intent on her surroundings. She wondered if the woman was Detta, who Oria had mentioned.

Raven dismounted without any help, not that her husband offered any, and her men remained standing behind her once they dismounted.

The man who hurried forward was shorter than most of the men around him and thick in size. He had blond hair that just touched his shoulders and a full, round face with numerous wrinkles at the corners of his eyes, yet he didn't appear old. But then that could have been from his smile that seemed perpetual.

"Welcome home, my lord," the man said.

Raven had forgotten that Wolf didn't only inherit the land and all its holdings, but the title as well.

"It is good to finally be home, Gorm." Wolf pointed to Raven without looking at her. "This is my wife, Raven."

"Welcome, Lady Raven," Gorm said and appeared to be sincere in his greeting.

"A pleasure to meet you, Gorm," she said with a smile and ignored the title. If she was going to learn anything from this man, she'd have to befriend him first.

Wolf turned to her then and perhaps reading her mind, though it was more likely knowing his enemy, said, "It would be wise for you to remember that my men are extremely loyal to me."

"Why should I think otherwise?"

"A thief always looks for opportunities. The only opportunity for you here is to serve me as a good wife. That's a warning you should heed and I'm sure it's the first warning among many to come until you learn your place," he said and turned away.

"I don't serve anyone," Raven said and none too quietly.

Wolf made sure his response was heard by more than his wife as he walked over to Gorm. "You'll learn." He stopped in front of the man. "Her men will need permanent lodging."

"It's been arranged, my lord," Gorm said, his smile never faltering.

"Good. Have them shown to their lodgings," Wolf ordered.

Raven had no intention of suffering any of his dictates. "First, show us where our horses will be sheltered so we may tend them."

"Your horses will be seen to," Wolf said, dismissing her request with a brief wave of his hand and turning as he spoke. "You'll come with me."

"NO!"

Her sharp response had him swerving around and the glare he sent her would have frightened most men.

The man definitely could intimidate with a look alone, but when it came to her men, she defended them regardless of the consequences. "My men and I will see to our horses first, then I will see where you intend to lodge my men."

Wolf approached her. "None of that need concern you."

"It is every bit my concern and until I see to it, I'm not going anywhere with you."

His steps were quick, but she was quicker, her knife out before he reached her.

"I'd think twice about forcing me," she threatened.

He saw that her men hadn't made one move to help her, but he could see on their faces they wanted to. Were they that confident in her abilities or were they somehow aware of when to help her and when not to? He had much to learn about this woman.

It wasn't lost on Wolf that some of his men had now seen his wife pull a knife on him twice or that Gorm had lost his smile, a rarity for him. He couldn't let it happen again.

"Pull your knife on me again and it will be the last time you do," he warned loud enough for those around them to hear.

"Don't threaten me and it won't be necessary," she argued and turned quickly to Gorm. "Let's get this done so my husband isn't embarrassed when he tries to take my knife from me and fails."

Gorm's mouth fell open and Raven's men chuckled.

"Tread lightly, *kona*, or you will be very sorry," Wolf warned and turned away from her, signaling the six warriors who had been by his side since yesterday to follow him and they did, the old woman opening the door to stand to the side then following in after they all entered the longhouse.

Gorm's smile returned, though not as strongly as before and Raven forced a smile to her face to help ease the man's worry.

"Follow me," Gorm said and Raven and her men followed after him.

"Who was the old woman?" Raven asked as she walked alongside Gorm.

"That is Detta. She tends the keep mostly and helps me if needed. She has been here before Wolf took ownership. She is a kind soul and keeps much to herself."

Raven filed that away in her memory. It meant she had much knowledge of the keep itself and of the surrounding land.

Gorm showed them to several buildings, some new, that housed various animals. She was pleased to see their horses would have a good, sturdy shelter. She and her men tended their animals before continuing on to their lodgings. None said a word about Wolf, nor would they dare do so in front of Gorm. Raven was surprised when Gorm led them to a grouping of six cottages and her men were each given a cottage of their own.

"The whole cottage is for me alone?" Iver asked.

"We don't all share one?" Fyn asked, just as surprised.

"No. You each have one of your own," Gorm confirmed.

George smiled. "That means we don't have to contend with your snoring, Iver."

Brod laughed. "We'll hear him straight through the walls he's so loud."

It was good to see her men smile, laugh, and tease one another. Life hadn't been easy and seeing some of that jollity they once shared return warmed her heart.

"Does someone occupy the sixth cottage that's grouped here?" Clive asked.

"That would be me."

They all turned to see a petite, thin woman, her long, blond hair in a braid and over it was a scarf that tied in a knot in the back of her head. She was dressed in the garments of a Northwoman, a dark linen underdress and an apron type tunic over it. Bronze brooches were clipped to each of the two apron straps at her chest and strung beads hung between them. She was pretty even with the scar that ran along one cheek. A small lad, about four years, with a thatch of thick blond hair, was plastered against her, his skinny, little arms hugging tight to her leg.

"This is Greta, our healer," Gorm said with a wide smile.

"I am pleased to meet you," Greta said hesitantly and slowly.

"You're just learning our language, aren't you?" Raven asked.

"I am," Greta said with a pleasant smile and again spoke slowly. "I hope to have my son, Tait, versed in his homeland language as well as your language."

"Wise of you," Raven said.

"We'll help teach him," Fyn said, "if his da doesn't mind."

"Greta is a widow," Gorm said.

"I'm sorry for your loss, Greta. My men are good men. You are lucky to have them nearby," Raven said, seeing the apprehension on the woman's face as she looked at each of them. She couldn't blame her. She'd be living surrounded by men who were strangers to her. In time, she would learn they were good men to have around. She also thought it wise of Gorm to place her men here. With people seeking the healer, many eyes could be kept on them. No doubt her men would realize the same, though she would mention it to them.

Greta nodded, but she still didn't appear convinced.

"Food for my men?" Raven asked, turning to Gorm.

"That is my task," Greta said, Raven's attention returning to her. "I will cook for them, though their task is to help provide the fish or game needed as the other men do. More is stored in the sheds for all to share and so none go hungry."

"We'll do our share," Clive assured her.

"I am cooking a fish stew and will let you know when it is ready," Greta said and took her son's hand to walk past them and enter her cottage.

"We should return to the longhouse now," Gorm advised.

"After I speak alone with my men," Raven said and Gorm made no protest. He nodded and stepped away to give her time with her men.

"These cottages are a bit of a distance from the longhouse, but I suppose it's better than a climb to the keep," Clive said with a nod to the stone keep sitting high on a hill."

"I'll make sure to see all of you throughout each day as we discussed," Raven informed them and lowered her voice. "Something has come up and I want to see what we can find out about it."

The men nodded, knowing whatever it was, it was meant to be spoken about in private.

"Don't get into any trouble," Raven said with a smile.

"Who us?" Brod said, his grin wide, and they all laughed.

Raven fell in step beside Gorm as they made their way back to the keep. She kept a keen eye on her surroundings, taking in everything she could. From what she could see, the two different cultures seemed to be blending well. People didn't appear to purposely avoid one another and smiles and talk were often exchanged among them.

"I hope you will find the longhouse to your liking," Gorm said.

"Does it hold enough heat in the winter?" Raven asked, the cold air feeling as if it had settled permanently into her bones.

"It has served us well in the frigid North," Gorm said.

"But will it serve well here in my homeland?" Raven questioned, but Gorm didn't answer.

She was glad yesterday's snow hadn't lingered into today, though she didn't think they'd seen the last of it. She entered the longhouse and stopped after taking only a few steps, Gorm continuing to the table where Wolf sat with only two of the six men he had entered with earlier. The room was large, the ceiling high with several wood posts appearing as if they not only supported the roof but held the structure together. On the posts were skillfully carved symbols that ran up the height of the posts. A large fire pit occupied the middle of the room and cast off strong heat. Narrow tables and benches were placed on either side of it. The smoke from the fire drifted up and out of a hole in the roof. The floor was rough wood, but that was better than it being a dirt floor. Furs hung from pegs in the wall, and weapons, spears, axes, and more hung in various spots along the wall as well, while others rested against it. It was obvious the Northmen were not lacking in weapons.

Gorm and the two warriors withdrew from the room quietly.

Raven didn't hurry to the table where her husband sat. She took off her cloak, dropping it on one of the benches and stepped close to the fire pit. She almost sighed with pleasure as the heat from it wrapped around and sunk into her. She closed her eyes and let the heat bathe her with its warmth. After a few moments, she hugged herself, hoping to trap the heat deep within her.

"You're cold?"

She turned, surprised to see her husband so close to her. She hadn't heard him approach, but then she'd been too lost in the luxurious heat to pay much heed to anything else. Yet, she had heard concern in his voice and that had surprised her.

"Not anymore," she said, though worried once she moved away from the fire pit, the cold would return. "I suppose this room serves as a Great Hall."

Wolf nodded. "It's our common room. Our quarters are at the other end with two rooms in between."

"What purpose do those other rooms serve?" she asked, noticing there was no bite of anger in his tone or a sharp scowl to his features. But then he was in familiar surroundings and had no need for worry.

"Whatever I wish them to serve?"

"Do they stand unoccupied?" she asked, wondering if others would share the space with them.

"No, we are the only ones who occupy the longhouse, for now."

She didn't know what he meant by that and she didn't intend to ask—yet.

Wolf extended his hand toward a nearby table. "Sit and have a hot brew and I will tell you not only your duties as my wife, but what I expect of you."

"And I will tell you what I expect of my husband," she said and walked to the table, a shiver running through her from the loss of heat or what she was about to hear, she couldn't be sure.

Raven sat with her back to the fire pit and she watched as Wolf took the seat opposite her. There was no denying he was a man of extremely fine features. A woman could get lost in his eyes alone they held such an appealing intensity and strength. She admired strength above all else. One did not survive without it.

He spoke with authority and confidence and a spark of annoyance rose up to poke at her. He expected her to bow to his command and that wasn't going to happen.

"A Northwoman's duties once she weds are not that different from those here in Scotland. She tends the house, sees to the food and drink, sees to the care of the garments, and tends the children. The home is the wife's domain and she takes great pride in it."

"And what does the husband's duties consist of?" Raven asked.

"The husband sees to foreign trade, the planting of the fields, hunts and fishes to provide food, and sees that his family is kept safe."

"So the Northmen wed for a fair exchange of duties," Raven said and was surprised he wasn't annoyed or affronted by her questions.

"There are different reasons we wed just as you Highlanders do. Marriages are arranged to gain wealth and land. Others are made to settle disputes. Most marriages are made to benefit both parties."

Her question slipped from her lips without thought. "Do any Northmen wed for love?"

"They do. Trevor and my sister Demelza wed for love. My father was angry when he found out. He had had other plans for my sister. It took some doing to convince him otherwise."

Curiosity had her asking, "What plans did he have for you that went astray?"

He held her glance as he responded, "I was to wed a maiden from a nearby tribe to strengthen our ties with them, then bring my bride here to expand our holdings in these parts."

"Was she even familiar to you?" she asked, wondering if it had been more than an arranged marriage.

"Eria and I have known each other since we were young."

"Do you love her?" Raven almost bit her tongue for asking. It didn't matter to her. Or did it? How much had they each sacrificed to end what the attack had started?

"I care for her," he said after a brief hesitation.

Had he hesitated not wanting to tell Raven the truth? Or did he have to think of how he truly felt about her?

"Love has no place in our situation. We are bound by an agreement and we shall honor it," he said as if he dared her to say otherwise.

"I will honor the bargain struck," Raven said.

"You will be a good wife?" he asked doubtfully.

"Define good," she challenged with a smile and she was surprised when he returned the smile, and annoyed that she felt a flutter in her stomach, his features turning far too intoxicating. That was something she would not tolerate. She would not allow herself to find her husband attractive.

"I have a feeling that it won't matter how I define good." His smile faded. "Will you see to the duties I explained to you?"

"You told me you would tell me of the duties and also what you expect from me. What do you expect from me, husband?"

He didn't hesitate to respond. "I expect you to share my bed and couple without complaint and give me many bairns. You're never to draw a weapon on me again and you are to hold your tongue when told and I'm sure that's just the start of my list of things I expect from you."

Raven didn't hesitate to have her say. "I slept well enough with you last night, so I don't think sharing a bed with you will be a chore. It depends on how good of a poke you give me as to whether I'll complain or not, and it's up to you to plant your seed good and strong in me so it will be no fault of mine if it doesn't take root there. Don't give me cause to draw a weapon on you and I won't. And to hold my tongue when told will never happen. I lack experience in any wifely chores and I would advise you to seek servants who can see to them. As far as what a husband provides a wife, I can hunt my own food and I can keep myself safe. I can even provide foreign trade."

"So what you're saying is that you don't need anyone to survive," Wolf said.

"I have all the skills I need to survive, but a bargain is a bargain and I will honor it." Raven stood and walked over to snap up her cloak off the bench.

"Raven," Wolf called out as she went to leave.

She turned to see him standing, the familiar tic at the corner of his eye catching her attention.

"You didn't tell me what you expect from me, your husband."

"I expect only one thing," she said and saw her response caught him by surprise.

"What is this one thing you expect from me?" he asked.

She called out her response after turning and heading to the door. "That you let me be who I am."

Chapter Six

Wolf stood by the stream that ran through the woods staring at the rapidly running water. He'd discovered the secluded spot after several visits to Learmonth. Actually, he couldn't claim the discovery as his. He had followed Burnell here one day and found him talking to the leper, Brother Noble. That was when he had first met the leper and oddly enough they had become friends after that, meeting here occasionally over the last couple of years.

He'd found the leper easy to talk with and he had challenged him with his opinions and his vast knowledge. He always got Wolf thinking more deeply and viewing things from a different perspective.

"How is it I find you here alone when you should be celebrating your return home? That's a foolish question since I know you seek the peacefulness of the woods when something troubles you."

Wolf turned with a smile and clasped Trevor in a tight hug and with a solid slap to his back. "At least you have not gone soft wed to my sister."

Trevor stood a bit shy of Wolf's tall height, with a fit build, but then they had fought many a battle together and had spent endless hours at practice with their weapons. His good features had stolen many a woman's heart but he had eyes for only one woman—Demelza, Wolf's sister. Wolf had never let it be known, but he was envious of his close friend. Love of a good woman was something he feared he would never know and his recent arranged marriage had proven that true.

"Your sister sends her love," Trevor said, after stepping away from Wolf.

"She is well and your son, Aric, he is well also?"

"They both do well and surprisingly life here is better than I thought it would be," Trevor said. "While the locals are still skeptical, they don't shun us, and Demelza could not be more pleased that she lives so close to her sister Oria. Demelza wanted to come see you when we received word you were home to stay, but your missive said I was to come alone, so I made an excuse. A poor one I'm afraid, since her eyes narrowed when I told her. So tell me what secret you harbor."

Wolf was quick to be done with it. "I wed Raven."

Shock kept Trevor silent for a moment, then it had him asking, "The lass you have searched for these last five years and sister to Royden and Arran?"

"That would be her," Wolf confirmed.

Trevor shook his head. "Why didn't I know this?"

If Wolf trusted anyone explicitly it was Trevor and he had disliked keeping the news from him. He offered the reason that hadn't set well with him. "The agreement was not to be made known until it was done. Once it was, I wanted to be the one to tell you about it."

"And explain why you did such a foolish thing? All was arranged for you to wed Eria," Trevor argued.

"You know all too well that not capturing Raven changed much and kept me from claiming complete victory. I wanted an end to it. I laid claim to a good portion of land that rightfully belongs to my grandmother and should rightfully be mine," Wolf said with a sense of pride.

"And with Oria wed to Royden, the Clan MacKinnon can be counted in that."

"The MacKinnon may hate me, but they will not go against me, especially now with me wed to their sister."

Trevor shook his head. "But at what price? You are stuck with the MacKinnon woman for life."

"And a challenge she is," Wolf admitted. "Though she is pleasing to look at."

"She submits to you willingly?" Trevor asked.

Wolf rubbed at his close cropped beard. "We haven't consummated the marriage yet. When I discovered that she lived and worked with a band of thieves, five men, these past five years—not a virtuous life—I decided I wouldn't touch her until I can be sure she doesn't carry another man's child."

"Does your grandmother know about this sacrifice of yours?"

"She does."

"You saying no more tells me what she thinks," Trevor said, shaking his head. "Your grandmother would choose you to know love rather than for you to be married to a woman who more than likely hates you."

"Sacrifices are made all the time. Raven presented an offer that would put an end to what I started, her brothers' freedom and a marriage to me so peace would prevail in this area. Though I know I have not seen my last battle, I could do with some peace for a while."

"I agree with you on that. I enjoy my days with my wife and son and see the clan you awarded me grow in number and strength. I will always serve you well, Wolf."

Wolf clasped him on the shoulder. "I have no doubt of that, Trevor. And I am glad you and my sister are happy. Now let us go drink to my marriage and pray my wife doesn't kill me before the month is done."

"What do you mean kill you?" Trevor asked anxiously as they walked toward the village.

"She pulled a knife on me twice and the first time I never saw it coming."

Trevor shook his head. "Tell me about it."

The two men continued to talk as they walked. Neither one of them spotted the wiry man who lurked in the words and hurried off not long after they left to tell Raven what he'd heard.

***

Raven watched her husband and the other man, who she knew to be a longtime friend of Wolf's and husband to his sister Demelza, walk through the village. Many women let their glances linger on them, appreciating their fine features, but the two men were oblivious to them, too busy talking and occasionally laughing.

Naturally, curiosity and instinct had become her constant companions over the years since both were necessities to survival. Now more than ever she depended on them both and both had her wondering if the two were scheming something.

She remained where she was, leaning on the side of a cottage, waiting for Brod. She had sent him after Wolf when she had spotted him walking toward the woods. She intended to keep a good eye on her husband to make certain she and her men were safe. Her husband might say he was an honorable man but until she could see that for herself, she would take no chances.

Raven smiled hearing a grumbling yawn behind her, though she didn't turn. She knew who approached.

"So your old bones are tired are they?" she asked with a slight chuckle.

Clive shook his head as he stepped to her side. "Do I complain about my old bones that much that you know what I will say before I say it?"

"Aye, endlessly," she said and laughed again.

"I tell you, age is a trickster. It sneaks up on you and settles in your bones to attack at the least provocation," Clive said, his glance following where she looked. "Wolf must have sent word to Trevor while we were still at your home."

Raven lowered her voice as Clive had done when speaking about Wolf. "Wolf's sister did not join her husband."

Clive let his opinion be known. "Perhaps Trevor ordered his wife to remain home. It is cold and though the snow stopped, it will return and probably soon."

"Or his sister wasn't invited, the talk being for men alone," Raven said. "Is Brod about?"

"I imagine he'll appear any moment now since his task is complete. Iver is already busy getting to know the woods. Fyn is busy getting to know Greta to see what he can learn from her." Clive grinned. "And it's no toiling task, since his eyes light when he's around her."

"Remind him that she could be there to do the same as him and also what I told all of you about people coming and going since she's a healer. It's a good guise for them to keep an eye on all of you," Raven warned. "And what of George?"

"Once Iver told him the carvings on many of the posts and numerous other things were the Northmen language and they told a tale, George got busy committing them to memory so he can draw them in the dirt with the expectation of Iver translating them for him. He intends to learn the tales and see if they tell us anything."

"It's good the men keep busy and alert," she said.

"Always." Clive lowered his voice to a whisper. "You wanted to talk with us about something."

"I do, but I fear if the six of us gather we will call unwanted attention to us. I will talk with you and Brod and you will share it with the others."

"I am ready to listen."

Both Clive and Raven jumped, not having heard Brod approach.

"Quit sneaking up on us," Clive scolded.

Raven smiled and shook her head. "I still have not mastered your skill of how silently you move about."

"You do well for the time you've had to learn," Brod praised.

"Brod is right," Clive agreed. "For the limited time you had to acquire several skills, you've done exceptionally well. Now let's go to my cottage and talk."

"In whispers," Brod advised. "We are being watched."

Raven huddled close with the two, her voice barely a whisper. "You were followed?"

"No. I spotted who watched—three—and avoided them, but we all need to be aware that eyes are on us all the time," Brod whispered.

"You both will make sure the others know," Raven ordered and followed along with the two to Brod's cottage.

"First, tell me what you learned?" Raven said after they settled in the confines of the small cottage.

Brod spoke in the same cautious whisper that Raven had, detailing the conversation between Trevor and Wolf.

So the Beast didn't think her difficult to look at. Raven shook her head. What difference should that make to her? What was important is that he mentioned again that she had been the one to approach with a proposal.

"That is the very thing I wanted to discuss—his reference to me instigating the proposal, and this is the second time now he mentioned it. I was told the Beast requested it."

"You could have waited, not accepted the proposal. We were close to having what was needed to free your brothers," Clive said.

"Another two years is not close and in that time I could have lost one or both of my brothers. And what of Oria? She could have been sent across the North Sea to her family never to see Royden again. And Purity had to be protected." Raven shook her head. "No. Time had run out. I gladly agreed to the offer. Only now, I wonder if neither I nor Wolf proposed it, then who conceived the offer, and why?"

***

Raven stood in the bedchamber trying to comprehend that this was where she would sleep for the rest of her days. It was a sizeable room with a bed that appeared more a box then the type of bed she'd once been used to. Two roughhewn posts were attached to the two top corners, a board with carvings on it fixed between them, and the same at the two bottom corners with a sizeable box stuffed with a mattress and a mix of blankets and furs sandwiched between all four posts. The posts were carved with a plethora of intricate symbols. The last five years her bed had been where she could make it, so she had no reason to complain about this one. And she had to admit that the bedding looked inviting and comfortable and had a pleasant scent to it.

She was surprised, though glad, to see a fair-sized fireplace on the far wall, roaring with flames. Chests sat to either side of the bed with several candles on top of each. A small table was tucked against one wall with two benches beneath and a larger chest sat in front of the bottom of the bed.

Raven turned when she heard voices approach the closed door and she stepped away from the bed just as the door swung open.

"A bath," Gorm announced and stepped aside as three servants struggled with a large wooden tub.

She had recently washed before arriving home and had made her men do the same. While she had kept herself relatively clean, there had been many more times that hadn't been possible. Grime was a necessary companion for someone who didn't want to be noticed or when thieving.

Ambivalent about the prospect of taking a bath, she watched as a cloth was draped inside the tub and bucket after steaming bucket was carried in to fill it. The more she watched the tub fill, the more her desire to strip and climb in it grew. She could almost feel its heat soaking into her, chasing the cold that forever settled into her.

She was ready to jump to her feet after the last of the buckets were emptied into the tub—when her husband entered the room.

The tub was for him, not her, and a heavy disappointment washed over her to the point she thought she would cry, an annoying thought. She didn't cry. She wouldn't let herself and hadn't let herself. A few days after the attack she cried copious tears while hiding in a small cave. When she'd finished, she swore to herself that they were the last tears she would ever shed and she would do anything and everything to survive and see her family reunited.

Raven stood. "I'll leave you to your bath."

"It's your bath as well. Go first while the water is hot," he said.

She stood staring at him, not trusting him.

"In!" he ordered sharply. "Gorm has told me how he has noticed how much you shiver. The heated water will warm you."

The thought of the hot water soaking into her had her quickly shedding all but her shirt. She had no intention of standing naked in front of him, not ever if she could help it.

She hurried to the tub.

"Your shirt," he cautioned.

"It could use a washing," she said and hurried into the tub before he could stop her. She quickly immersed herself in the luxury of the wet heat. A deep, satisfying moan slipped slowly past her lips as she buried herself up to her neck in the deliciously hot water. She rested her head back against the tub and closed her eyes, not caring about anything at the moment than the heat that infused her.

Desire struck Wolf like a punch to the gut, hearing her drawn out moan that aroused his shaft much too swiftly. Damn, even clothed he found his wife far more appealing than he ever imagined he would. And damn if he'd never get that tempting moan out of his head, not until he heard it spill from her lips as he pounded into her and brought her to—he shook his head.

He had to wait. He had to be sure she didn't nourish another man's seed.

It was good he would wait and bathe when the water was cold. The sharp chill would rid him of the ache in his stiff shaft.

Raven let herself drift in the comforting heat of the water until she felt the heat dissipating, though it still remained warm enough. She had learned the importance of sharing while with her men. Sharing could often be crucial to survival and they had often cuddled close to a campfire at night to make sure none of them froze.

It was the reason she gave no thought to her words before she spoke. "Join me before the water grows too cold." She had no fear of him poking her since he had made it clear he would wait until he was certain she wasn't with child.

Wolf hesitated. He hadn't been with a woman in quite a while and didn't know if his resolve would hold. After all, she was his wife and he had every right to couple with her. Still, he had to be sure when he planted his seed inside her it was his that would grow.

"Do you fear you're not strong enough to resist me and will lose your resolve not to poke me until you discover for yourself no seed grows within me?"

Not only did he grow angry that she realized his thought, but also what she insinuated. "You call me a coward?"

"Your action—or inaction—do that for you."

Wolf stripped and climbed in the tub.

One look at his hard shaft as he entered the tub had her smiling. "Your protruding shaft speaks loudly."

"You would be wise to learn to hold that tongue of yours, wife," he said and settled across from her, bending his legs and planting them on either side of her bent ones.

"And I advise you to grow accustomed to it."

The warmth of the water calmed him some and her snappish tongue managed to cool his desire. The woman was insufferable. She'd probably take command in bed, a place he preferred to command.

"You show no signs of discomfort of me being naked in front of you or joining you in this tub. Is that because you've grown used to seeing naked men?" he challenged.

She laughed and flung her own barb at him." I spent the last five years with six men. What do you think?"

His brow narrowed. "Six men? There are only five with you." He leaned forward, the water splashing past her chin. "Where is the sixth man?"

A foolish slip of the tongue on her part. "He's dead."

Wolf leaned back, though eyed her skeptically. "How can I be sure you speak the truth and he doesn't lurk some place in wait."

"He does lurk someplace—in my heart. I will never forget him. He was the most wonderful man," she said and her chest grew tight with painful memories of losing the man who had been like a father to her.

This was something he never expected and he found himself asking. "You loved him?"

"More than anything," she admitted and the ache in her chest grew.

"Do you carry his child?" he demanded.

"No," she said and after ducking her head to wet her hair completely, she began to scrub it with the slice of soap she had swiped off the stool next to the tub before getting in.

"How do I believe you after you tell me you loved him?" he asked though the question was more for him to contemplate.

"You don't. It's impossible to believe someone you don't trust. Which is why you would never believe me if I told you I've never been touched by a man."

"You claim to be a virgin after telling me you loved a man?" he asked, his chest rumbling with laughter.

"See, you don't believe me," she said and hurried to finish washing, the warmth leaving the water. "And you will wait to discover the truth because you don't trust me."

That she was right annoyed him and that she might be telling the truth annoyed him even more since he would deny himself the pleasure of his wife and the consummation of their marriage until he could satisfy his worry. But he couldn't take the chance—he couldn't trust the word of a thief.

She glared at him. "Can't trust the word of a thief, can you?" The familiar tic at the corner of his eye let her know she was right. "Don't be so surprised that I know what you think. I've seen that look far too many times before not to know what it means." She stood, dropping the slice of soap in front of him. "I am who I am, like it or not, husband."

Wolf watched her climb out of the tub, her shirt clinging to her, showing the outline of a narrow waist and curved hips. Water dripped down her slender legs and her every step, her every movement, was more graceful, more powerful than the next. She grabbed two towels from the stack by the tub and walked over to the hearth slipping one towel beneath her shirt to tuck around her before she slipped the wet shirt off. She dried herself with the other towel. Once she was done, she rinsed her wet shirt near the hearth, the stone hissing where the water hit, then she moved one of the benches in front of the hearth to lay the shirt on it to dry. She went to the bed and snapped up the nightshift that had been left on the bed for her and slipped it on, the towel falling away as the shift drifted down to cover past her knees, allowing no chance at a peek of what lay beneath.

That she had enticed him without seeing a hint of her naked annoyed him, "I won't touch you until I know for sure," he said, condemning himself to ache possibly needlessly for days or weeks, he didn't know.

She turned a cunning smile on him. "I know, and so my virginity continues to remain intact." She went to the bed and snuggled beneath the heavy blanket and furs, cold down to her bones once again.

His wife played well with words that left him wondering, frustrated, and aroused. She talked about trust, but how was he ever to believe anything she said?

When you discover if she is a virgin or not.

The thought haunted him well into his sleep.

Chapter Seven

Raven walked through the quiet village in the pre-dawn light, leaving tracks in the snow that had fallen on and off for the last two days. She had left her bedchamber both days before her husband woke. She hadn't slept well either night, not since she had woken in the middle of the night and found herself pressed against her husband's back, his heat having drawn her to him. She had quickly moved away to hug the edge of the bed.

The memory still haunted her since his warmth had felt so good and so comforting, which bothered her even more. He was her enemy. How could she find comfort in him? But how could she go on thinking him her enemy when the rest of her days would be spent with him?

Life had changed in a single day all those years ago and she had learned to adapt. It had changed again and she needed to adapt once more.

She glanced up at the keep as dawn broke with an overcast sky, painting the keep solemn and gloomy. It would be a good day to explore the place.

First light would have her men up and about and since her husband had been avoiding her, he wouldn't care to her whereabouts. She turned, eager to see if she could spot her men when she spotted a dark figure, his hooded cloak concealing most of him, standing a distance away staring in her direction.

She saw it then, the bow in his hand primed with an arrow. He raised it and she had only a moment to make a decision. She ran since she remembered well that a moving target was more difficult to hit. The arrow missed her but not by much and she had a few feet to go before she reached a cottage she could duck behind. Her walk had taken her away from the village and toward the keep and the sufficient gap between the two left her vulnerable.

Her dark cloak also made her an easy target against the white snow. She whipped it off and let it fall as she ran. The next arrow completely missed her, spiraling well past her, and with not far to go to reach a cottage she hoped she'd make it.

Another arrow flew and missed her again and she knew the assailant only had time for one more shot before she reached cover. She didn't run in a straight path until she had no choice and she knew that was when he'd take his last shot and that was when she'd be the most vulnerable.

She picked up as much speed as she could and dove the last few feet to the side of the cottage. The arrow caught her arm just before she hit the ground.

She barely had time to cringe or see that the arrow looked to have lodged in the upper part of her arm. Pain or blood, she could let nothing stop her from getting to her feet or she'd leave herself vulnerable. Once on them, she ran, darting between cottages, not sure if the assailant followed.

A few people had emerged from their cottages and spotting her stared in shock. She saw one take off in a run and she knew where he was going—to alert Wolf. She preferred the trust and protection of her men and that's where she headed.

Fyn was outside, his arms raised in a strong stretch and his mouth open in a wide yawn when she reached the cottages. His yawn turned into a roar when he spotted her and had the other men spilling out of their cottages, weapons drawn.

Fyn had already reached her, stepping in front of her as his eyes searched the area.

The other men circled her, so she no longer was a target.

"A dark cloaked figure between the keep and village," she said with a wince, finally allowing herself to feel the pain in her arm.

Iver and Brod took off while Clive, George, and Fyn remained with her, Fyn helping her to sit on a bench near his cottage.

Greta had emerged from her cottage and once Raven sat she hurried to her. "I can help."

Fyn blocked her with his body. "We'll see to her."

"No you won't—MOVE!" Wolf bellowed as he approached them, fury in his eyes.

Fyn looked to Raven.

"This isn't her choice and don't make me tell you again to move," Wolf warned, the commanding timbre in his voice enough to make any sane person obey.

"Do as he says, Fyn," Raven said, before it escalated into an unreasonable situation.

Wolf's fiery glare turned to complete rage when he saw the arrow that protruded from his wife's arm and the blood that soaked her shirtsleeve.

"I should go for Wren," Clive said, stepping forward.

Wolf looked to Greta.

"She is a far more experienced healer than I am," Greta said, "but it will take her time to get here and the arrow shouldn't wait that long to be removed."

"Go and fetch the woman but take George with you," Wolf ordered with a nod to Clive, then looked to Gorm, who stood not far from his right. "Send six warriors with them."

Clive went to protest but the flair in Wolf's dark eyes warned him against it. He gave a nod and he and George followed after Gorm.

Fyn moved from Raven's side to step behind her as soon as Wolf stepped toward her.

Wolf lowered himself to rest on his haunches in front of her. "You will keep your eyes on me and tell me what happened as Fyn helps Greta remove the arrow from your arm."

"I don't need to be distracted from the pain," she argued.

"Believe me, wife, you do," he said and reached out and took her hand.

Raven glanced down at his hand wrapped tightly around hers, its strength strangely comforting. She looked up at him ready to tell him she didn't need his help, and yet there was something about the way he held her hand, that to her surprise, she favored.

"Don't waste your breath. I'm not letting go," Wolf warned.

It struck her odd that he was staying with her. He didn't have to. He could have gone off to search for the culprit, and leave her alone to deal with her wound, but he hadn't. He stayed. He didn't leave her to face this alone. His thought was of her and that puzzled Raven.

"I need to get some clean cloths, then you'll need to break the end of the arrow off so that you can pull it out," Greta said to Fyn. "If you could tear away her sleeve while I fetch what I need, that would help."

Fyn nodded and saw to the task.

Wolf was pleased that Fyn was gentle in ridding Raven of the bloody sleeve, while he kept her occupied with talk. "I spoke briefly with Iver and Brod, both impatient to chase the culprit that wounded you. The only thing they could tell me was that a dark cloaked figure shot at you when you were in the open space between the keep and the village."

Raven nodded, still baffled by his actions. She didn't know if his talk would distract from the physical pain she was about to suffer. However, she had found physical pain easier to bear than pain that touched the heart. A wound healed sooner or later. A pain to the heart never truly healed. It lingered and would open unexpectedly and you would suffer the hurt all over again.

She would suffer the pain of the arrow and be done with it. It was the pain Wolf had caused her family and scarred her heart that had yet and perhaps never would heal. And yet she found herself confused by him. He treated her well enough and had eventually helped her clan. What enemy does that?

It concerned Wolf that she was so quiet, not saying something to annoy him. It meant that she was in more pain than she would say. So he said something he knew would annoy her.

"I will make sure one of my warriors remains with you at all times from now on," he ordered.

"You will not," Raven snapped. "I need no one following me about."

"Why? Are you up to something I don't know about?" Wolf challenged.

"With a husband that ignores me, I need to find something to do around here," she quipped.

Her tongue was quick and her barbs could sting more often than not and Wolf felt that one, but he tossed it back at her. "I will make sure to spend more time with you."

"Oh, joy!" she said and rolled her eyes.

Greta returned and placed a basket of clean cloths on a small bench she had Fyn fetch for her.

"It would be wise to hold her still," Greta said to Wolf.

He surprised Raven when he lifted her gently in his arms and sat on the bench, his one arm remaining around her waist to hold her tight against him and his other hand latching onto the forearm of her wounded arm in a firm grip, keeping it from moving.

Once settled, Wolf turned his face to her and he hastily stopped the catch in his chest before it fell from his lips in a sharp gasp. However, he failed to stop the words that hurried out of him. "You have the most stunning blue eyes I have ever seen."

She stared at him, speechless. Men had commented on her eyes before, but never the way he did. There was something intimate about the way he'd said it. And she had no response for him.

"Tell me about the culprit," he said, his lips not far from hers.

She felt him tighten his hold on her, which meant Fyn was about to break the tail of the arrow off. She focused on her husband's dark eyes, full of strength and actually found comfort in them.

"He was small in size." She clamped her eyes shut and gasped at the pain that shot through her arm. She felt his brow rest against hers.

"Small in size, you say," Wolf said to distract her.

She nodded, glad for the feel of his warm breath whispering across her face. He was closer than anyone had ever been to her and for the first time in what seemed like forever she didn't feel alone.

"And fast, so fast," she whispered.

His breath faintly brushed her lips. "I'm going to find him and make him pay for hurting you."

His grip grew tight again and this time Raven latched on to his arm around her waist, needing to hold on to him for what was to come next.

"I've got you, wife. I won't let go."

He whispered so softly Raven could barely hear him and she thought, for a brief moment, his words sounded as if he actually cared for her.

The pain stabbed so sharply that it caught her unaware and her eyes went wide before everything went black.

"It's good she fainted," Greta said, I can clean the wound before she wakes."

"Be quick if you can," Wolf ordered and looked down to where his wife's head rested on his shoulder. He had been surprised at the shot of fear that had rushed through him when her head dropped like a stone on his shoulder. He didn't know why it had upset him so, he barely knew Raven. She could annoy him endlessly and yet he also admired that about her. She hadn't shown him an ounce of fear or submitted to his every word. And she defended her family and her men regardless of what she might suffer. If she did that for the family they would have together, then she would make a better wife than he had expected.

Wolf felt the slight stir of her body against him and knew she was fighting to wake. "She's waking. Are you almost done?"

"Aye, just a bit more," Greta said. "The bleeding is but a trickle which is good."

Wolf watched as Fyn gently kept Raven's arm aloft for Greta to tend it. He hoped Greta would be done with it before Raven woke, but feeling her stir more strongly he doubted it.

"Stay as you are, wife. It is almost done," he said softly.

Raven managed to look up and finally get her eyes open to gaze upon Wolf's face, and winced as a cloth was wrapped around her arm. She let her head rest on his shoulder, not having the strength or will to do otherwise. After a few moments, she felt him stand, holding her firm in his arms.

"I'm taking you to our bedchamber. You will rest and Wren will be here soon," he said as he walked.

A bit disoriented, she said what she thought. "You are kind to me."

"You are my wife. It is my duty to see you protected and see you kept safe."

She thought, but once again spoke her thought aloud. "We are enemies."

"Only if we allow ourselves to be," he whispered.

Once in their bedchamber, he laid her on the bed, removed her boots, but left the wool socks on her that he had made sure were tucked in her boots for her to use, and her plaid, leaving her in her shirt. He eased her under the blankets, brushed her hair away from her face and ordered, "Rest. It won't be long before Wren arrives."

"We need to talk about why someone tried to kill me," she said, grateful for the warmth and comfort of the bed.

"We will, but for now rest."

She closed her eyes, the pain in her arm taking all of her focus. She heard the door close and knew she was alone. She allowed herself to drift, to find a way to cope with the pain. She found something nagging at her more than the pain, something about the arrow in her arm, something she had caught when she had first glanced at it. She let herself drift to see what she could find and after some time her eyes opened wide.

Raven paid no mind to the pain in her arm, she got dressed with some difficultly, wincing each time she moved her injured arm too much and opened the bedchamber door to the sound of arguing voices. They grew louder as she approached the common room.

"This is how you protect my daughter? You might not value her as a wife but you pledged to honor your agreement and that means keeping Raven safe."

Raven recognized her da's angry voice and hesitated along the narrow hall that ran from the bedchamber to the common room with two rooms off to either side of the hall.

"I will see my wife kept safe," Wolf argued.

"Yet she suffers an arrow through her arm."

That was Royden and he was as angry as her da.

"He could have killed her." Her da pointed out.

Raven didn't want to think of that. After fighting these last five years to return home to her family only to die was an unbearable thought.

"I will find the one who did this and the reason why, and he will suffer for what he did," Wolf said with a confidence that didn't have Raven doubting him.

"You all should temper your tone. You will disturb Raven."

Though the voice was softer, Raven recognized it. It was Oria.

"Oria is right. Raven needs rest right now."

That female voice was stronger and easily recognizable. It was Wren. Raven was glad to hear them both and proceeded into the room.

"What are you doing out of bed?" Wolf cautioned and went to her, his arm quickly circling her waist.

"I remembered something about the arrow that lodged in my arm," she said.

Wolf nodded, knowing what she would say. "A Northmen symbol was carved near the tip of the arrow."

"You tried to kill my sister," Royden accused with a shout.

"That ends it. Raven returns home with us," her da demanded.

Wolf's hand shot up when Royden went to approach and Oria was quick to grab her husband's arm.

"My wife stays with me and no one from here tried to kill Raven," Wolf said with the strength of a man who spoke the truth. "Many Northmen engrave their arrows in the hope that they will claim many lives. Some tribes use the same symbols, but the one on the arrow that struck Raven is a common one and refers to no particular tribe."

"One thing it does tell us," Royden said, "is that the arrow belonged to a Northman."

"Or the one who used it wanted us to believe that," Wolf said.

Wren stepped forward. "You can speak or argue about this all you want but Raven's wound needs tending."

Wolf looked to see the cloth covering her arm had turned bloody. "You shouldn't have gotten out of bed."

"As much as I don't want to admit it, he's right," Royden said.

"Enough!" Raven snapped and foolishly raised her wounded arm to wave her hand at her brother. A fierce pain shot through her arm and had her going limp and leaning against her husband, who immediately lifted her in his arms.

"Sit her at the table so I can tend the wound," Wren ordered and Wolf did as she said.

Wolf remained near his wife's side, his hand on her shoulder while Wren gently unwound the cloth covering Raven's wound.

The door to the common room opened and two of Wolf's warriors entered along with Brod and Clive.

"We lost the tracks," Wolf's warrior said once he came to a stop in front of him. "And we weren't able to find any evidence of anyone camping in the immediate area. I have extended the search, but have found nothing so far."

With Iver not there, she knew the man continued to follow the culprit's trail, but said nothing. She wanted to see what he might find before confiding anything to her husband.

"See that our best archers are assigned to the battlements in the keep," Wolf ordered.

The warrior nodded and both warriors left. Clive and Brod remained.

"You do well?" Clive asked.

"Minor pain nothing more," Raven said. "I will speak with you later."

"You will speak with them tomorrow and don't bother to argue with me about it," Wolf warned, a glare in his dark eyes challenging her.

"Tomorrow is soon enough," Brod said. "Rest well."

Raven watched the two men go, understanding the message. It would take until tomorrow for Iver to return, so it could wait until then for them to talk. And it was a good reason for her not to argue with her husband.

"You disturbed the wound that was doing nicely, causing it to bleed once again," Wren said. "You need to rest it for a week or more so it may heal properly. You were lucky it caught such a small portion of your arm. That arrow could have done far more damage than it did."

"Are you going to listen this time?" Royden asked with a glare at his sister.

"She'll listen," Wolf said.

"You don't know her," Royden warned. "She won't listen."

"I know the way of a warrior and your sister is a warrior. She is wise enough to know that if she does not let her arm heal properly, she'll never skillfully wield her weapon again."

Royden appeared annoyed but nodded. "You're right about that."

"Come, Oria, help me get Raven settled in bed where she will spend the rest of the day," Wren said in a tone that warned of a lecture if her words weren't heeded.

***

It wasn't until later that night that Wolf joined his wife in their bedchamber. Her family had lingered long enough to be satisfied that Raven was safe and for Wren to be done and promise she'd return in two days to check on Raven.

He found her standing by the fireplace in a nightshift that had been provided for her and went to admonish her.

She held up her hand, keeping her injured arm close to her side. "Don't scold me. I needed out of that bed if only for a little while."

"A short reprieve," he said and proceeded to disrobe.

She didn't turn her eyes away, having grown accustomed to seeing him naked and not at all uncomfortable with it. How that had happened, she didn't know. She hadn't given much thought to coupling with him when the agreement had been made. It hadn't been important then. What had mattered to her was her brothers' freedom and reuniting her family. Now faced with the prospect, it seemed more daunting.

She went to turn away from the hearth and moved too fast, a pain shooting through her arm and turning her lightheaded. She did the first thing that came to her mind, she called out to her husband, "Wolf."

He turned and it took only a few short steps to reach her side, seeing she had paled. His arms went around her and she dropped her head on his shoulder to rest and allow the lightheadedness to pass.

"Should I fetch Greta?" he asked, worried over her.

"No, some lightheadedness, that's all," she assured him.

"You are sure?"

"I am. It's already passed," she said turning her face up to look at him, not realizing he had lowered his head, leaving it far too close to her face.

Wolf tried to ignore her stunning blue eyes, intent on his lips, and a hint of passion sparking in them. He warned himself to look away, but the tip of her tongue stole out between her lips to roam slightly over them, and all was lost.

His hand went to the back of her neck, gripping it as his lips came down on hers with a need he had to satisfy—her need.

Chapter Eight

Raven gripped his arm, needing something to keep her on her feet, her legs losing some of their strength as the most exquisite sensations rocked her body. His kiss was as strong and commanding as he was, taking charge, demanding she respond, and giving her every reason to willing do so. And she did. She didn't want to resist or deny him. She enjoyed the feel of his lips and when the tip of his tongue teased her lips apart, she opened her mouth to welcome him.

Lord, but she was drowning in the most sensational pleasure. If a kiss was so pleasurable, she couldn't imagine the immense pleasure coupling would bring. Instinct, curiosity, or need, she didn't care what it was that had her pressing her body against his, she wanted to experience more. His arm went around her waist and pulled her tighter against him and when his hard shaft rubbed against her, it set off a sensation in her that sent a wicked shudder through her.

He silently warned himself to stop, no good would come of it. It could go no further. But he didn't want to stop. He found immense satisfaction in the kiss, in feeling her pressed against him, of knowing she had a need for him.

Or was it for him? Or was it a need of hers that hadn't been satisfied in some time?

The sobering thought had him ending the kiss and taking a hasty step back. Her hand fell loose of his arm and seeing her unsteady on her feet, he reached out and held her arm until her legs turned firm, then he moved away from her.

Annoyance or frustration had him lashing out at her. "Your kiss tells me you're not inexperienced when it comes to a man."

Raven kept the hurt of his barb from showing. While she had enjoyed the kiss, he evidently thought otherwise about it. And she decided the truth would strike much sharper than any barb she threw.

"Or it could be that it was my first kiss and I found it more pleasurable than I ever imagined it would be." Truth was a powerful arrow and she was pleased to see her husband couldn't hide the sting it had caused him.

Wolf shook his head. "I doubt the man you loved didn't kiss you. Now go to bed."

She could correct him, tell him the truth, but she didn't think he'd believe her. Besides, she was tired of defending herself. Let him think what he would. She shivered and hugged herself, rubbing her arms.

Seeing her tremble, he thought on what Gorm had told him about how often she shivered or how she would mention the cold.

"You're cold more often than not. Why is that?" he asked curious, knowing this region had its fair share of cold winters and that most of the people had adapted. Why not her?

"The first winter on my own was a difficult one. If it hadn't been for—" She stopped abruptly.

"The man you loved?" Wolf snapped, thinking she had shared more than kisses with the man and feeling the fool for thinking it could be otherwise.

"Get in bed," Wolf ordered, pointing to the bed.

She wasn't about to argue since a deep shiver had taken hold of her. She eagerly slipped under the covers, hoping warmth would chase the chill and the horrid memories. But the shivers didn't stop and without the distraction of talking with her husband, the pain in her arm made itself known. Between the pain and the cold, she remained restless until she thought she had no other choice than to plead for her husband's warmth. She turned her head to find him standing beside the bed.

"Are you in pain?" he asked.

"I've suffered worse."

"That's not what I asked," he snapped. "Are you in pain?"

"A bit of pain but more cold," she admitted, seeing his determination to get an answer and though his rebuke had been curt, it also held concern.

She was relieved when he slipped beneath the blanket. She told herself it was warmth she needed from him, nothing more, but she knew his arms would also bring a sense of comfort and she longed to feel that more than anything.

He eased his arm under her shoulders and lifted her gently to move her to lie against him.

Raven shivered as the heat of his body began to seep into her. And when he turned wrapping himself around her, his leg going over hers and his arms easing carefully around her so as not to disturb her wound, she sighed not only from the heat that embraced her, but from the comfort that seeped into her.

"Thank you for sharing your warmth," she said, resting her head on his shoulder.

"You need only ask if you want something from me, Raven. If I can give it to you, I will."

"A good thing for a wife to know," Raven said, feeling sleep sneak up on her.

"And will you do the same for me—give me what I ask?"

Her words echoed his. "If I can, I will."

"Good, then when Iver returns from tracking the culprit you will bring him to me so together we can hear what he has learned."

"You have a sharp eye, husband," she said and yawned while reminding herself to tell her men to be more vigilant around him.

"Something you would do well to remember," he cautioned.

"Believe me, I will," she said as her eyes closed and sleep claimed her.

Not so Wolf. Though he felt a strange satisfaction holding his wife in his arms and keeping her warm, sleep eluded him. He couldn't stop thinking about the man she had loved. He could see and hear, when she spoke about him, how much she not only loved him, but admired him. Why that should annoy him, he didn't know, but it did. He supposed with her now being his wife, and belonging to him, he didn't want to think of her ever having belonged to another. Yet she continued to claim she hadn't known any man intimately. He couldn't believe that possible after hearing that this man continued to live in her heart.

He admonished himself for lingering on a matter that made no difference to his present situation. It should not matter to him at all. But for some reason it did.

The kiss.

He hadn't expected to enjoy kissing her so much. Hadn't expected to get lost in the kiss as much as he had. Hadn't expected to feel something stir deep inside him that he'd never felt before with any woman. Strange. Compelling. Enticing. He wasn't sure how he'd describe it since it left him with a deep desire for more and he knew he'd explore it again.

At the moment though, he had something more important that needed his attention.

Finding the man who had attempted to kill his wife.

***

"My wife is all right, Greta?" Wolf asked when he entered the common room, alarmed that she had requested to see him.

"She does well, my lord. Her arm continues to heal and she wisely follows Wren's instructions. Wren is pleased with how well it has healed in only a week's time and feels the scar will be the only reminder of the incident."

"So Wren told me. Why then did you request to see me?" he asked. "And have you seen my wife?"

"She walks with Clive, Brod, and Iver," Greta said. "Fyn and George mind Tait for me. You wanted to know when the leper visits. He's in the woods and I am having food and drink prepared for him now."

"I will take the food and drink to him," Wolf said, glad to visit with the leper since it had been a while since their last visit, and he always enjoyed talking with him.

"I will have both brought to you as soon as it is ready," Greta said and took her leave.

Wolf sat alone in the common room. While his wife had brought Iver to him the day after the attack for him to tell them both what he had found, he still harbored doubts that she and her men were as forthcoming as they should be.

He had to admit that Iver had been open about what he had discovered. He had tracked the culprit who had harmed his wife to an area where signs of a campfire confirmed that men had been camping there, no doubt in wait for their cohort. It had been difficult to track after that since the various tracks had gone in different directions.

At least it confirmed what Wolf had surmised. The man had not acted alone. There were others involved. He had thought to assign some of his warriors to follow Raven but it proved senseless since he had seen for himself that her men had taken it upon themselves to make sure they followed wherever she went, except when she entered the longhouse. He felt she was safe with them so he didn't have his warriors follow, though he had told them to keep a good watch when she was around. He'd also placed more warriors on the battlements. From there they could see a group of men coming from afar except where the forest was the thickest.

Once food and drink for the leper were brought to him, Wolf took it to the woods, to the spot by the stream where he had met with him several times.

Wolf left the sack of food and skein of wine near the tree where he'd always left it and moved to sit on a stump a good distance away. When the leper didn't appear, he called out, "Brother Noble."

A cough sounded before a brown-robed cleric, slightly stooped, emerged from behind a thick tree. His hood hung down to hide his face and gloves covered his hands. There wasn't any part of him that wasn't covered.

"How are you?" Wolf asked, still surprised at their friendship, since they had little in common and held different beliefs. But perhaps the link that connected them as friends was their differences.

"Kind of you to ask, Wolf, I do well enough," Brother Noble said in his raspy voice. "And you? Have things finally settled for you?"

"Not as I expected, but for now there is peace—I think. I wed Raven of the Clan MacKinnon."

"Don't you consider her your enemy?"

No judgment, no disparaging remark, or condemnation, a question that simply gave thought and that was what Wolf enjoyed about the leper. His words always gave him pause to think and he did so now aloud. "I actually never gave thought to her before the attack. She was meant to wed a Northman of my choice after my warriors conquered her clan, just as I had done with the other conquered clans. I never expected her to escape and become a thorn in my side these last five years. Though I will admit she was constantly on my mind and not in a good way. I couldn't understand how she avoided capture. Now I know. She dressed like a lad and joined a band of thieves." He shook his head. "But you must grow tired of hearing me complain about her."

"Not at all. I hoped to see peace brought to this area once again and it would seem your unselfish act in marrying Raven has answered my prayers."

"It wasn't my unselfish act. It was Raven's. It was her unselfishness and courage to seek a marriage with me as a solution to freeing her brothers and regaining some of her land for her family."

"Raven proposed this odd union?" Brother Noble asked.

"That was what I was told when I was approached about the agreement, though I did not take kindly to it at first. After some thought and discussion with my grandmother, I realized it was for the best. I could finally settle and live with less strife."

"She is a good wife then?"

"I haven't determined that yet," Wolf said.

"She is troublesome?"

Wolf scratched his close-cropped beard. "She has a mind of her own which can prove troublesome at times. She also has a fierce loyalty to those she cares for and loves."

"And she has neither for you?"

"I don't believe so," Wolf said with a scrunch of his brow.

"It sounds like you aren't sure," Brother Noble said.

Wolf shook his head. "I don't know what to make of her sometimes."

"If you don't know what to make of her, how then do you feel about her?"

"I don't know," he admitted as if the answer surprised him. "I'd been angry with her for foiling my plans, though angrier at myself that a young woman could do what powerful men failed to do… defeat me. There are few who can claim victory over me and that she has done so with nothing more than a band of common thieves was a solid blow to my reputation. And—"

"Something more, you hesitate to admit?" Brother Noble asked after Wolf abruptly stopped speaking.

Wolf ran his fingers through his dark hair, pulling it away from his face and turning his head for a moment as if he wasn't sure if he should answer the leper.

"Tell me what troubles you, my son," Brother Noble encouraged, his voice raspier than before.

Wolf didn't hesitate this time. He felt the need to rid himself of the frustration. "She is a beautiful, appealing woman, and I find I desire her far too much."

"Is it that you desire her that troubles you or is it that you find yourself feeling something for her that presents the problem?"

Wolf thought a moment. "As usual, you've given me something to think about."

"It is good to allow things to ponder in your thoughts when possible. It often lets you see things more clearly and make wiser decisions."

A soulful blare of a horn echoed through the woods and had Wolf bolting to his feet.

"What is that?" Brother Noble asked.

"Someone from my homeland arrives. I must go," Wolf said. "You are welcome to remain here as long as you wish. Shelter will be provided for you."

"I am grateful for your generosity, but I have a mission for the monastery I must see to."

"Until next you visit, travel safe, Brother Noble," Wolf said, letting the leper know he looked forward to seeing him again.

"God go with you, my son, and may patience be your friend when dealing with your wife."

Wolf shook his head. "There is not enough patience in the land to deal with Raven."

Chapter Nine

Wolf was surprised to see Lars entering the village along with six Northmen from his tribe. Lars was like a brother to his father and the one man his father depended on most, trusted the most, and he wondered why his father had sent him.

Wolf braced himself when Lars drew near. He was a man of generous girth, with the strength of three men, and his hug could crush a man. His long hair burned as bright as the sun and flames combined and was braided in several places, and his thick beard was braided in two places and reached past his chest. He was draped in leathers and furs with a battle-axe hanging from the belt at his thick waist, his favorite weapon and one he wielded with extreme skill.

"WOLF!" Lars cried out and grabbed him in a hug that lifted him clear off the ground.

After Wolf was back on his feet, he offered, "Drink to quench that thirst your journey has cost you and food enough to fill your belly."

Lars slapped his sizeable stomach and laughed. "An offer I can't refuse."

Wolf spotted his wife as they got near the longhouse. She was with Iver and from the look of them both, dirt clinging to their garments and pine needles poking out of her hair, they'd been in the woods.

"Raven!" he called out and when she turned his way, she smiled and it was like a touch of sunshine on an overcast day. He felt a catch in his chest and silently berated himself for letting her smile affect him. But if he was honest, it wasn't only her smile that played havoc with his heart and tormented his loins. It was her beauty that shined through the smudges of dirt and the way she held herself erect with such confidence.

"She's a beauty even though she's a bit messy," Lars said as she approached them. "You and she will make fine looking babies together."

A reminder that it was not yet a possibility poked at him annoyingly. He had wanted a marriage with little angst, the main reason he had agreed to wed Eria. She was sweet and kind and would have made a good, obedient wife. She was the complete opposite of Raven.

"And who is this giant of a man?" Raven asked when she stopped beside her husband.

Lars stepped forward, his arms reaching out to grab Raven in a hug.

"Stop right there, giant," she ordered, her knife in her hand, warning him off.

Wolf glared at the knife. How did she do that? The knife was suddenly there in her hand. He hadn't even seen her reach for it and he was right beside her.

Lars' hands went up, but his generous smile stayed steady. "Impressive. I didn't even see you reach for your weapon. You are lucky to have a warrior woman for a wife, Wolf. She will serve you well."

"What's a Northman doing here?" Raven asked, returning her knife to its sheath without taking her eyes off the large man.

"I've brought important word from Wolf's father."

While Wolf would have preferred Lars hadn't shared that information, he understood why Lars hadn't hesitated to respond to his wife. Any good warrior responded without question to an authoritative command, and Raven certainly had spoken as one accustomed to such status.

"Let's retire to the longhouse and while you fill that large belly of yours with food and drink you can tell me of my father's message," Wolf said.

Raven followed right along with them, having no intention of being left behind. Besides, she was curious as to the message.

"Detta!" Lars yelled, seeing the elderly woman and ran to swing her up into a hug.

Raven remained silent as she walked alongside her husband. The quick way his eyes had traveled over her and the disapproval she'd seen there of her appearance all but confirmed it wouldn't be long before he said something to her. At the moment though, she was more curious as to why Lars was greeting Detta like a long lost friend. With all that had been going on, she hadn't paid much heed to Detta, the woman doing as Oria had told her—keeping to herself. But seeing the way Lars greeted her poked Raven's curiosity.

"What were you doing in the woods?" Wolf demanded.

She saw no reason not to tell him the truth. "Iver was teaching me how to track and there's no need to remind me about my arm. I'm cautious with it and it heals nicely."

Something he already knew since he had insisted at taking a look himself when Wren was last here. But he hadn't been the only one, her da had insisted as well. But her da had done so out of love and worry for his daughter. What had been Wolf's reason?

Before he could chastise her like her brothers once did, she said, "Lars seems to know Detta."

"He's been here before."

A hasty response, at times, could be suspect. That's what the old man used to tell her. She grinned and called out, "How long has it been since you've seen Detta, Lars?"

The way the giant of a man froze told her what she thought and she turned to her husband. "You lied to me."

"Detta is from my tribe."

The news brought Raven to an abrupt halt. "Are you telling me you planted an old woman here to spy for you?"

"And what of Clive?" he shot back. "His visits here as a merchant weren't meant to acquire information for you?"

"You compare—equal it to—Clive visiting as a traveling merchant to sending an old woman to live away from her family for years?" she asked.

"All in my tribe do what is necessary and without question," Wolf said. "A lesson, as my wife, you should learn."

Raven didn't follow right away when he walked off. Something poked at her. Why send an old woman here to spy? And why leave her here after he'd laid claim to Learmonth? Didn't she have family to return to?

Her husband and Lars had disappeared inside the longhouse, but Detta had turned and was walking off toward the keep.

"Detta," Raven called out and the old woman stopped and turned to face her.

"Lady Raven," Detta said with a gentle smile.

Raven could see past the years that had aged her to the beauty she must have once been, years that hadn't robbed her lovely, soft green eyes of their luster. "We've yet to actually meet."

"My duties are at the keep, yours are at the longhouse, but if you should need me for anything—"

"I do need you," Raven interrupted and caught the slight rise of the woman's brow.

"How may I help?" Detta asked.

"I'll let you know. You can go now," Raven said purposely dismissing her as one would a servant and once again caught the slight rise of her brow. There definitely was more to the woman than she was being told.

Raven hurried into the common room to take a seat next to her husband. Lars was already busy eating from the wealth of food on the table.

"You're cold?" Wolf asked, seeing she kept her wool cloak on and hugged it around her.

"Snow is in the air," Lars said between bites. "I can smell it."

"He's right," Raven said with a shiver. "The animals are restless in the woods. They sense something is coming."

"Ida," Wolf called out to the servant lass who lingered nearby. "Bring my wife a hot brew."

As the lass hurried off, Wolf got up and went to the table next to theirs, retrieved his fur cloak and brought it back to drape over his wife's shoulders and tuck around her.

His thoughtful actions stunned Raven and he surprised her even more when he sat close enough for their sides to touch and for his leg to lean against hers under the table, sharing his heat with her as he did each night in bed.

"It is good you care for your wife. Marriage is much better when you care for each other," Lars said.

Raven was surprised when her husband smiled.

"My wife does have very strong feelings for me," Wolf said and turned a wide grin on her.

She grinned back at him. "I certainly do have strong feelings for my husband."

"Wonderful. Your father thought for sure one of you would kill the other before you were wed for a full moon cycle." Lars shook his head. "Not so your mother. She insisted you would make a good husband and you would treat your wife well." He laughed. "She's proved your father wrong again."

Raven hugged the tankard of hot cider Ida had brought, warming her hands, and wondering how his mother could think that when she knew Raven had reason to hate her son. Or did his mother know something she didn't?

"What message do you bring from my father, Lars?" Wolf asked to turn the subject away from how he and Raven felt toward each other. It was a thorn in both their sides, one he feared might prove impossible to remove.

Lars rested his beefy arms on the edge of the table. "Brynjar is seeking a union with Eria."

Raven felt her husband's anger surge, his arm muscles growing taut against her.

"Her family can't be serious to agree to such a dreadful union," Wolf said, trying to keep hold on his anger. "Eria wouldn't last but a day with the brutal man." He shook his head. "Brynjar doesn't care about a union with her tribe. He does this to see what I'll do."

"Eria's family asked that she be sent here to you, fearing he'll abduct her, leaving them no choice but to yield," Lars said.

"That's exactly what Brynjar wants," Raven said. "The perfect excuse to return here and finish what he started." She looked at her husband. "He wants his revenge on you. Maybe his men are already here and it's one of them who pierced my arm with an arrow. It did have a Northmen symbol carved in it."

Lars eyes spread wide at the news. "Someone attempted to kill you?"

"She was too fast for him, the arrow caught the flesh of her arm," Wolf said. "I sent trackers but whatever men the culprit met up with had dispersed in different directions, leaving it difficult to follow from there. The men continue to search to see if anything can be found."

"Well it certainly was no Northman from our tribe," Lars said and gave a nod to Raven. "You're safe with us."

She liked to believe she'd eventually be able to stop looking over her shoulder, but she wasn't sure about that.

"Since Brynjar expects you to bring Eria here, she'll stay where she is," Lars said.

"No!" Wolf and Raven said in unison.

Lars smiled. "You think alike. That is good, means less arguing between you both."

Wolf doubted that and from the way his wife rolled her eyes, he knew she thought the same.

"It would be easier to battle Brynjar on land unfamiliar to him," Raven said.

Lars asked what Wolf had been thinking. "You are familiar with Brynjar?" Lars' fingers disappeared into his thick beard, giving his chin a good scratch as his eyes settled on her in question.

"All foreigners on my home soil are suspect to me," she said, glaring at Lars.

Lars smiled and looked to Wolf. "I like your wife."

Wolf ignored Lars's remark and turned a scowl of his own on his wife. "Brynjar is not only a dangerous man but an evil one. If he should show himself here again you will keep your distance."

"What do you mean if?" Raven challenged. "You know he will come after Eria, though that will be just an excuse and do you not also use it as an excuse for him to come here, so you may finish what was started between you both?"

Lars saluted her with his tankard. "A quick mind as well, and she's right. It must be finished between you and Brynjar. His evil ways disturb the peace in our homeland. He needs to die."

"So where did you leave Eria?" Raven asked and shook her finger at him. "And don't look at me like you don't know what I mean. All knew Wolf wouldn't hesitate to protect the woman he was to wed. And his father would send the man he would trust the most to bring her safely here. So where is she?"

Lars shook his head. "Your wife's mind works far too quickly. There'll be no secrets between you two."

"There better not be," Raven said.

"That works both ways," Wolf warned, leaning his head down so their faces almost touched. "That means later you will tell me the actual reason you were in the woods." He lifted his head and gave a quick nod to Lars. "Where is she?"

"Eria wanted to see her best friend," Lars said.

"She's with Greta," Wolf said and Lars nodded. "And if I know my father, he's ordered you to remain here to help me."

"You wound me, Wolf," Lars said, with a pound to his chest. "Your father didn't have to order me. I want to be here."

"I have no doubt of that, Lars, and I'm glad you're here," Wolf said.

Raven stood. "I'm going to visit with Eria."

"Sit. You'll wait for me," Wolf ordered.

Raven laughed. "You forget so soon that I don't take well to orders?" She dropped his cloak beside him on the bench and turned to leave.

He reached out quickly and grabbed her arm and cursed when she cried out. He dropped his hand off her, realizing he had grabbed her wounded arm, and hurried to his feet. His arm shot around her waist. "I didn't mean to hurt you."

She rested her forehead on his chest, squeezing her eyes shut tight against the sharp pain piercing her arm.

"Raven," he said softly, gently rubbing her back while keeping his other arm around her waist. "Are you all right? Should I send for Greta?"

Raven raised her head, a wince on her face. "No, but we should go see her to be sure you didn't disturb the wound."

"Is this a ruse to get your way?" he asked, but seeing the pain in her eyes he didn't believe so, though he didn't doubt she'd used it to her advantage.

"No, husband, it's an opportunity I intend to take advantage of."

Lars let loose with a loud laugh. "I really like your wife." He waved them off. "Go. I intend to sit here and enjoy the food and drink and the heat of the fire."

Wolf grabbed a fur off the pile near the door and draped it over his wife's cloak, bringing it snug around her shoulders before opening the door. He wasn't surprised to see a light snow falling, though it had yet to cover the ground.

"Eria is a gentle woman and could use another friend," Wolf said as they walked.

"Warning me to watch my tongue and be nice to the woman you love?" She bit her tongue too late. Why should she care if he loved Eria? Or that she was again seeking an answer to that question. And yet for some unexplainable reason she wanted to know if he did love the woman.

His thought was the same as hers. "Why should you care if I love Eria?"

It slipped out then, and damn if she could make sense of it. "Because I will not suffer a cheating husband. You dally with Eria and I'll find a man of my own to poke."

Wolf stopped and grabbed her arm, making sure it wasn't the wounded one. "Don't ever dare threaten me with that. I'll have no wife of mine seek another man's bed. I'm the only one you'll have slip between your legs."

"And I'll have no husband of mine dip his shaft into anyone but me," she said, jabbing him in the chest.

Wolf brought his face near hers. "Since you honor your word, make sure you remember that and you don't deny me when I want to dip my shaft in you."

Raven yanked her arm free, though she knew he let her go, his grip far too strong for her to free herself if he chose otherwise. "You'll be lucky if you can keep me satisfied."

Anger caught him unware, his response sharp. "How many men did it take to do that?"

Raven felt the slap though he never raised his hand and that she allowed it to sting her, upset her even more. She tossed her chin up. "None as I've repeatedly told you. But that doesn't mean I've never craved a man and I doubt you have the stamina and skill to satisfy all that pent up craving." She turned and walked away from him annoyed at the ache in her heart, but pleased at the tic in the corner of his eye.

His wife was beyond frustrating and he cursed himself for losing his temper, which he did far too often around her. But damn if her quick barbs didn't leave a mark.

He shook his head, mumbling beneath his breath as he hurried after her, and his anger rumbled at the thought of her ever being with another man.

Raven stopped when she spotted Eria. She stood talking with Greta, Fyn, and George. One look told Raven everything. Eria was everything she wasn't. She was petite with pale blonde hair and an angelical face that could easily steal a man's heart. She wore a pleasant smile and from the adoring smiles on Fyn and George's faces, she spoke sweetly. The little lad Tait was even enthralled by her, staring up at her with a smile, from where he stood next to Fyn.

Eria turned then and her face lit with joy and Raven knew the loving smile wasn't meant for her. Eria took off in a run and ran right past her into Wolf's arms.

Raven felt an unusual jolt to her chest. Why should it matter to her if the woman hugged her husband and that he returned the hug, lifting the petite woman off the ground? Eria obviously cared for Wolf, while she didn't care what happened to him. He'd been her enemy for the last five years, but now he was her husband and that changed things. Her brothers were happy with their wives and even her father had found happiness with Wren. What was done was done. Did she want to continue living with her husband as a foe or should she at least try to establish a friendship with him? Otherwise what would life be like for her?

You have two choices. You make the best of what you've got or you strive for something better. That's what the old man had taught her. Raven recalled asking him what you did when life delivered a severe blow. He'd told her you recover the best you can, though not always in the way you'd like, and you get your revenge by living life fully in spite of it all.

Did she make the best of the husband she got? And hadn't she enjoyed his kiss and wouldn't mind kissing him again? And what about sharing a bed with him. He did keep her warm.

"Eria, this is my wife, Raven," Wolf said, yanking Raven out of her musings as he walked with Eria to his wife.

Eria stepped forward once they got close. "I'm so pleased to meet you and so grateful that you allowed me to come here."

Raven didn't mind her tongue. "You puzzle me. How can you be pleasant to the woman who robbed you of the man you love and were to wed?"

"Raven!" Wolf warned with a sharp tongue.

"It's all right, Wolf," Eria said softly. "I can understand how Raven must feel." She turned to Raven. "Wolf makes whatever sacrifice he must for the benefit of his tribe as you did to benefit your family. And though he will not be my husband as planned, he still continues to protect me, see me kept safe, as he does for you, and for that I am grateful. And I am relieved you do not object to that or me being here."

"I don't need Wolf to keep me safe. I can do that myself. And as for you being here, I have no objections, but a warning,"—Raven stepped close to her—

"attempt to poke my husband and I'll take a knife to you."

Eria paled and stepped closer to Wolf.

Raven turned but not before she saw Eria tuck herself against Wolf, while his dark eyes looked as though he was ready to kill her. "Where's Iver?" she called out to George and Fyn.

"In the woods," Fyn said.

"Don't you dare go in the woods, Raven," Wolf warned.

"Take care of Eria. She needs you, I don't," Raven said and walked in the direction of the woods.

Chapter Ten

Raven had not seen her husband since she had left him with Eria earlier and she braced herself before entering the longhouse to face him. To her surprise and annoyance, he wasn't there. No one was there, though a servant hurried forward when she spotted Raven.

"I can serve you when you're ready, my lady."

Raven recalled her husband calling the young woman… "Ida, where's my husband?"

"He won't be long," Ida said.

"That's not what I asked, Ida. Where is my husband?"

"He'll return soon," Ida said with a smile that faltered.

"Did he order you not to tell me where he was?"

"I do what Lord Wolf tells me, my lady," Ida said, her hands clenched tightly in front of her.

She'd had enough of the title. "I'm not my lady or Lady Raven. You are to call me Raven."

"I do what Lord Wolf tells me," Ida repeated.

Raven was glad she didn't bother to address her either way, and she understood the lass's loyalty to Wolf.

"Let me get you supper, my lady," Ida said.

Annoyed the servant addressed her that way again, her tongue turned snappish. "I'm not hungry. You're dismissed."

Ida didn't move.

Raven shook her head. "What other orders did my husband give you in regards to me?"

"Lord Wolf instructed me to remain with you and see that you had whatever you needed."

Raven didn't say what she thought, that it sounded like he wouldn't return until late. She didn't bother with any more questions since Ida wouldn't answer them anyway. She turned and walked to the door.

"Where do you go, my lady?" Ida called out.

"That doesn't concern you, Ida," Raven said and left the longhouse. Once outside, she hurried to the one end and ducked around the side, staying in the shadows. The snow had turned heavier and covered her tracks behind her.

She didn't have to wait long. Ida hurried out the door, whipping on her cloak, and looked one way and then the other. Frantic at not spotting Raven, Ida hurried off, and Raven followed. She stopped by the end of a cottage when Ida continued on toward the keep.

So her husband was at the keep.

Doing what?

Raven made the climb up the steep slope, staying in the night shadows so as not to be seen. She was close enough when Ida opened the door to hear loud laughter, and Lars's voice ring out.

"It's good to be reunited with family."

So that was why she wasn't invited to feast with them—she wasn't family. At that moment, she ached to be with her own family, her brothers, their wives, and her da. But she also had another family right here with her—her men—and that was where she headed when she turned and began her trek back down the slope, anger gnawing at her.

Raven had taken only a few steps when someone grabbed her from behind and she cursed her own foolishness for not staying alert. The man was about her height and from what she could feel of him being plastered back against him, he was thin in the chest, but his grip was strong.

She threw her head back hard and heard the crack to his nose and his arms loosened enough for her to slip out of them, but his fist connected with the side of her head and it stunned her enough for him to deliver another blow, catching her jaw and sending her tumbling to the ground.

He was on her before she could respond and his fist came down at her again, but she managed to block it with, thankfully, her uninjured arm. He was quick, a sharp slap catching the other side of her face. She caught his broken nose with her fist and he screamed in pain, but his hands were quick again and this time they were at her throat, squeezing.

She had to do something fast or she'd soon lose all breath and strength. She went for his eyes, but he managed to block her efforts.

Your small blade.

She heard the voice in her head and blessed the old man for reminding her. She clawed at his hands with one hand so he didn't see her struggle to get her other hand to her blade. She fought with every ounce of strength she had to keep from losing consciousness. Finally, her hand wrapped around the handle of her knife and as she pulled it from its sheath, the man was suddenly ripped off her as a mighty, bone-chilling roar filled the air.

Raven grabbed at her neck, choking to regain her breath as she watched her husband bounce the man off the ground, then grab him around the neck with one hand to hoist him up and leave his feet dangling above it.

"I'm going to enjoy making you suffer before I kill you slowly," Wolf said and the man's eyes bulged with fear.

By then they were surrounded. People had poured out of the keep and her men, along with others in the village, came running up the slope. Raven struggled to get to her feet, still trying to regain her breath.

Her men hurried to her, but Wolf threw the man at Lars to subdue, which he did with his meaty hand clamped around his arm and a knife to his throat, while he went to his wife.

"Out of my way," Wolf ordered and Raven's men stepped aside.

Wolf hunched down in front of her, his eyes bright with fury as he looked upon her face blooming with bruises and a touch of blood. He didn't say a word, he scooped her up in his arms and looked to Lars. "See him tethered good and keep guards on him until I return." His eyes turned to the crowd and he called,

"Gorm." The man appeared. "See to the sentinels. Make sure they are all accounted for, then post more."

Iver spoke when Wolf stood and turned to him, knowing what he would ask. "The snow would have covered any tracks that mapped his journey here. I can try in the morning if the snow has stopped, but if the snow falls heavily all night it will be impossible to track anything." He stepped closer to Raven, her other men doing the same. "Are you all right?"

"I am good." She smiled. "Not so my pride."

They laughed, her humorous response and smile letting them know all was good.

"Do you need me, sir," Greta called out.

"No, Greta. I can see to my wife. Return to the feast and enjoy," Wolf said and she walked off as he turned a nod on Raven's men. "Go and enjoy with them and help calm the women and children."

They looked to Raven for her approval. "Go, enjoy, and offer help any way you can."

Everyone dispersed, though several warriors followed Wolf as he carried her to the longhouse.

"You need not carry me. I can walk and there is no reason for you to miss the feast. My wounds are nothing. I can tend to them myself," she said, though it wasn't what she truly wanted. She wanted to stay in the comfort and peace of his arms, though she didn't understand why.

"I had no intentions of remaining at the feast. I had supper prepared for us at the longhouse so we would have time to talk alone."

"Why didn't you tell Ida to have me wait there for you?" she asked.

"And would you have waited?"

"You're getting to know me."

"Unfortunately, I can't say the same about you when it comes to me."

He didn't think she knew him. Was he right? She knew about him, but that wasn't truly knowing him.

"Did he hurt you?" Wolf asked when he placed her on her feet in their bedchamber.

"I got my own punches in," she said proudly.

"That's not what I asked," Wolf said, his dark eyes intent on her.

Raven understood. "He intended to kill me, no more than that. And understand one thing, husband, I would let no man take me by force."

Wolf's eyes sparked with fury, his nostrils flared, and an angry growl rumbled in his chest. "I would tear any man's heart out of his chest if he attempted to do so."

The sincerity and fierceness of his words stunned her and what he did next stunned her even more. His hand gripped the back of her neck and his lips came down on hers. She responded to his hungry kiss without hesitation, not realizing she needed it just as much as he did. It was a deep, binding kiss drawing them closer together, not in body but in something much deeper that Raven had no explanation for and yet accepted without question. Never had she a wont or felt a need to kiss a man, but she realized she had a wont and need for Wolf's kisses.

Wolf rested his brow to hers after ending the kiss. "I grow angry at the taste of your blood on my lips.

This should not have happened to you. I failed to keep you safe."

"You didn't fail," she assured him. "You reached me just in time."

"You placate me, wife. I saw the knife in your hand when I yanked him off you. You were about to give him what he deserved."

"And who then would we have to question?" she asked, her hand going to spread along his neck and jaw, feeling his taut annoyance locked there.

A woman's hand was a familiar touch to Wolf, but none had affected him the way Raven's touch did. It sent a spiraling shot of passion racing through him that poked at his heart and his shaft. How could this obstinate, challenging woman do that to him? How was it that he desired her so fiercely that she was forever on his mind? And when he saw the man on top of her, he'd felt a rage like he'd never felt. It had ripped at his gut and twisted at his heart until he thought he'd explode in a fury nothing could stop.

"You can't die on me, Raven. You committed to this union and I will hold you to your word," he said and brushed his lips across hers.

The light shiver tingled her senseless. "And I will honor my word, husband."

He fought against kissing her again, not trusting himself. He had a need for her that he couldn't explain. It had started with their first kiss and had grown, and kissing her again only ignited that need that had lingered and tormented him.

"Your lips need tending and your bruises deepen," he said and heard her stomach rumble. "And you are hungry."

Raven held her tongue, though there were things she was eager to ask him, but she didn't want to spoil this moment where peace existed between them.

His touch was gentle as he wiped the blood from the corner of her mouth, after he sat on the bed beside her. Then he ran his hand down along her neck and across her throat, left slightly bruised from her attacker's hands. His anger had calmed, though seeing her bruises growing ever deeper wouldn't let it fully abate. His urge to kill the culprit grew, but first he had to get information from him. And that was something that couldn't wait.

"I can tell you're anxious to speak to the culprit who attacked me. So am I. Let's go." She stood.

"Can you tell that's my thought or is it what you would do?" he asked.

"What difference does it make? If you ask me if it's what I wish to do, I would tell you no. I would prefer we remain here and talk as you had planned for us. But that's not a wise choice. It is more important the prisoner be questioned." She shook her head. "It troubles me that the darkness may hold more surprises. The night doesn't allow those in the battlements to see anyone approach."

"So more men may lay in wait," Wolf said, admiring his wife's sharp mind. "Which is why you will remain here in the safety of the longhouse while I see to this."

"You don't really think I'm going to do that, do you?" Her confident smile said it all.

He stood, shaking his head.

She gasped, caught unaware by his arm that sneaked around her waist to yank her against him.

"One day you will learn to obey me, wife."

"How boring that would be," she said and surprised herself when she stretched her head up to kiss his lips with a strength she hadn't intended.

Wolf rested his cheek next to hers after the kiss ended and whispered in her ear, "Be careful, wife, you might find something you like in this marriage."

She assumed he meant their kisses, but she asked anyway. "And what might that be, husband?"

"Me," he whispered, then left her side and went to the door. "Hurry, if you're coming with me." She hurried over to him and he stilled her with a hand to her shoulder. "You would tell me if you suffered more injuries than I see?"

"Aye," she said softly. "I have suffered far worse and still fought."

His hand went to her face, his finger faintly running over her bruised cheek. "You need not do that any longer. That is for me to see to."

He took her hand and led her through the longhouse. He grabbed a fur cloak from a pile on a chest near the door to drape over her shoulders before collecting his own cloak and slipping it on.

"What makes you think I would like you?" She couldn't help but ask, his remark having lingered in her mind.

"Why wouldn't you?"

"I can think of many reasons."

"That once may have been valid, but are they now? Do they truly serve either of us any purpose?" he asked.

"I can think of some that still do."

"Then we will discuss them and see them finished," he ordered.

"There is one that will never be finished," she said, stepping away from him to open the door. "Your love for Eria." She was out the door before he could say a word, not sure if she wanted to hear his response, yet disappointed when he hurried outside to walk alongside her in silence.

He took the lead, taking her hand and directing her to a shed not far from the longhouse. Several guards circled it and they parted as Wolf approached, then closed the circle once he stepped past them.

Lars waited inside with the prisoner. The thin man was secured to a wood pole secured in the ground in the center of the shed. Blood was caked around his nose and mouth and bruising was already deepening under both eyes.

"You're a strong woman to witness the torture your husband will inflict on this man," Lars said.

"Do what you will to me. I won't say a word, since you will kill me anyway," the man said and spat on the ground near Wolf.

"You're right I intend to kill you, but the choice is yours whether you suffer or not," Wolf said. "And believe me when I tell you I can make you suffer greatly. Tell me who sent you and I'll spare you the suffering."

Tears filled the man's eyes. "I'm ready to die."

"No need for him to die. I know who sent him," Raven said with a confidence that had Lars and Wolf turning raised brows on her. She walked closer to the prisoner. "There would be only one reason for you to suffer torture at Wolf's hands. You're more frightened of betraying the man who sent you than the man who holds you prisoner. That means Brynjar sent you."

The man couldn't stop his eyes from turning wide.

Raven smiled. "You just confirmed it."

"Then kill me fast. Please, I beg you. They will know I failed again and come for me if they learn I live. Please. Please. Kill me and be done with it."

Raven went to her husband. "You can't kill him now. He can tell us much."

"That he can," Wolf agreed and turned a scowl on the man. "Why does Brynjar want my wife dead?"

"I don't know. I and a few others were given the task to kill her and were told if we failed or betrayed him we'd suffer at his hands. Not his warriors' hands but his hands." The man shuddered. "He takes great pleasure in inflicting endless pain. I've heard the screams of men begging to die. I will answer all your questions, but please kill me fast when you are done with me."

"How did you come to join Brynjar's group?" Raven asked.

"He raided my tribe in the far north and took some of the men prisoners. I and some others were lucky enough to hide our families just in time. I haven't seen my wife and son in seven years. I dare not try to escape and return to them for fear what Brynjar will do. I am better off dead."

"That's not true," Raven said. "Your wife and son wait and pray for your return."

"You can't believe his tale," Wolf said. "Brynjar warriors have been taught to lie, to do anything necessary to accomplish a mission for him."

"I tell the truth," the man pleaded, "though there are some with me I wouldn't trust and one from a neighboring tribe."

"Whether you lie or not, I don't care. You attempted to kill my wife twice and for that you will die," Wolf said, condemning the man.

"I have a better idea," Raven said.

"Of course you do," Wolf said, shaking his head. "Tell me and be done with it."

Raven smiled and proceeded to detail it.

Chapter Eleven

Wolf sat atop his stallion, riding alongside his wife, and shaking his head the next morning. "I can't believe I let you talk me into this or that I let you join me."

"You realized the wisdom of my words and as for letting me join you," —Raven laughed— "that wasn't an option."

"You do know he could be leading us into a trap," Wolf warned.

"Sten, his name is Sten," Raven corrected. "And I don't believe Sten will do that."

"And what makes you think that?"

"I offered him something no one else has given him."

That fired Wolf's blood. "And what exactly did you offer him?"

"Hope," Raven said.

Wolf caught the sudden sadness in her eyes that faded quickly. He had learned how adept she was at hiding her hurt or any pain she suffered and it troubled him. She had her family and her men who kept watch over her and yet he got the feeling that she felt herself alone.

"How did you give him hope?" he asked.

"I told him that you would see him reunited with his wife and son if he helped us capture the other men with him. He did ask that Toke, a friend from a neighboring tribe who had been taken captive with him and was on this mission, be reunited with his family as well. I assured him it wouldn't be a problem."

"And you continue to think what he tells you is the truth?"

"What I know is that people will do anything to protect and reunite with a family they love," Raven said, a glare in her bold blue eyes that defied him to disagree with her. She never expected the response he gave her.

"Would you do the same if taken from me?"

"I would move heaven and earth to return to you." Her response stunned her, not knowing where it came from. She quickly added, "I am honor bound to you and my honor will always return me to you."

His breath caught at her words and though she followed with talk of honor he paid little heed to it. She had spoken quickly, not a trace of hesitation to her words. Had it come from someplace deep inside her that she couldn't fight against. It made him wonder if his wife was beginning to care for him.

"Nothing would keep me from finding you, wife," he said with a fierceness that brought a smile to her face.

"Of course you would—you're honor bound to me."

"You're right. You belong to me now and always and I'll let no one take you from me," he said, again with such fierceness that it broadened her smile.

"Oh, joy! A husband who will rescue me," she said with a teasing laugh.

Wolf's words stilled her laughter. "Only if you let him."

Brod approached them, ending their conversation. "Iver says the camp is just as Sten described. The man you asked about, Toke, sits off by himself and has a badly bruised eye. The other four drink and talk about what a failure Sten is and it was time they did away with the fool before he damaged their mission."

"Toke probably suffered the bruised eye for defending his friend," Raven said.

"That is a strong assumption," Wolf agreed. "The fools have no one standing watch?"

Brod shook his head. "From what Iver heard, they believe themselves superior to other warriors and believe they will not be discovered."

"They foolishly believe that because they are Brynjar's warriors they are invincible. They are about to find out otherwise. Let Iver know the attack is imminent," Wolf ordered and Brod took off. He turned to his wife. "You will remain here with your men."

"Iver already lies in wait and Brod will join him shortly. I go where my men go."

"That is your way no more. I am your husband and you will obey me on this," Wolf said, a fiery warning to his command.

Raven remained silent.

"I mean it, Raven," he said, glaring at her.

Still, she remained silent.

Wolf looked to Clive, George, and Fyn who approached and settled their horses directly behind Raven. "Make sure she stays here."

He didn't wait for a response, didn't expect one. And he wasn't fool enough to think his wife would obey him. The only thing he could do was to see it done before she joined him.

Wolf had his men leave their horses behind and circle the camp on foot, trapping the unsuspecting men. Brynjar thought himself unfailing, superior to all others, and he had instilled that in his warriors. It was one reason they charged ahead into battle, believing death could not touch them. He had seen the shock in their eyes when a sword pierced them or an axe severed them. At that moment, they realized they were not as invincible as Brynjar claimed them to be.

Wolf watched the four warriors talking around the campfire and he caught a quick glance of the man who cowered away from them, his eye swollen shut and a bruise to his jaw. He'd seen hatred enough to recognize it and it was evident on the man's face as he stared at the four.

The four men suddenly rushed to their feet.

"You got her," one said with excitement.

Wolf cursed low beneath his breath and looked to see his wife enter the camp area with Sten. His temper soared and he was ready to charge in after her, but he wisely refrained. He shook his head when he heard his wife laugh.

"Actually, I got him and I'm here to accept your surrender," Raven said, laughter mixing with her words.

The four appeared dumbfounded, but his wife had a way of doing that to people. He held his hand up for his men to remain as they were and the signal was passed on to the other warriors who circled the camp.

Clive, George, Fyn, Iver, and Brod stepped out of the woods to fan out to either side of Raven.

The larger of the four men laughed. "You think five men and a mere woman have a chance against six of Brynjar's warriors?"

"Six men," Sten said and waved at Toke to join him.

"You join him and you're dead," the large man warned.

"Trust me, Toke," Sten said and the man went to hurry to his friend.

The large man reached for the knife at his waist and before his hand could brush the hilt, he screamed out in pain. He looked down to see a knife embedded in his hand. He raised it to see that the blade had gone through, the point sticking out of his palm.

"Now there's only three of you," Raven said and took the sword George handed her, before drawing his own.

Wolf roared, the signal for his men to attack and they did. He went directly for the large man, seeing him head for Raven, a sword in his good hand. He had seen some women skilled with certain weapons, but never had he seen a woman as skilled with a sword as his wife. She made the man look a fool, the way she skillfully avoided him while her blade, sliced his arms, chest, leg. It was like a cat playing with a mouse, tormenting him before going in for the kill. But his wife didn't plan on killing the man. She wanted more information.

Raven delivered a swipe of her blade to his sword hand and the weapon fell loose to land on the ground. "Surrender," she ordered and too late realized his intentions.

The large man grabbed his knife from its sheath and rammed it into his chest before anyone could reach him.

His last words were, "He'll see you dead."

Raven hurried a glance around and saw that all four men lay dead, then she spotted her husband. The deep lines in his scowling face warned of his anger. She smiled to combat it. "My plan worked."

Wolf took hold of her arm, then turned his head to order, "You know what to do." He then hurried her off under a large pine tree. "NEVER! EVER! Do that again."

"You refused to even give my plan thought," she argued.

"You're right. It was a foolish plan that put you in harm's way."

"And yet it was victorious," Raven said with a proud tilt of her chin.

"It could have proven otherwise."

"But it didn't," Raven continued to argue.

"You constantly fail to realize one thing."

"What's that?" she asked.

"I am in command, not you." His hand rushed to her mouth, his fingers keeping any response from slipping past her lips. "I don't want to hear another word out of you. You took an unnecessary risk today."

He shook his head when she mumbled against his fingers. "Still, you argue."

She shoved his hand away. "My life. I defend it."

He brought his nose so close it nearly touched hers. "My wife. I protect her. Do it again and I'll see you go without food for two days."

"I've gone without food longer than that. You can threaten me with starvation, beating, lock me away, take away shelter, and it won't matter."

It struck him then what she might fear the most. "What if I threaten you with love, Raven? What will you do then?" He kissed her, gently, lovingly, then whispered, "Don't ever frighten me like that again."

Her mouth fell open as he walked away. He couldn't mean that. He couldn't ever love her. Or did she fear she'd be foolish enough to fall in love with him?

***

"I'm going to beat him senseless," Arran said, seeing his sister's bruised face.

"Wolf didn't beat me, Arran," Raven said, sitting in the Great Hall with Purity and hugging a tankard of hot cider in her cold hands. She was grateful that Princess, Purity's large dog, had decided to lean her big warm body against her leg. The ride here had chilled her to the bone.

"Then how did you get those bruises?" Arran demanded.

"You need to know those responsible were sent by Brynjar," she said and reluctantly told him the rest.

Arran clenched his hands. "I'm going to put an end to that evil man and I'm still going to beat Wolf for failing to keep you safe. And I don't care if your men came with you. He shouldn't have let you come here with the amount of snow that covers the land."

"I didn't let her. She snuck away."

Raven turned along with her brother, Purity, and her men, who sat warming themselves at another table near the hearth, to see her husband standing in the entrance that led from the kitchen into the Great Hall. He was swathed in furs and leather with a battle axe at his side and a scowl on his face that made him appear a mighty Northman ready to plunder and conquer.

"She also didn't obey me when I went to trap four of Brynjar's men yesterday. She and her men beat me to it."

"You didn't!" Arran said, turning a furious glare on his sister. "Whatever is the matter with you?"

Purity was about to defend her friend when she saw Raven's men cringing and shaking their heads. She held her tongue and was glad she did.

Raven jumped to her feet. "ENOUGH! I am a grown woman, not a child to be scolded."

Arran bolted to his feet and yelled, "THEN ACT LIKE ONE."

Wolf was at her side in an instant, his voice a loud command. "DON'T EVER RAISE YOUR VOICE TO MY WIFE." He turned a sharp glare on Raven when he saw her ready to speak. "And don't tell me you can defend yourself. I am well aware that you can, but that doesn't mean I will leave you to do it alone."

Purity stood. "Raven and I should have some time alone. You two enjoy some food and drink." She hurried around the table to Raven and with an arm around her urged her out of the room and up the stairs to her small solar, relieved neither men stopped them.

King, Purity's cat, followed them and parked himself in her lap once she sat. "Do you want to tell me what truly troubles you?"

Raven stared at the flames in the hearth. "I don't know how to be a wife."

***

"Your sister is maddening. She never obeys me and does as she will," Wolf complained before downing a good portion of ale.

"Raven has always done what she pleased, I warned my father time and again to curtail her foolish behavior." Arran shook his head. "He spoiled her. Let her do whatever she wanted and now she's grown into—"

"A woman brave and selfless enough to set you free," Clive said, sending both men an evil look. "A woman who leads us with skill and courage. A woman who has survived death twice and saved all our arses more than once. A woman who went hungry more times than she should have and had to survive the cold too often. A woman who lives honorably and loves fiercely. And you," —Clive gave a hasty nod to Arran— "don't deserve to have her as a sister." He turned another evil glare on Wolf. "And you certainly don't deserve to have her as your wife."

"What do you mean she almost died twice?" Arran asked, worry creasing his brow.

"She wouldn't want me saying anything. "You want to know, then ask her yourself," Clive said and took a swig of ale.

Fyn offered a clue with his remark. "Raven fiercely protects those she cares for."

It was obvious to Wolf and he could see from the way Arran's brow went up that he understood as well. Raven had suffered near fatal wounds protecting her men and somewhere the scars he had yet to see on her body would tell the tale.

George added his own words as well. "Raven has been free for the last five years. What do you expect her to do when you want to replace that freedom with a cage?"

***

"I don't know how to be a wife either," Purity said with a laugh.

"You certainly make it appear as you do."

"It helps that Arran and I love each other. I used to dread the prospect of my father arranging a marriage for me. All I could think about was what would I do if I didn't like the man. It was a thought I was told never to question. I was to accept whatever man my father chose, even if he was the cruelest man in the world. It was why all those years ago I begged your brother to wed me. I knew Arran would not treat me cruelly, as many did because of my deformed hand. But I know now that a marriage is much better when a husband and wife have a mutual love and respect for each other."

"Something Wolf and I don't have," Raven said, a sudden sadness creeping up to tug at her.

"There must be a touch of something—concern, caring—since he made a point of coming after you."

"More like annoyance for me not obeying his word," Raven argued. "He cares not a whit about me. A good, dutiful wife is what he looks for and Eria fits that perfectly."

"The woman you mentioned that Wolf was to wed."

Raven nodded. "She's everything I'm not."

"Would you want to be like her?"

"Good Lord, no!" Raven said.

"Then what should it matter. You make a far better wife for such a powerful and fearless man. And from what Wren told me, Wolf was genuinely concerned about you when you suffered that arrow to your arm."

"He sent his men after the culprit, but he stayed with me while the arrow was removed from my arm," Raven said, recalling how it had surprised her.

"You sacrificed much for your brothers' freedom, don't sacrifice anymore," Purity warned.

"What else is left for me to sacrifice?" Raven said with a defeated laugh.

"A future," Purity said softly. "It does us no good to continue to think of Wolf as our enemy. He has helped not only Royden rescue Oria, but helped Arran protect our clan against Brynjar. Some of us may not be able to forgive, but we can adapt. You may never love your husband, but at least make him your friend rather than your foe so you can share a good life together and finally know some peace."

Raven gave her words thought.

"One other thing you must always remember," Purity urged. "You are not alone. You have your family and you have your men who have become family to you. You are well loved, Raven."

***

"That was a foolish thing you did today, wife," Wolf said as he stripped off his garments in their bedchamber.

Raven stood by the hearth warming herself, the cold having seeped and settled into her bones on their return ride home earlier. He hadn't spoken a word to her the whole way home, but she expected his chastising tongue to strike sooner or later.

She remained silent, too tired to exchange barbs with him tonight.

"I would have taken you to see your brother if you had asked."

"I doubt that," she said. "You would have told me it was too dangerous."

"So you admit to it being dangerous but not foolish."

She walked right into that trap. "Think what you will of it. I do as I please."

"And that's the problem, especially with your life in danger," he said and walked over to her.

Raven was growing accustomed to seeing him naked, though she wasn't happy how her body had been responding to it. At first it was just a stirring in her, then it expanded to more of a tingle that rushed over her and enticed. Lately, however, she had felt herself grow wet in the most intimate of places and that had upset her. How could she desire her enemy?

Adapt.

The old man would advise that and Purity had advised it today as well. And she should know better than anyone that sometimes that's the only choice left to one.

"We need to come to terms with each other," he said.

He stood far too close to her and damn her thoughts, since all she wanted to do was rest herself against him, have his arms wrap around her, and let his warmth seep into her. She shivered at the thought.

"You're cold. You need to get in bed where you'll be warm," he said and his hands went to her plaid and began to unwrap it.

Raven stood there stunned for a moment, her eyes on his fingers, long and lean and powerful, as they worked on stripping her of her plaid. She should stop him, tell him she could undress herself, but she said nothing. She let him undress her, ready to stop him if he should try to slip her shirt off.

"Do you realize the repercussions if you should die shortly after we wed?" he asked but didn't bother to wait for her response. "Your brothers would wage war against me. Once again people—family and friends—would die." He dropped her plaid to the floor. "And if you've forgotten, I have more warriors. The odds wouldn't be good for your family."

His fingers curled around her hand with a firm possessiveness, nearly capturing all of it, and led her to the bed. He rested his hands on her shoulders and eased her to sit, then hunched down in front of her. His hand reached for her leg and she went to pull it away but she wasn't fast enough, he captured it in his hand. His fingers curled firm around her calf.

"I can do that," she snapped, uncomfortable with the unexpected sense of intimacy between them.

"I know you can, but you're going to let me do it for you to show that we can work together without difficulty or protest." His hand moved to her boot and he pulled it off along with the sock and the other boot and sock followed quickly. "Under the blankets," he ordered.

She hurried to obey that command, needing a bit of a distance between them, his innocent touch disturbing her in far too many ways she couldn't explain.

He walked around to the other side of the bed and slipped beneath the covers. "You understand the wisdom of my words, don't you?"

"As much as I don't want to admit you're right, I do understand the wisdom of your words," she said, annoyed it made sense.

"I am pleased to hear that and now there is something we need from each other for this to succeed."

"Trust," she said before he could.

He turned on his side, his hand going to the curve of her waist to ease her on her side to face him. "Tell me what I must do for you to trust me, wife?"

Her skin tingled where he touched her and she did her best to ignore it, but it was far from easy. "First I'll hear what I must do for you to trust me."

His response was delivered without a bit of hesitation. "Confide and share all with me as you do with your men. There will never be trust between us if you don't."

She might have argued with him if she hadn't learned to trust enough to confide and share. "I will agree to that if you agree to what I ask?"

"Tell me," he urged, eager to seal their agreement.

"Trust my word that I've been with no other man and do not wait to consummate our vows."

Chapter Twelve

Raven walked to the village, dawn just breaking. It was quiet and cold, her boots sinking into snow just below her ankles. No flurries fell, but the snow wasn't finished with them yet. She had woken almost an hour ago snug and warm in her husband's arms. It continued to surprise her how comfortable and peaceful she felt with him wrapped around her. He'd been her enemy for so long, it was difficult not to see him any other way. And yet she didn't feel that way when sleeping in his arms. She tried over and over again to make sense of it, but it eluded her.

Last night when he spoke of trust, she had no argument with it. They were wed and would spend the rest of their days together. And as Purity suggested, wouldn't she rather her husband be a friend than a foe?

Unfortunately, they had failed to seal the bargain Wolf had offered, more precisely he had failed to agree. He had failed to say anything after she had told him what she expected from him if he was to trust her. She couldn't say it hadn't hurt—it had. And that in itself had surprised her. Why should she care what he thought? But for some reason it mattered to her.

Perhaps the sting of his failure to agree was a silent statement of what he actually thought of her.

A woman not worth trusting.

The thought stung. Had his words that they work together meant nothing more than empty promises? She had seen enough of that as her journey as a thief. She had learned there was more honor among thieves than nobles and that wasn't saying much. How then did one truly trust?

She wished the old man was still alive. She missed him so much. They had spent endless hours talking, debating, arguing. He had taught her well and his knowledge continued to help her survive.

The glow of a fire caught her attention as she approached the cottages where her men stayed. She shook her head and corrected with a whisper, "Live. Where they now lived." She had to remind herself this was permanent—unlike most places they'd been—this place was now their home.

A cauldron hung over the fire pit, no doubt brewing something her men would be grateful for and they showed their appreciation in many ways to Greta for seeing them fed. She had noticed Fyn spent much time with Greta and her son Tait. The men teased him about it and he gave as good as he got, but never once had he denied it. It made her realize how much they had all sacrificed the last five years. This was their chance of finally having a permanent home and more if possible. She couldn't deny them that, just as she shouldn't deny herself.

But how did she do that wed to Wolf?

Raven approached the cauldron, needing the heat from the fire to warm her some, when Greta stepped out of the cottage and gasped.

"You startled me," Greta said as she went to the cauldron. "No one stirs yet, though soon they will." She added a handful of leaves to the cauldron.

"What has you up early?" Raven asked, though from Greta's creased brow, Raven surmised worry was the culprit.

"Concern that Brynjar's men are here. They are an evil lot." She shuddered. "Brynjar hates failure in any form. His agreement with the old chieftain of the Clan Macara to wed his daughter Purity failed. He will not let his plans, whether agreeable or not, to wed Eria fail. He will come for her, though it is truly Wolf he wants."

Raven needed her curiosity settled. "Why is that? Why does Brynjar hate him so?"

She stared at the cauldron a few moments. "Brynjar doesn't need a reason. He's a vile man."

Her brief hesitation had Raven sensing that the woman knew more than she was saying and she was completely caught off guard with what Greta said next. "Eria is a good woman and not your enemy. You should be kind to her."

The words flew right out of Raven's mouth. "Does Eria love Wolf?"

"No. Eria cares for him as she would a friend just as he cares for her as a friend. Their parents arranged their union, wanting to unite two powerful tribes, and both felt it was their duty to submit to their parents' command. Wolf may be called the Beast, but he is far from one, except, of course, when he battles, then he is more ferocious than a wild beast."

Fyn came out of his cottage stretching and broke into a smile as soon as his eyes fell on Greta, and she returned the same enthusiastic smile.

"Fyn is a good man," Raven said.

Greta's smile grew. "I know. Tait adores him."

Tait wasn't the only one who adored Fyn, and Raven was happy for him. He deserved a family, a home, love.

"You all right, Raven," Fyn asked when he joined them.

That he looked to her first, asked how she was, when he obviously was eager to talk with Greta made her think how dedicated her men were to her. How much they had sacrificed for her. That had another question looming large in her mind. How long did she expect them to sacrifice for her?

The thought startled her and made her realize she had some thinking to do.

"I'm good, Fyn, a bit bruised and sore, but nothing that I haven't felt before," she said with a chuckle.

He laughed. "Haven't we all been there and more than once."

Raven saw Fyn's laughter fade along with his smile when he looked to Greta. She had paled and her hand rested on her scar. He hurried to take the woman in his arms and Raven walked away, giving them their privacy. If it was anything she should know Fyn would tell her, though would he if Greta asked him not to?

Change was in the air, she could feel it, smell it, almost taste it. It was inevitable.

Raven headed back to the longhouse wondering over more than her husband and the bargain they had yet to strike.

"One of these mornings I will wake before you."

Raven admonished herself silently for letting her mind wander and not paying attention to her surroundings. Then she spotted the two warriors off to her sides and realized she'd been followed since she'd left the longhouse earlier. She had to remember that.

"Few stir this cold winter morning," Raven said and stopped when her husband's steps brought him to her.

He reached out to snatch hold of her hand. "Come and warm yourself by the fire while we eat."

"I'm not very hungry," she said and saw his eyes turn suspicious. Was he thinking her ill due to the possibility of her being with child? The thought annoyed her. "I thought to speak to the two captives again."

"They've told us what they could. What they know. Brynjar trusts few men and even less women."

"I think they may know more, but fear saying anymore," Raven said. "They worry what Brynjar might do to their families if he discovers they didn't die with the other men. It would be good if you could bring their families here. Then they would be overjoyed with the Beast's generosity and be eager to help him in any way they can. Or perhaps we will find that the men's tales are just that—nothing more than tales."

"Plans have been implemented to bring both families here, if they exist. Until then, the two men will be kept imprisoned."

More and more he was finding they thought alike. He'd never had that strong of a bond with anyone and had only seen one couple who shared a bond like it… his grandmother and grandfather. His grandmother insisted it was their deep love that forged their strong connection. He and Raven far from loved each other. Surprisingly, though, he had found himself growing comfortable with her in ways he never expected. At least it was a start for them to get along and hopefully be friends rather than foes.

"A decision I would have made," Raven said, pleased they thought the same on the situation. She let her eyes linger on his. They were filled with such power that they could overwhelm if gazed upon too long. It was no wonder they called him the Beast, he was as forceful as one. She turned her eyes away. "I could use a hot drink to warm me."

He kept hold of her hand as they walked toward the longhouse.

Not one to measure her words or wait for the right time, she blurted out, "You never answered me last time when I told you what you must do to trust me."

"I have no answer—yet," he said.

"Aye, you do. By not answering you confirmed you don't trust me." She slipped her hand out of his and walked to the longhouse, leaving him standing there.

Wolf had the overpowering urge to hurry after her, scoop her up and over his shoulder, and rush off to their bedchamber and see this settled. But that would mean he surrendered and he never surrendered to anyone, and he wouldn't start now.

He took steps to follow after her, but by no means rushed.

His wife stood by the fire pit, her hands stretched out to the heat.

Wolf walked up behind her, his arms encircling her as his hands captured her two in his to rub warm. Only when heat returned to her fingers did he release her hands and turn her to face him, wrapping his fur cloak snug around them both.

"You are forever chilled. What happened to leave the cold forever in your bones?" It wasn't just curiosity that had him asking. He was concerned at what may have happened to her. Even more concerned that he'd been to blame.

Memories began to flood her, memories she kept tightly tucked away. Memories she didn't want to relive.

Wolf felt her reluctance to speak, to share her past. Her body tensed against him and a familiar shiver ran through her. He walked her to the table nearest the fire pit and ordered hot brews to be brought to them. He kept his arm around her and his cloak as well.

Her silence said more than words. She obviously didn't trust him enough to share but then he hadn't given her any reason to.

She shivered beside him. "That first winter alone was harsh. It set a cold in me I don't think will ever leave."

He rubbed and squeezed her arm, forcing warmth into her, glad she was sharing with him.

"Threadbare garments. Shoes with holes so large nothing would fill them. Food once a day if I could find it. Though it was shelter I mostly sought, desperately needing out of the cold. Death stalked me. I could feel its presence. Sometimes I thought I saw it lurking near, dark and frigid ready to swallow me whole. I'd managed to get a fire going, only it didn't last long. It tempted, its tendrils of heat reaching out to tease me before it flickered out and left me in the cold darkness once again. If it wasn't for—"

He waited to hear his name fall from her lips, the man she loved, but it never came. She kept it tightly hidden away, not wanting or unable to share it.

"That winter infused my bones, not with heat, but with a frigid cold and it seared my soul in a loneliness I never knew existed until…"

Again she wouldn't say his name, this man who saved her, this man whose child she might carry. She eased herself away from him. Did she think she betrayed his memory by being in his arms? The thought annoyed him. She was his wife whether she wanted to be or not.

"You're mine now," he said, to him a response that meant she'd never suffer any of that again.

She glared at him a bit stunned. "I don't belong to you."

The strength of his response confirmed otherwise. "You do belong to me and you have my word that I will never see you go hungry, suffer the cold, or be lonely again." He waited, ready for her protest and was surprised when it didn't come. It wasn't like her to be silent and he wondered over it.

She cupped her hands around the warm tankard, enjoying the heat that trickled through her at first, then began to flow strong. The warmth of the tankard hadn't done that. It had been his words. She could argue she didn't need anything from him, but seeing Fyn with Greta had changed something in her. Maybe too, it was seeing her brothers and da happy with the women they loved. The Mighty Beast would never love her and she wouldn't need him to, but he would look after her. And she would owe him the same. Was that enough to build a reasonable marriage on?

Adapt.

She had no choice and hadn't the old man reminded her of that often enough?

A hardy laugh entered the room before Lars did, a broad grin on his face. "I'm starving and have you smelled how thick the air is with pending snow?"

Raven was glad for the interruption, since she had no words for her husband, but she did have much to think about.

"More snow by nightfall for sure," Gorm agreed, having followed in behind him.

Raven hadn't spoken much with the man since her arrival, though she had planned to. He was always busy, directing workers, giving orders, keeping everything running smoothly. He also took the time to talk with people, share a smile or a laugh. He was well respected by all.

"A hunting party goes out today," Gorm said.

Why?" Wolf asked. "The storage sheds are full."

Gorm smiled. "A wolf has been spotted."

"A new fur for our leader," Lars boasted proudly. "Wolf and I will join them."

"Leave the wolf alone," Raven commanded like one in charge.

Lars' brow knitted. "Why?"

"We don't bother the wolves here and they don't bother us. Harm one and you'll bring the wrath of their leader and pack down on us," she warned.

"Much like our own Wolf," Lars said with a laugh that shook his thick belly.

Raven looked to each of the men as she spoke. "The last time a wolf was killed in these parts its leader and pack almost decimated the whole clan responsible for it. The wolves hunted them over time until only a few were left. The clan almost died off, while the wolves grew strong."

Lars readily dismissed the claim. "That's probably nothing more than a tall tale, told on cold winter nights."

"Lady Raven speaks the truth."

Raven looked to see Detta wrapped in a fur-lined cloak, standing just inside the door.

The old woman approached them slowly. "Ask those here in Clan Learmonth. They will tell you the tale in much more detail since Learmonth is the clan that killed the wolf."

Several eyes widened in surprise.

"There'll be no killing of wolves here," Wolf ordered and Gorm acknowledged his command with a nod.

Detta did the same as if approving and appreciative of Wolf's decision.

"What brings you here, Detta?" Wolf asked.

"I thought Lady Raven might enjoy a tour of the keep today." Detta turned to Raven in wait of a response.

Raven shrugged. "Does it matter, since we won't be residing there?"

"See for yourself," Wolf offered. "If you feel you would be more comfortable there, I'll consider it."

Though she wore a smile, sarcasm dripped with Raven's every word. "Oh joy, how generous of you."

Wolf ignored her intentional jab but he didn't ignore her when she stood. He grabbed her arm. "You will stay and have your meal, then you can tour the keep."

She tugged her arm free. "I'm not hungry and I will do as I please." She heard it then, the complete silence, not even the fire crackled. She had blatantly defied her husband in front of his people. She looked to see everyone staring at her and also to see the slight tic at the corner of her husband's right eye. She shook her head and kept her voice strong. "Good Lord, you all better get used to me… I'm not an obedient wife and I never will be." With a quick slide off the bench, Raven was on her feet and walked over to Detta. "Let's go."

Detta didn't move.

Raven wasn't surprised that the woman remained as she was and that her eyes were focused on Wolf, waiting for his command. She, however, had no intentions of waiting. "I'll take the tour myself," she called out as she headed to the door. "Enjoy your meal, husband."

Annoyance sparked in her when she stepped outside and spotted the two warriors that had followed her earlier lingering nearby. She'd had enough. It wouldn't take much to lose them, though with the snow on the ground it would make it easier for them to track her. She'd have to think differently.

She ducked behind a cottage, then another and another, until she found the one she needed. She climbed the sturdy pine tree with ease and haste and watched below as the two warriors who'd been following her almost collided as they rushed around opposite sides of the cottage. She kept herself from laughing and giving away her hiding spot. From what she could hear of them talking, they both feared telling Wolf that they had lost her. In the end, they bravely went together to let the Mighty Beast know they had lost his wife.

It always paid to be cautious, so Raven waited several minutes after they left and was glad she did. They returned to scout the area one more time, then hurried off. She knew they were gone for good this time and got herself down out of the tree and made sure to keep herself from being spotted before reaching the keep.

She entered straight into the Great Hall, smaller than the few she had been in, but carefully maintained. A fire raged in the large hearth and a pine scent was heavy in the air, and she saw why. Branches of pine had been placed along the top of the mantel. The tables and benches appeared freshly scrubbed and newly made candles flickered with flames. What caught her attention the most were the tapestries hanging on the walls. They depicted defeated and victorious battles and in the middle of one battle scene, if one looked close enough, a wolf could be spotted, his head held proud.

"How did you lose my men?"

She really had to remain more alert to her surroundings. She turned with a smile to her husband. "With ease."

"If you care not what I think, then take pity on your poor men and how they worry when you disappear," he argued.

She laughed. "My men know when to worry."

"Do they?" he challenged. "Ease their burden and mine as well and don't lose the men I assign to follow you."

"I'm no burden on my men," she snapped, the thought alone disturbing.

"This needs to stop, this constant battle between you and me."

She shrugged. "It can when you trust me."

"Tell me his name?" he demanded, still trying to comprehend why it mattered to him.

Her brow creased. "Who?"

"The man you love."

"The man I love?" she repeated and saw that his hands were clenched at his sides.

"The man who saved your life," he nearly shouted.

"Why does that matter to you?"

"Answer me," he demanded.

Her chin went up. "I'll answer you when you do what is necessary for me to trust you."

Chapter Thirteen

Raven roamed through the keep after her husband all but stormed out of it. She decided to start at the top and work her way down. The more she explored, the more the place disturbed her. She entered the master bedchamber, surprised at how small the size. Actually, the whole keep was small in size and she wondered how Oria had managed to survive here for five years. It felt more a prison than a home.

She tried to imagine herself sleeping here with Wolf and a chill ran down her spine. It was far too confining. The whole place was much too confining. She'd feel trapped if she had to live here. Oddly enough, she found the longhouse more to her liking. Of course, if an attack was imminent, then the keep would prove useful.

This time she caught the light footfalls on the stairs and was well aware of who approached the room.

"Your friend Oria was a good wife to Lord Learmonth even though he was old enough to be her grandfather," Detta said from the open doorway.

"A marriage of convenience until her true love returned," Raven reminded.

"Aye, but still, it was nice having her here. Oria is a kind and gentle woman. I admire her and I do miss her," Detta confessed.

Raven was surprised by her heartfelt words. The old woman truly favored Oria, but who wouldn't? She was as Detta said, kind and gentle, not qualities found in Raven's nature.

"Many a Learmonth has been born in this room," Detta said. "It would be good to see another born here."

Raven wanted to yell '*hell no*' but refrained. Detta didn't need to know her thoughts on the keep. She also recalled something Wolf had told her and was quick to ask, "How do you know that many a Learmonth has been born in the room when Wolf planted you here to spy?"

Detta folded her aged hands to rest against her apron-like tunic. "I did my job well and found out all I could. Now, what else may I show you?'

Raven was itching to leave as fast as she could, feeling far too confined, but she had questions to ask. "How long have you been here?"

Detta smiled. "Long enough."

An answer yet not an answer.

"Not many speak of the wolf tale. How did you hear about it?" Raven asked as she stretched her hand out for the old woman to precede her out the door.

"I heard whispers of it until one day someone told me the whole tale."

Another untruth. It was known that the clan rarely spoke of it, fearful it would somehow bring the wrath of the wolf down on them again. Or perhaps they believed it already had with the arrival of Wolf the Mighty Beast.

Raven was glad she had gotten a chance to speak with the old woman. She had deduced much from their brief talk and Detta's demeanor, the results burning her curiosity even more. The old man had taught her to observe people, having insisted one could learn a lot about a person by just watching them. And if there was one important thing that she had learned about Detta, it was that she wasn't who she seemed to be.

"Whatever your decision, I will be pleased to have you live here in the keep," Detta said when they entered the Great Hall.

"Thank you, Detta. You have been more helpful than you know," Raven said and the woman turned to leave.

"Detta."

The old woman stopped and turned to face Raven.

"By now you know I speak my mind and I make no apology for it. So I will speak it to you… you're no simple servant. You're much more. Maybe one day perhaps you will trust me enough to tell me the truth."

Raven didn't expect a response. The reaction on the old woman's face was enough to confirm her thought. She stepped outside without saying another word and pulled her wool cloak around her against the cold. A snowstorm would hit soon, and as she approached the village she saw everyone rushing around preparing for it. Food was being distributed to the cottages, shovels rested next to doors, smalls animals were brought inside and other animals were secured in shelters. She imagined her brothers would be doing the same, recalling the many times it had been done when she'd been young. Of course, sometimes a snowstorm would catch them unaware, but not often. There was just something about snow you could sense and feel.

The snowflakes started falling as she made her way down the hill to the village. A horn suddenly sounded and people started rushing about and that had Raven running. She ran even faster when she saw that people were congregating near Greta's cottage. Fear slammed into her chest that something had happened to one of her men.

Wolf was issuing orders when she got near, but her eyes went to Fyn holding up her bow and cache of arrows, which meant a hunt, and the look of fury on his face meant only one thing… Greta or Tait, or both were missing.

Iver's attention was on the ground tracking and he soon disappeared into the woods. Clive, Brod, and George weren't standing far from Fyn and they all had their eyes on her. She knew why. They waited for her.

Wolf's warriors were gathering as were many of the villagers. With the snow coming, time was their enemy. They would have to move fast.

Raven knew what she had to do. She flung off her cloak and raised her hand as she drew near and Fyn let out a wild roar that had everyone jumping away from him and unknowingly clearing a path for her. She didn't halt her speed, she increased it and as she drew near her men, Fyn threw her bow to her and she caught it with ease as she rushed past everyone, her men following behind her, and they disappeared into the woods.

Fyn hurried up alongside her as they kept pace with Iver, tracking fast thanks to the snow already on the ground.

Fyn explained as best he could as they rushed along. "The prisoner Toke managed to escape. He's got Tait."

She grabbed the cache of arrows Fyn held out to her, her injured arm sore and protesting no doubt from climbing the tree, but she ignored it, and flung the strap across her chest as she kept a few paces behind Iver. Any questions she had, and she had many, could wait until later. Right now all that mattered was rescuing the young lad.

***

"That's some warrior woman you have there," Lars said with a huge grin. "Did you see the way she didn't even stop or hesitate to catch that bow? And her speed," —he shook his head— "I've never seen a woman run that fast."

Wolf was furious, proud, and jealous. She trusted her men without question. She had had no idea of what was going on and yet she never stopped and questioned. Her hand shooting up in the air had to have been a signal that she was ready to join them in whatever it was and Fyn's roar confirmed they would join as one to see it done. Each of her men stood steady and waited and followed her lead.

He wanted that kind of unwavering trust from her.

"The men are ready," Gorm said, a sword at his side.

"I'm leaving Lars here with you in case it's a trap," Wolf said.

"We're prepared," Gorm informed him.

Greta approached. "Please, Wolf, I beg you, please bring my son back to me."

"You have my word I'll bring Tait home," Wolf said.

"No matter what, Wolf," she pleaded.

He spoke with a fierce command that no one could deny. "No matter what, Greta, your son will be returning home with me."

She nodded, tears streaming down her cheeks and Eria stepped forward to offer what comfort she could, her arm going around Greta.

Wolf turned away knowing Greta wanted her son brought home alive, but also letting him know that he was to be brought home no matter what condition they might find him so she could hold her son in her arms again, even if only for one last time.

Wolf led his troop of warriors into the woods, following his wife's tracks and sending a tracker ahead to see what he could find. He worried over her. She might be a skilled warrior but that didn't mean she couldn't be harmed. Or that this was somehow a trap she was falling into and he'd be too late to save her. Her men would protect her, as she would them, making his worry grow.

He thought he would have a docile wife in Raven. Someone who chose to unselfishly surrender to set her brothers free. Someone who would be obedient, grateful, possibly a bit fearful of him. She was none of those. And while she certainly wasn't easy to deal with, he found her not only more interesting than any other woman he had known, but no woman had ever challenged him the way Raven did.

The thought of his wife charging into danger before him jabbed at his gut. If she got herself hurt one more time, he was going to lock her in their bedchamber. The ridiculous thought sobered him. He'd never do such a terrible thing to her and she'd never allow it. She'd raise hell if he tried and he wouldn't blame her. He didn't wed her to make her a prisoner.

Let me be who I am.

That was what she had told him she expected from him and he was just beginning to understand the depth of her request.

***

Iver suddenly slowed and so did Raven and the others. When Iver stopped and dropped down to examine the ground, Raven went to him, though remained silent. Iver would speak when he was ready.

After a few moments, Iver stood and kept his voice low. "Toke grows tired. He no longer carries the lad. I don't think he's far from us. We go slow from here."

Raven signaled the men and they proceeded with cautious steps.

Iver held his hand out to her and she scrunched her face annoyed, understanding what he expected of her, and she reluctantly surrendered the bow and cache of arrows to him.

"You're a skilled archer," he said, slinging the cache of arrows over his chest. "But your arm has yet to heal."

"I was carrying them for you," she said with a grin. "And we both know I'll never be as talented as you."

"You've come close," he said with a pride in his student that was easy to see.

Raven followed alongside him grateful for all that Iver had taught her.

It wasn't long before they spotted Toke, his breathing laborious and with a grip on the back of the little lad's garment. The lad was crying and shivering. He must have run out of the cottage with intentions of returning quickly when he'd been scooped up since he wore no cloak or wrappings over his regular garments.

It angered Raven beyond measure and within a matter of seconds she determined the best action. She didn't wait, she drew her dagger and hurried into the small copse of pines where Toke had taken shelter.

***

Wolf had slowed his warriors' pace when his tracker had discovered what Iver had and he came upon his wife and her men just in time to see her advance on Toke.

Toke drew his dagger and turned it on the lad.

Raven didn't hesitate. She threw her dagger, catching Toke in the shoulder with such force that he stumbled back, releasing the lad.

Fyn had followed behind her and ran straight to Tait and the little lad flung himself into Fyn's arms, sobbing. Fyn held him tight and hurried him safely away.

Toke steadied himself fast and went to throw the dagger he still held, but Raven had already drawn the other dagger she carried. She was far too fast and skilled for the man. Her dagger landed in his throat and his eyes turned wide with shock as he gagged and dropped to the ground.

Wolf stared, amazed at his wife's skill. His warriors' whispers told him they thought the same. He went to her, annoyed yet proud.

"Spare me a tongue-lashing," she said when he stepped alongside her.

"At least you are wise enough to know that your arm isn't healed enough for you to use a bow and arrow."

Raven caught Iver's grin.

One thing Raven never did was to accept praise that didn't belong to her. "That was Iver's doing. Besides, he's a better archer than me."

"Then my thanks go to you, Iver, for being wise when my wife was foolish," Wolf said with a nod to the man.

"Raven has her faults," Iver admitted, "but foolishness isn't one of them."

Wolf tried to keep the command out of his tone, but he was eager for an answer. "Tell me one fault of hers."

Iver answered without a glance to Raven and without hesitation. "Raven loves with all her heart and soul and would do or give anything to keep those she loves safe, even if it means she suffers."

"But you already know that, don't you?" Brod asked, with a touch of sarcasm, having stepped up behind Iver.

Wolf's warriors circled the two men, but Wolf raised his hand and waved them off. "We all sacrifice in some way."

"Some more than others," Brod said and looked to Raven. "We're going to follow Fyn and Tait home to make sure no one else lingers about."

"Wait a moment and I'll go with you," Iver said and hurried to retrieve Raven's daggers, wiping them on the dead man's garments before returning them to her.

Wolf raised his hand and made a gesture that had a few of his warriors following after Raven's men.

"Don't trust them?" Raven asked.

"Extra hands to fight if needed."

She had learned he could be as blunt as she often was, so she acknowledged his considerate gesture with a nod. "Appreciated."

Wolf took hold of her arm and walked her away from the body that his men were wrapping to take back with them. "I won't deliver a tongue-lashing, but I will have my say."

"I'll at least listen," she agreed.

"I would advise that," he cautioned.

"Is that a warning? A threat?" she asked, stepping closer, unafraid… mostly. The man could intimidate with a glance and there was his strength to consider. She wasn't foolish enough to believe she could break free of his hold. His grip was like a shackle clamping around her arm and her waist at times. The crazy part was that most times his strength comforted her.

"Must I make it one? Will you forever argue with me? Can you not just once—once—pay heed to my word?" he argued, trying not to raise his voice.

She looked puzzled. "You gave no word."

"You never gave me a chance," he clarified.

She offered a reasonable explanation. At least she thought she did. "I saw the terror on Fyn's face and knew something had happened. There was no time to question or debate."

He slapped his chest. "That's *my* decision to make. I command *my* people, *my* clan, not you."

She didn't understand why his words stung her at times, though that didn't stop her from unleashing her tongue on him. "*Your* people. *Your* clan. I should have expected those words from you, but I'm glad you made it clear, what was obvious anyway, you'll never accept me as your wife."

He groaned in frustration. "*You* are part of my people. My clan. And never doubt that I accept you as my wife. But *I lead*. Not you. And you and your men need to learn that." He could tell by the sudden gleam in her eyes that he had somehow walked into a trap.

"I'm not your wife until you seal our vows. And I, nor my men, will pay heed to your word until you trust me… and you know what you have to do to prove you trust me. If you need reminding, it's the same thing you need to do to officially make me your wife."

Chapter Fourteen

Raven was surprised to find herself on the verge of tears watching the way Greta hugged her son and Fyn, the little lad refusing to leave Fyn's arms. But no tears came, she wouldn't let them.

"He's found a family for himself," Clive whispered, standing beside her and poked her in the arm with his elbow. "I think George is about to do the same."

Raven saw what Clive did, the concern on Eria's face for George upon his return and the gentleness in the way George reassured her.

"They'd make a good match," Clive said. "They are both gentle souls, though George can be fierce when necessary. When Eria discovered his interest in Northmen symbols, she was only too pleased to discuss them with him. They spend much time together."

"Things are changing, Clive," Raven said.

"We all knew it would. It was just a matter of whether it would be for the better. I'm glad to see that it is, especially since my old bones—"

"Are too tired for all this," Raven finished with a smile. "You've talked about Bethany enough through the years. Isn't it time you did something about it? I can attest that she's a warm-hearted, loving woman. I don't know what I would have done without her when I was young. She was the closest thing I had to a mum. If you wait too long, some other man might scoop her up."

"Angus," Clive grumbled. "He's had his eye on her since his return home."

Raven tilted her head, casting a glance at the gray sky. "The snow falls lightly but that will soon change. We'll probably be stuck inside for days or possibly longer. Wren won't be able to get here to see how my arm heals. I want you to leave now and take a message to her. Let her know I'm doing well and she's not to worry about me. And don't dare try to return home today. Bethany will see you provided with shelter. You stay with my clan as long as necessary."

"Raven," Clive whispered, tears shining in his aged eyes.

She gripped his hand. "I don't want to lose any of you, but it's not fair to keep hold of you."

"You'll never lose us, Raven," Clive said, sniffling back tears. "We're family."

"And families grow as they should." She nodded toward Fyn, Greta, and Tait.

Clive elbowed Raven again. "Brod has an eye for Ida and I believe the interest is mutual."

She looked at the way the two stared at each other from a distance. Clive was right. There was interest there."

"You didn't only free your brothers to live their lives," Clive whispered, squeezing her hand. "You freed us all and gave us a chance at a good life."

Raven felt the tears build deep inside her, but stamped them down. "Then you better get living yours. Bethany probably has a hardy stew brewing to warm everyone during the snowstorm and honey oat cakes as well."

Clive's eyes lit with delight, then faded.

Raven let go of his hand. "You've done all you can for me, Clive. It's up to me to do the rest. If Bethany feels about you as you do about her, then stay with her. You've more than earned your own happiness."

"He was right about you. You're unique, like no other." Clive wiped at his wet cheeks. "I still miss him."

"So do I," Raven admitted, thinking about the old man and wishing she had him to talk with.

"I'll talk with the men, then be off. And God willing all goes well, I'll be back to visit or whenever you need me."

Raven's chest tightened in pain as Clive walked away and began to talk with Iver and Brod. Family was growing but it was also separating and that was the difficult part of change. But she wasn't losing anyone and she had to keep hold of that thought.

Gorm approached her and she wondered what dictate he brought from her husband.

"Lord Wolf is speaking with Sten. He asked that you join him."

She nodded, surprised at the invitation, not that she had intended to wait for one. She knew he wouldn't waste any time in speaking with Sten. It was something she would do and it was growing more obvious that they thought alike more often than not.

She followed alongside Gorm. "You do a lot here, Gorm."

"It's no chore," he said. "It pleases me to serve Wolf. He is a good man and an exceptional warrior."

That Wolf's tribe thought highly of him had become apparent since her arrival here. Their view of him was in sharp contrast to what she had thought of him the last five years. It wasn't easy seeing beyond the vicious warrior she had believed him to be. All she had to do was recall that day his warriors had attacked her clan and remember the carnage left in its wake, including her brother losing his hand and her family being ripped apart.

A sudden thought narrowed her brow. He hadn't participated in that attack. Why?

Her eyes went straight to her husband when she and Gorm approached the area where Sten was being questioned. Her husband was a fierce warrior but not a vicious man, nor a cruel leader. He was commanding yet tolerant when needed and from what she had seen so far of him… he was fair in judgment with his people. She had chosen to wed him and it was growing more apparent by the day that it was time to make the most of her marriage.

"Nothing? You know nothing?" Wolf asked the man on his knees in front of him.

"I tell the truth, sir," Sten pleaded. "Toke said nothing to me about an escape."

Wolf shoved Sten to the ground with his boot and planted it on his chest. "You claim to know him well and yet he says nothing to you about his intention to escape?"

Sten continued to plead, his body shivering and not from the cold. "I'm truly sorry, sir. I don't know if Toke intended to escape or just took advantage of a moment? The look in his eyes a few moments before he ran made me think he decided at that precise moment, but why that precise moment, I couldn't say. I beg you, sir, please believe me. I speak the truth. If I knew anything I would tell you."

"Or I could have the truth beaten out of you," Wolf said and Sten paled when Lars stepped forward.

Lars fisted his hands and his nostrils went wide with a snort. "I say we beat him."

Sten paled and the pitiful plea in his eyes fell on Raven. She couldn't say why but she believed Sten told the truth. If Toke had known something, he hadn't confided it to Sten. But why not?

She walked over to her husband and looked down at Sten. His shivering had increased and he was pale with fright. "Did Toke trust you, Sten?"

He went to respond and stopped, a sadness so heavy descending over him it was difficult not to recognize it. At least for Raven, since she was familiar with the heavy burden.

"I thought he did," Sten said. "But now I wonder if either of us trusted anyone anymore."

"Time with Brynjar can do that to you," Lars said as if he understood.

"Toke never had a loose tongue. He listened more than he spoke. Now and again he would tell me what he heard, snippets mostly, unless he heard more and didn't say."

"Would fear hold his tongue?" Raven asked.

Sten didn't have to think on that question. "Fear held us all prisoners, especially our tongues. Dare to utter a single word against Brynjar and he'd somehow find out and you weren't the only one made to suffer for it and suffer badly." He looked up at Wolf. "You are feared because you are a courageous and a ferocious warrior who knows victory more than defeat. Brynjar is feared because he is pure evil."

Wolf moved his boot off Sten and the man sat up slowly.

"Can you think of any reason why at that moment Toke may have chanced an escape?" Raven asked.

Sten shook his head as he spoke. "He looked around as we worked just as I did, it all reminding me of home and my family. Though, Toke did seem focused on your men." He nodded at Raven. "When the guards left us to finish the task at hand, Toke pulled his hood up and walked off, blending in with everyone."

Wolf contained his fury upon learning the escape was his guards' fault. His warriors would be punished for their neglect. "How long before the guards returned?"

"Maybe about twenty minutes," Sten said.

"Gorm," Wolf said with a distinct growl in his voice.

"I'll see to it, my lord," Gorm said, understanding he was to gather the guards responsible, and left in haste.

Sten shook his head again. "I don't know where he thought he would go, seek shelter or find warmth, when the scent of a snowstorm was so heavy in the air. It makes no sense."

Raven heard the question she was about to ask come out of her husband's mouth.

"Could he have been meeting someone?"

"There were no other men that traveled with our small group that I was aware of, but there were other men on the ship that brought us here. And Brynjar rarely lets anyone know his true plans. All I was told was that—" Sten paled again.

"You were to see my wife dead," Wolf said, anger twisting his gut and growing his muscles taut.

Sten nodded, fearful of saying any more.

Gorm returned with four fierce looking warriors. "They volunteered to guard the prisoner."

"You don't need that many," Raven said and the scowl that spread across her husband's handsome face showed he thought otherwise. She ignored it and voiced her opinion. "There's a small storage room in the keep that would serve as a better cell and would prove more difficult to escape, though I don't think Sten has any intentions of doing so. And one guard at a time will suffice, freeing your other three warriors."

His wife was right, though he didn't openly admit it. "See it done, Gorm."

"One last question, Sten," Raven said as the largest of the warriors grabbed his arm and swung him up off the ground and held him firm. "Were you and Toke together the whole time you were held captive by Brynjar?"

"No, we were separated and only came together a couple of months ago."

Raven directed her order to Gorm. "See that he is fed well and kept warm. He'll do us no good dead."

Gorm looked to Wolf and he nodded, giving permission for Gorm to carry out her order.

"I could use some food myself," Lars said, as Sten was carted away.

"Then share the meal with Sten. A full belly may encourage him to talk more," Wolf said.

"And ale… lots of ale loosens tongues," Lars said, his hardy laugh trailing after him.

As soon as everyone departed, Wolf turned to her but she spoke before he could. "I know… your clan, your people, your command."

"I'll always have the last word in matters, wife. That won't change. But I respect your opinion."

Raven smiled and poked him in the chest. "So what you're saying is… I'm not allowed to give orders to your men like I do to my men."

"That's exactly right," he said, returning her smile. "And what order did you give Clive that had him leave?"

She wasn't surprised that he knew. He had either seen him leave or someone had told him.

Raven's smile grew with her response. "Love."

"Explain, *kona*," he said, doing his best to hide the jolt the word had delivered.

Raven detailed why she sent Clive to her clan and also mentioned Fyn and Greta as well. It was too early on with George and Eria or Brod and Ida to mention them.

"My men have served me well and I want them to be happy," she said.

"I wish Clive well and I'm glad that Fyn is planting roots here. He will make a good mate for Greta, and

Tait seems to care a great deal for him. No wonder your men are so faithful to you—you're an unselfish leader, a rare quality in one who leads."

"I was taught well," Raven said, thinking how she often did as to how the old man's teachings had guided her and helped her survive.

That she continued to hold the mysterious man she loved in high regard continued to annoy Wolf. Even in death she was devoted to the man. That strong of a love was difficult to find and he couldn't deny he continued to be envious of it.

Wolf's tongue was sharp when he spoke. "I go to reprimand the warriors who neglected their duties. Go and see to a wifely duty instead of getting into any trouble."

Raven laughed. "I will see to a wifely duty when you see to your husbandly duty."

He was left with the sting of her barb as she walked away and he grumbled to himself as he went to see to his other duties.

His warriors were known for their exceptional skills and he made it clear that their neglect—their failure—had reflected on themselves and him. And it wasn't a pleasant reminder since the Beast had delivered the reprimand and punishment. The two warriors were left shivering when he finished with them.

The snow wasn't falling heavily when Wolf headed to the longhouse, hoping to find his wife there. He had to admit that he enjoyed talking with her, even though she challenged him at times—most times. He discussed things with her that he had never thought he would discuss with a wife, nor did he ever think her opinion would be of value to him. But it was impossible not to pay heed to her words, since she spoke with a wisdom unusual for a young woman. Though the last five years had probably aged her beyond her young years.

Wolf spotted one of the guards he had assigned to follow his wife headed to the longhouse. Leif was one of his most trustworthy warriors, the reason he had assigned him to watch over Raven.

"My wife is in the longhouse, Leif?" he asked as he got near.

Leif halted and turned. "No, my lord. She is with Brod and Iver in Brod's cottage. Hagen stands guard outside while I fetch food for her men and Greta, at your wife's suggestion, since Greta is busy seeing to Tait, fright still having a hold on him."

Hagen was another trustworthy and exceptional warrior, easing Wolf's concern. "She intends to share the meal with them?" He didn't care for the thought. Their meals together could be contentious at times, but he enjoyed them.

"No, my lord. I heard her tell her men she would be eating with you later."

Wolf was pleased to hear that.

They were both about to enter the longhouse when Ida stepped out wrapped in a cloak and a covered basket hooked on her arm.

"I was about to look for you, my lord," Ida said. "Brother Noble is here and I was about to take food to him."

"Take the food to the small cottage no one uses and set a fire in the pit so Brother Noble may have a warm place to eat and wait out the storm." Wolf turned and hurried off after a nod from Ida, eager to talk with the leper. He'd been a voice of reason at times and Wolf could use some reasonable advice right now.

"Brother Noble," Wolf called out when he arrived at their usual meeting place. "Food and heated shelter waits for you."

The leper stepped from behind the tree. "Your people will not want me near."

"My people know I won't put them at risk," Wolf said, seeing a dark cloak draped over the brown cleric robe that usually covered the leper. He appeared more stooped than usual and his steps slow.

"You are well?" Wolf asked.

"My illness takes its toll."

His voice was raspier than usual and Wolf was concerned for him. "These missions are too much for you, especially in the cold."

"Abbott Thomas says the same."

Wolf was relieved to hear that. "I am glad the Abbott looks after you."

"Enough of me, tell me you've found, if not love, at least peace in your marriage."

Wolf laughed. "I hope peace is possible between Raven and me since we are stuck with each other. She is more of a challenge than I realized."

"Is there anything you find you like about her?" Brother Noble asked, a cough disrupting his words.

"She is brave for a woman, too brave at times, placing her life in danger when she shouldn't. She's also quick in mind and word, her barbs stinging." Wolf laughed again. "I do enjoy talking with her, though our conversations can be prickly at times. And—"

"Something you're not sure of or you don't want to admit, my son?" Brother Noble asked when Wolf suddenly paused.

"I like that she seeks my embrace at night when we're in bed. She feels good—somehow right—in my arms. It may be only the heat she seeks from me, but I favor her there nonetheless."

"Perhaps there is room for love to grow between you and Raven," Brother Noble suggested.

"Love isn't something I've given much thought to. I've had no time for such foolish notions. I would wed to benefit my tribe which in a way I've done—"

"Again you pause," Brother Noble said and when Wolf hesitated, he encouraged. "Tell me what troubles you, my son."

The need to confess hastened Wolf's response. "I've never told anyone that love has lingered on my mind, due mostly to the way my grandmother talked and continues to about the love she still has for my grandfather even though he is gone. She sacrificed much to be with him and never once regretted it. I never saw two people so much in love, so caring, so understanding of each other, then my grandparents. My mother and father have a good, loving marriage, but it isn't anything like my grandmother and grandfather's was. They shared something rare. I suppose if I were honest with myself, the true reason I've paid no heed to love is because if I can't have what my grandparents shared, I don't want to love at all." Wolf paused but not for long. "I think my wife already found that rare kind of love. You can hear the love in her voice when she speaks about this man who taught her and helped her survive these last five years. I don't think she will ever love another man that way and oddly enough I find myself envious, and also annoyed that she won't at least confide his name to me."

"Perhaps trust is an issue with her."

"You're wise, Brother Noble. Trust is the very thing she asks of me."

"You don't trust her?"

"She tells me she's never been intimate with a man and yet she was, from my understanding, deeply in love with a man. How then did they stay apart? And what if she carries his child?"

"The child would need a father. If you like how this woman feels in your arms, you must care somewhat for her. Wouldn't you then care for her bairn who was part of her, help him grow into a strong man or if a lass, keep her safe since her da couldn't? Or are you too bitter you were forced to wed Raven?"

Chapter Fifteen

Wolf couldn't get the conversation he'd had with Brother Noble out of his head, especially the question he had no answer to. Was he bitter that he'd been forced to wed Raven? Had he been forced? He could have refused the proposal, but on further thought, it was a solution that seemed the best at the time. He had wanted to settle and establish a good life, put down roots in a land that was his heritage.

It seemed Raven's men wanted the same. He was pleased for Fyn and Greta, and little Tait deserved a good father. Greta had barely spoken about Tait's father, when she had arrived at his tribe seeking safety and shelter. The wound on her face had yet to heal and the only thing she would say was that the father of the bairn she carried wasn't a good man. He was glad she and Tait finally had a good man. And it meant that Fyn would plant roots here and being in love and loyal to Greta would make him loyal to the tribe. He had also noticed how Eria was spending time with George. And he hadn't missed the glances exchanged between Brod and Ida.

Raven's men were settling nicely in the tribe, establishing roots that would keep them here, keep them loyal. That was what he needed to do with Raven, establish roots and loyalty with her. Unfortunately, that wouldn't happen until they trusted each other.

He'd been so lost in his thoughts he hadn't realized the snow had turned heavy, coating the ground. Bairns ran around squealing with delight as they tried to catch the snowflakes as pups nipped at their heels, and parents were busy making sure they had all they needed to weather the storm. Gorm was seeing that food and firewood were generously distributed and shovels were available to those who were assigned to digging pathways.

Wolf made a point of stopping and speaking with various people, seeing they had what they needed, though he had no doubt they did. It wasn't that he never heard a complaint, the tribe had its share, but being prepared for a snowstorm wasn't one of them. Snow was something they dealt with often in their homeland.

He wasn't far from the longhouse when he spotted his wife with her head bent and her eyes cast to the ground as if searching for something. He headed her way wondering what she may have lost. She suddenly bent quickly, whipping something up out of the snow that had coated the ground.

Her cloak.

All this time she had gone without it and he hadn't taken note of it. He'd been too angry over the escape, too annoyed that she had taken matters into her own hands, and too intent on talking with Sten, to see that his wife had lacked protection from the cold, something that plagued her too often.

He whipped off his fur cloak as he drew near her, snatched her damp wool cloak from her hands, and hurried his warm cloak around her. "There are several fur cloaks in the longhouse. You will wear one of them from now on."

"Is that an order?" Raven asked, shuddering as she drew the warm fur around her.

He framed his words carefully. "It's a wise choice."

Raven smiled. "Wise response."

Her smile brought his own. "I am a wise man."

Raven laughed. "I could argue that." She held her hand up when he went to respond. "But I won't, since I appreciate the warmth of your cloak."

And the scent of you on it.

She pursed her lips to make sure those words didn't slip out, growing uncomfortable with the unexpected thought. Or did she? She had grown accustomed to his alluring scent. It wrapped around her like his arms, bringing comfort and strangely a sense of safety. The thought troubled her, it feeling like a sense of surrender. She couldn't surrender, not ever. She had to stay strong, always strong or she wouldn't survive.

Wolf grew concerned when her brow seemed to crease with worry. "Something wrong, Raven?"

She brushed it off with an excuse. "The day grows long and I grow hungry."

She lied, that was obvious, but why? What didn't she trust telling him?

Trust.

That stood between them, divided them, and he knew what he had to do to change that. But did he dare take a chance? Or did it matter? She was his wife and Brother Noble was right. If she did carry another man's child, the bairn would need a father.

"Sir," Gorm called out as he hurried toward Wolf. "A man stalks the area. The sentinels spotted him and Iver found his tracks and says he hides them well."

"Gather the men, we search," Wolf ordered and turned to his wife as Gorm rushed off. "You are to remain in the longhouse."

She said nothing, her intent blue eyes focused on him.

"I mean it, wife. You will seek the safety of the longhouse while I see to this," Wolf commanded.

"You know of this because I sent Iver to see if he could find anything," she argued. "From what I've learned of Brynjar, he leaves a mission to more than one man."

"The reason I spread sentinels out wider."

"We both had the same thought," Raven said. "Brynjar didn't rely on Sten's group to carry out the mission. He sent someone to follow and make sure of it."

"And there may be others that follow, Brynjar is not one to accept defeat." Wolf gave a nod to the longhouse. "Now go and wait for me where you will be safe."

"I will not sit idly by while you hunt the man intent on seeing me dead," she retaliated. "My men and I—"

"Your men are welcome to join me. You will remain here," Wolf said, the strength of his voice sounding like a decree.

Raven went to argue, having no intentions of being left behind, but her husband grabbed hold of her arm and yanked her against him, his brow coming to rest on hers.

"There is much to be settled between us, wife, and I will not have you taken from me before I see that done."

His warm breath fanned her face like a gentle kiss and she closed her eyes for a moment, lingering in its gentle caress. And while she should have been surprised when his lips touched hers, she wasn't. She enjoyed his kisses as much as she didn't want to admit it. There was something about his kiss, a closeness of sorts she had never experienced. She didn't quite understand it, since when her men had talked about their experiences with women they had never mentioned it. So, it had left her puzzled.

When he brought the kiss to a gentle end, a sudden tug to her heart had her asking, "What of you? I don't wish to lose you." Her remark was strange to her own ears and she thought to clarify it, but found no words that could explain it.

"I'm the Beast. I need no one to protect me," he whispered.

His mouth had remained close to hers and the faint whisper of his words once again caressed her lips. "We all need someone."

Her words hit him hard, thinking she referred to the man she loved and he shoved her away. "You will obey me on this and stay here."

His sudden anger startled her and sparked her own ire. "Until you are truly my husband, you have no say in what I do." She went to turn when she spotted a dark figure in the snow, slinking past one of the cottages. Her eyes went wide and she took off after him.

Wolf didn't hesitate, he followed.

***

The heavily falling snow made it difficult to see, but Raven had braved such weather before so it didn't frighten her. She was no fool and it wasn't long after that she realized the man she followed was leading her away from the village. That could prove fatal in this snowstorm, especially with the cat and mouse game he was playing with her. She had to consider he was leading her into a trap, not that she held much credence with that. Her thought was that Sten's group had one man in it who reported back to another of Brynjar's men who had probably waited along the way. When the man failed to meet, the warrior came to find out why and if he failed to report to the next man, then another warrior would follow after him. Brynjar had no intentions of giving up.

Why though?

Was this man here to see her dead? Or was this another matter entirely? Was he here to get the woman whose parents refused Brynjar's offer of marriage? Her questions needed answers, which meant the man had to be taken alive. Not an easy task if he was there to kill her, but she was certain her husband hadn't hesitated in following her. And no doubt Gorm would dispatch warriors as well.

It was time she took command of the situation. She waited until she was sure he caught a good glimpse of her then she turned away from him and headed back to the village, not the least worried he wouldn't follow.

The heavy snow made the task more difficult. Visibility grew worse and made it almost impossible to see anything. She was relieved when she caught the outline of a cottage and followed it. She kept her eyes peeled as best as possible and her ears alert, surmising that it wouldn't be long before he attacked if she was truly the target.

She caught a dark blur out of the corner of her eye race her way and turned knife in hand, but the man never got a chance to reach her. She scrunched her eyes trying to make out what was happening only a short distance from her. Her heart caught in her throat when she heard the distinct growl and saw the blur of fur sail through the air.

A wolf?

It took a few moments to see clearly enough and realize it wasn't a wolf, though in a way it was… it was her husband, the Beast. Though the heavily swirling snow prevented a clear view, she was able to see enough to know why he was called the Beast. He fought like one, relentless, unforgiving, determined to conquer. His prey didn't stand a chance.

Her husband's warriors appeared as if they had materialized from the snow and formed a circle around their leader. Her men joined her, standing at her side.

Fyn was the first to speak. "His name fits him."

Iver added his own thought. "He tears at his prey like a beast."

They were right. It was as if he unleashed a wild animal and she hated to admit that watching him sent a bit of fear rumbling through her.

When the fight ended, the man appeared as if he'd been torn apart, though there was enough life left in him to speak. At least her husband had been wise enough to let him live long enough to question.

The man lay on the ground and struggled to speak. "You'll not stop him."

Wolf's breathing was ragged, his anger still strong, and his hands fisted at his sides, fighting the urge to finish the man. "I will," he affirmed as if pledging a vow.

"Not before he has his way," the man said and managed to grin. His movement was so rapid no one caught it before it was too late. The man grabbed the knife that his fingertips faintly touched and slid it across his throat. His blood quickly spilled out along with his life.

Wolf stared at the man, an angry growl rumbling from him, then he looked to Gorm. "See that he's tossed in the woods for the animals to feast on."

A chill ran through Raven when he turned his eyes on her. She suddenly felt like the wolf's prey, his dark eyes looking as if they waited to stalk her every move. He raised his arm and pointed. "The longhouse now!"

She wasn't about to be dictated to and went to protest.

Wolf was ready for her. He raced at her so fast that it had her men jumping out of his way. He scooped her up, dropped her over his shoulder, and headed to the longhouse.

Fyn went to follow and George stopped him. "It's time they worked this out between them."

Fyn nodded. "You're right."

Brod agreed with a nod. "No more can be done with this snowstorm bearing down on us. Time for the heat of a roaring fire, tankards of ale, and plenty of food."

"Snow doesn't stop a Northman," Gorm said, coming up behind them.

"Join us in food and drink and tell us Northmen tales," Brod offered with a grin.

"Join me in the keep where there is heat, food, and drink a plenty," Gorm invited and looked to Fyn. "Lord Wolf has already instructed that Greta, Tait, and Eria seek shelter there while this snow rages. It's also an easier place to keep them safe."

"I'll go escort them there," Fyn said.

"I'll help," George offered and the two hurried off.

"Women can turn a man's head to mush," Iver complained shaking his head.

Brod and Gorm laughed and the three men headed to the keep.

***

Wolf deposited his wife in the common room near the fire pit and slapped his hand over her mouth before she could speak. "Listen well, wife. If you ever chase after danger again, I will throttle you senseless." He pressed his hand firmer to her mouth when her eyes widened as if she was about to argue and he was well aware of what that argument would be. "I know you can take care of yourself, but you no longer have to. You have me now. I will see you kept safe."

Her blue eyes betrayed the battle she fought with herself and he knew what stopped her.

Trust.

She didn't trust him.

Wolf's hand fell away, giving her a chance to speak.

Raven shook her head. "Until trust exists between us, I trust myself and my men to keep me safe."

It rankled Wolf that she put such trust in her men but had not an ounce for him even after he had made sure to protect her from this attack.

Raven raised her hand when he went to respond. "I don't want false promises or empty words. Trust—true trust—I learned comes from deep within. A place where someone would never think to betray."

"You had such a trust with the man you loved?" Wolf asked, knowing her response would annoy him.

"I did, though we both earned it just as I earned my men's trust and theirs mine. I have hidden nothing about myself from you. You see and hear for yourself who I am. You either accept my word as truth or you leave us to forever doubt each other."

Wolf turned away from her, his mind in turmoil. Surrender was not something he ever considered. He had fought every battle, every engagement large or small, to the end and had emerged mostly victorious. He had retreated a couple of times to regroup and when he'd reengaged, victory proved easy.

This engagement was different. There'd be no retreat. Once he entered battle, her word would prove true or false, which meant either certain victory or defeat for him. Unless he didn't think of it as a battle to win or lose. He'd actually come to favor his wife. She challenged him in words and action, and he couldn't deny he was attracted to her. She invaded his thoughts endlessly and dreams as well. He loved having her in his arms at night, wrapped snug around him. And she aroused him far too easily, a sign he had tried to ignore that he was eager to make love to her.

L*ove.*

That word had surfaced far too often in his head of late when it came to his wife. Could he truly feel more for her than he would admit? Was he failing to trust what his heart was trying to tell him? How would he ever know if he didn't give it a chance? How would she ever trust him if he didn't believe her word?

Wolf whipped off his cloak, tossed it aside, went to his wife, and scooped her up in his arms. "It's time we settle this. It's time we seal our vows and I make you my wife."

Chapter Sixteen

Raven wasn't sure what to do when her husband set her on her feet in their bedchamber. She had wanted this—his trust. But the hundreds of butterflies fluttering in her stomach had her thinking twice about it. She may have learned about coupling from listening to her men but it was from a man's perspective. She had no idea how it was for a woman. That she was about to find out both thrilled and frightened her.

There was one thing she wanted to know before anything happened between them. "So you chose to see if I tell the truth."

Wolf's hands halted, having already partially disrobed, and his eyes found hers. "I know you told me the truth, that's why I do this."

He shocked her speechless but not for long. "Suddenly you believe me?"

"I believe you, I trust you, and I care for you." His response was unexpected and unintended, but it felt right.

Only a few words of what he'd said stuck in her mind and she had to be sure she had heard him correctly. "You care for me?"

"I do," he said, feeling comfortable with admitting it. "You can be troublesome at times, stubborn as well, and definitely foolish, but you have courage, strength, and you are loyal to those you care for, and you will stop at nothing to keep them safe. I know you will protect our bairns as fiercely as a wolf protects her cubs, and I hope someday you will come to care for me as well."

Words failed her. She never expected to hear such kind and caring words from him. She thought they would forever be at odds, never even become friends, never truly care for each other. It touched her heart to think that they could actually have if not a loving marriage then at least a caring one.

She had a chance here not only to make the most of her situation as the old man used to advise her to do, but to make a better life for herself. One where she would have a husband who cared for her and one day maybe, just maybe dare she think, they could find love with each other.

Raven spoke what she felt. "I thought I would hate you forever, but I don't. You are different than I thought you'd be. Of course, I was right about you being overbearing and that you dictate to me far too much, but you're not the barbarian I expected." She turned a teasing smile on him. "You're a good leader, fair with your people, and a warrior of exceptional skill. I believed I would have to tolerate you in more ways than one. I was pleasantly surprised to see that your features are more than tolerable as are your manners. While I don't need you to keep me safe, I have no doubt, when necessary, you will keep me safe. And surprisingly and completely unexpected, I've come to care—*somewhat*—for you."

Wolf smiled at her confession. "You care for me."

"Somewhat," she corrected, his teasing smile driving the butterflies in her stomach wild.

"It's a start," he said and was glad for it.

"Aye, it is," she agreed, and like him, she was pleased they had found some common ground.

Wolf quickly finished disrobing and when he looked to his wife, he was surprised she still wore her shirt as she did each night in bed.

He would remove it for her, but he sensed it was better she did so herself. "You'll need to take that off."

Her worry had her words rushing from her mouth. "I have scars."

Wolf stretched his hand out to her. "It matters not to me. Come and let me see them."

Raven hesitated. The old man was the only one who had ever seen her partially naked since he had tended her wounds. She had never stood naked in front of anyone and while Wolf was her husband and had the right to see her unclothed, she found herself hesitant to do so.

He saw the uncertainty in her eyes and he thought to go to her, but he knew it was better for them both if she came to him freely. He knew of only one way to accomplish that.

"You are no coward, wife."

Raven's chin shot up and she walked over to him and took tight hold of his hand as if needing his strength, his reassurance.

"No scars can mar your beauty, Raven," he said and brought his mouth to hers in a gentle kiss. He was quick to add, "I speak the truth so don't challenge me on it."

She smiled since she had been about to do just that. "You know me too well."

"And we are about to know each other more intimately," he said, his hands going to her shirt to slide it up along her body. He kept his eyes on hers, her shirt reaching her waist. "Raise your hands, wife." He thought she might protest, but she didn't. He hurried her shirt over her head and tossed it aside, something he had ached to do shortly after they had begun sharing a bed, but had refused to admit to himself.

A sudden chill raced a shiver through Raven.

Wolf hurried her into his arms and rubbed her back to send warmth through her. He felt it when his hand rubbed her shoulder—a scar. She stiffened and he grew angry thinking of how she must have suffered.

"Scars are the sign of a brave warrior," he said, hoping to ease her worry.

"I haven't noticed any on you," she said, raising her head to look at him.

He released her and stepped back, spreading his legs and pointing to a spot on his right inner thigh.

Raven did her best to ignore his protruding shaft, though it was impressive, and she couldn't help but smile when she saw the scar on his leg, not far from his groin. "A dissatisfied lover?"

He chuckled, then teased playfully, "You can judge that for yourself soon enough." He grew serious when he explained, "I got the wound saving Trevor from a deadly blow."

Raven looked down, her hand going to her left side just above her waist to rub the scar there.

Wolf stepped closer to her, easing her hand away to touch the puckered flesh while taking in the slimness of her waist, the gentle curve of her hips, and the dark thatch of hair that hid her treasure.

Knowing his curiosity would have him asking, she said, "Death almost claimed me with this one, but I had no choice. I had to help Iver or he would have died."

Wolf's fingers brushed across the scar as if he could make it disappear. "Iver owes you his life."

"He owes me nothing. We are family," she insisted.

He spotted another scar just above one of her breasts and his hand went to it. He didn't have to ask, he knew the danger of a wound there, but he asked anyway, "This one could have proved deadly."

"It almost did," she confessed.

"Who did you save this time?" he asked, understanding what Clive had meant when he said she had earned their respect and obviously their loyalty.

"Fyn," she said, though offered no more and was glad he didn't ask for more.

Wolf ran his hands down along her sides to rest at her waist and looked down at the small scar he felt on her right side. He turned her slightly to have a look and though it was small, he could see by the look in her eyes that it was the scar that pained her the most.

"Did you get this one saving the man you loved?"

Raven shook her head, lowering it as she whispered, "I couldn't save him."

He slipped his hand beneath her chin and raised her head. "Those scars cause the most pain, a pain that never leaves us. My most painful scar can't be seen, but it remains never-ending."

"Tell me," Raven urged, wanting him to share it with her so she would be more comfortable sharing her pain with him.

"Later," he said. "Now is not the time to recall sorrows. I want this night to be memorable for the both of us." He lifted her in his arms, her flesh cool against his warmth and he walked to the bed.

She slipped her arms around his neck just before they reached the bed. "Wolf."

He rested his brow to hers. "I know, wife. You've never laid with a man."

"You do believe me," she said, startled.

"I do and I feel the fool for not realizing it sooner, since I've lost precious time in making love to you."

That he actually admitted to feeling a fool stole a bit of her heart and brought her a strange sense of comfort, but that he regretted not making love, not simply coupling, but making love to her sooner stirred her passion.

"We begin anew?' she asked with hope. Hope that they could share a decent life together regardless of the past.

"Aye, wife, we begin anew," he agreed and she brought her lips to his.

"Let it be so," she whispered before sealing their agreement with a kiss.

Wolf placed her on the bed and followed down to lie beside her. He ran his hand with a feather-like touch over her shoulder and down along her arm, and loved that her skin prickled with gooseflesh from his teasing touch. "I thought of this moment many times." His hand roamed over one of her breasts, cupping it. It weighed firm in his hand and he ran his thumb over her hard nipple, sending a shiver through her. "I wondered if you would submit or refuse me, but never did I imagine I would favor you, want you with a raging passion that pains my shaft."

Raven's hand went to rest on his hand that squeezed her breast gently. "I don't want to submit—I want to *share* this night with you."

"And all the days and nights to come?" he asked as if it were a vow he asked of her.

"And all the days and nights to come," she repeated, his intimate touches sending a flurry of tingles rushing through her.

How was it his touch could awaken passion so quickly in her? How was it that she actually ached for his touch and his kiss? And how was it that it felt so right and not at all like she surrendered?

Love!

No, she couldn't love him. It wasn't possible. It was a need she felt, like the need her men had spoken about. She had never felt a need before Wolf's touch. She had never let a man near her, not after the fright she had suffered at the hands of a stranger. But this was different. She wanted Wolf to touch her.

Love strikes at the strangest times and in the strangest ways. That was what the old man had told her. Could love have sparked between them?

"Where do your thoughts go?" Wolf asked, seeing she had drifted away from him and thinking another man had come to haunt her thoughts and interfere with their night together.

She moved her hand off his to run her fingers over his cheek and down into his beard and along his strong jawline. She faintly rested her fingers along his lips, amazed at how perfectly they were shaped. They weren't too full or too slim. They were perfect to kiss.

Her delicate touch played havoc with his passion. He ached to slip one of her fingers in his mouth to nip and suckle, but first he wanted a response from her, and he demanded, "Truth, wife."

She turned a slightly confused look on him, having not believed where her own thoughts had drifted. "Love. I was thinking about love."

"With another man?" he demanded again, though this time none too gently.

She shook her head, confusion still evident in the slight scrunch of her eyes. "No, I wondered if love would ever be possible between us."

"Once again we think the same, wife," he said, glad another man would not come between them tonight. And he couldn't wait any longer to do what he'd ached to do. His mouth captured one of her fingers, drawing it into his mouth, nipping at it with his teeth and suckling at it with a teasing slowness.

He was pleased to feel an intense shudder rock her body and a soft moan spill from her lips, lips that were in desperate need of a kiss. He released her finger with one last nip and claimed her lips with his.

Wolf never imagined he'd be more than eager to kiss and intimately touch Raven, but he couldn't deny the exquisite pleasure it brought him. Touching her silky soft skin was like tasting fine wine and not being able to get enough of it. He had to explore every inch of her, touch all of her, taste all of her, claim all of her.

His lips followed his hands, nibbling, tasting, kissing her delectable skin, and that he had elicited moans of pleasure from her made it all the more enjoyable. His touch grew more intimate, his fingers making their way to the little nub of pleasure that nestled in her dark thatch of hair, and she gasped when his fingers began to play with it.

Raven couldn't quite comprehend it all. His hand, mouth, tongue did things to her that sent sensations through her that she never knew existed or even thought possible. She thought she had had a good understanding of what went on between a man and a woman. Not so, she was a complete novice when it came to coupling. A quick decision had her doing what she always did when she wasn't quite sure of something. She allowed her instincts to rule. Or was it her passion that took charge and had her reaching out to touch her husband?

With his mouth doing deliriously wonderful things to her nipple, she ran her hands through his hair, grasping his head. The more he pleasured her the more she ached to do the same to him. When she finally got the chance to take hold of his rock-hard shaft and feel the power pulsating through it—he grabbed hold of her wrist.

"Not tonight. It will be over much too soon and I want us to linger in pleasure." He hated to see disappointment in her eyes, though his pleasure grew knowing how much she ached to touch him. "Another time, I promise," he assured her and himself.

Her disappointment soon faded as he continued to work his magic on her and she was soon lost in a haze of pure pleasure. Her skin prickled with a maddening desire, her nipples were so taut they ached, the spot her husband had tormented with his touch and mouth throbbed unmercifully and the ache between her legs was just as relentless and made her want to plead with her husband.

Instead, she threatened, "NOW! NOW, husband or I will take my dagger to you."

Wolf rose up, stretching over the length of her, laughing. "You'd cut off the appendage of mine that would bring you the greatest pleasure?"

She scowled. "You would torment your wife senseless?"

He lowered his face to hers, his hands braced to either side of her, and kept himself just hovering over her. "I intend to pleasure my wife senseless so I may linger in the joys of her moans that grow me harder and harder."

Raven's scowl disappeared. "I have that power over you?"

He brought his lips down near hers. "You'll not use it against me, wife."

She grinned. "Of course not, husband." She grabbed his face, her fingers settling in his beard and loving the feel of the mixture of roughness and softness, then she kissed him.

Her passion-filled kiss pushed Wolf to the edge and he tore his mouth off hers. "Hold on to me," he ordered.

Raven clamped her hands on his arms and instinctively spread her legs. She wiggled her bottom to meet his shaft that probed at her entrance.

"This is it, wife. This makes you mine," he said as if giving her one last chance to deny him.

"It makes us one," she corrected.

His heart swelled with a joy that was foreign to him, a joy he had never felt. "Aye wife—one."

He entered her slowly, careful not to hurt her. Her sheath was snug and it hugged him tight as he slipped his thick shaft deeper into her. Her moans grew as did the way she moved beneath him, arching up, seeking more of him.

She gave a sudden thrust that had him instinctively plunging into her and he came to an abrupt halt when she gasped in pain.

"Good God, don't stop now," she cried out.

He smiled and did as she ordered, keeping his eyes focused on hers as he did, enjoying the passion that struck like lightning in her brilliant blue eyes.

Raven had felt a moment of pain that had passed quickly. All she cared about was the intense pleasure of his mighty thrusts and she matched each one with the thrusts of her hips while keeping her eyes locked with his.

She bit at her lower lip as an intense sensation grew far more powerful than she felt she could contain.

Her moans grew as well and she feared they would soon turn to screams. She was going to explode, she wanted to explode.

"Wolf!" she cried out, slamming her hips against him again and again.

"Let go, wife!" he commanded.

And she did, screaming out his name as she burst in pure pleasure.

Her screams as she climaxed finished him, sending him hurtling over the edge and erupting in a climax with a forcefulness he had never experienced with any woman. And he let loose with a powerful groan.

Wolf was left so spent that he dropped off her to lay flat on his back, fearful if he didn't he'd collapse on top of her. His breathing was as laborious as hers and they both laid side by side in the aftermath of an exceptional climax.

When he was finally able to speak, he turned on his side toward her and hurried a blanket over them both, worried she would suffer a chill like she often did. "I didn't hurt you, did I? I saw the pain in your eyes and—"

She pressed her fingers to his lips, silencing him. "It was nothing." She smiled. "Everything else was—amazing." She tapped his chest. "And so you know, I won't mind doing it as often as you'd like."

Wolf laughed and kissed her quick. "Often. I'd like to do it often." His laughter faded, along with his smile and he dropped down on his back.

Raven turned on her side toward him this time. "I know what you want to ask, but you don't want to spoil this moment, this new start, between us."

Wolf turned on his side to face her. "It shouldn't matter and yet it plagues me. What man would love a woman so strongly and yet not want to make love with her?" His brow shot up. "Unless he didn't love you in return."

"Or he loved me... like a father loves a daughter," Raven said.

He shook his head, feeling a fool. "I never gave that thought."

"I suppose I didn't make it sound that way," she said, knowing he wasn't all to blame for the misunderstanding. "I am grateful every day for Charles finding me when he did. He came upon me as a man was forcing himself on me. I fought, but the man was large and bulky, and I was weak from lack of food and the cold. I didn't have the strength to fight him off."

Wolf grew enraged at the thought. "Please tell me Charles killed him, or I will hunt him down and kill him myself and none too quickly."

The anger in her husband's dark eyes left no doubt he would and she realized then what a staunch champion he would be for her.

Raven nodded. "He did, and then he told me he would teach me how to protect myself so no man could ever force himself on me again."

"The reason you are so skilled with a knife."

"Aye, Charles taught me well."

Wolf ran his hand tenderly along her cheek. "I like Charles."

Raven sighed softly, glad for his touch. "He was a good man, an honest man. He lost his wife and son to an illness that swept through the clan he belonged to, leaving few survivors. He had only his daughter left, and from what Charles said she was far too sweet and caring. A new chieftain arrived and he was a mean man. Unfortunately, he favored Charles's daughter." Sadness filled Raven's every word. "Charles made plans to leave with his daughter but the chieftain found out and locked Charles away in a cell. When he was freed, it was to bury his daughter. She had died at the hands of the chieftain. Charles left and having nothing, he became a thief and planned his revenge."

"Tell me he got his revenge," Wolf said, anger brewing in him for what the man had suffered.

She shook her head, her sadness growing, her hand going to the small scar at her side. "I was too late to help him when a band of evil thieves hit us. He died from his wound, but before he did I pledged my word to him that I would see it done. That nothing would stop me."

"I can see to that done for you, wife," Wolf said, not taking the chance of letting her do something so dangerous.

Her blue eyes darkened and a sinister look crossed over her lovely face. "I already did and I made the chieftain well aware of why he was about to die."

"If there is anyone else you must avenge, you will leave it to me," he ordered, just the thought of the chance she had taken sent a fright through him he felt clear down to his bones. "And don't bother to tell me you can see to it yourself. I'll not have you taking such dangerous chances."

"We can discuss it," she said.

"There is nothing to discuss. You will obey me on this," he ordered once again and braced himself for her protest.

"I told you about Charles. Now tell me of this scar that pains you that no one can see."

That she ignored his order and changed the subject told him she had no intentions of obeying him. He'd let her think that for now.

"It's my fault Oria was taken from our family," he said, something he had never told anyone.

"What do you mean? You could have only been a young lad yourself."

"Near seven years and tasked with seeing to staying with the slave who watched over Oria that day. I was impatient. I wanted to join the other young lads on the practice field. The slave told me to go, that she didn't need my help. I left and gave her the opportunity she needed to abduct my sister. I thought only of myself and my sister paid dearly for my selfishness."

"You did what any young lad would have done. If the woman hadn't abducted her that day she would have found another day to do it. She'd probably been planning it and she took advantage of the moment and your vulnerability. This scar is not for you to carry. But I would share that with Oria. She should know how you feel. It will make a difference in how she feels about you."

"I don't know if I would agree with that," he said and heard his wife's stomach grumble. "You're hungry."

Raven wasn't about to deny it. "I am."

"I'll have Ida bring food to us," he said and turned to leave the bed.

"Wolf," she said softly and he turned. "I can't be someone I'm not."

He didn't respond. He got out of bed, partially dressed, and left the room to find Ida, the question she didn't ask echoing loudly in his head.

Can you ever accept me for who I am?

How did he accept her independent, spirited nature that was sure to get her into endless trouble and that would drive him completely mad with worry?

He stopped abruptly when a response resonated in his head.

Love her. Simply love her.

Chapter Seventeen

Raven stood by the hearth in her shirt, staring at her sleeping husband. She had become accustomed to every little sound waking her. It was how one stayed alive while traveling the dangerous roads. If one slept too soundly, you could wake to find a knife at your throat or what little belongings you had gone.

She turned her eyes to the flames in the hearth. The wind whipping around the longhouse had been responsible for waking her. Though it hadn't startled her awake like most sounds had done. Instead it had poked at her sleep until she woke in the warmth and comfort of her husband's arms. A smile woke along with her, recalling last night and the three times they had coupled. The two quick ones had been as enjoyable as the lingering one. Even now she felt ready to couple with her husband again. She feared she would never get enough of him. But first there were some things they needed to discuss. If this was to work between them, trust and truth were essential.

"Regrets, wife?"

Raven's eyes went quick to her husband lying on his side, his hand stretched out to her.

She went to him, though stopped before she got close enough for him to touch her, not trusting herself. She'd be distracted too easily if he touched her and while she would welcome that, she first needed to talk with him.

"We need to talk," she said, reluctantly keeping her distance.

He lowered his outstretched hand. "I'll ask again, regrets, wife?"

"Never," she said with a smile that confirmed her word as truth.

Wolf bolted out of bed, yanked her shirt off her, without little protest from her, and had his wife up in his arms before she could make a fuss. Though, he realized if she had wanted to make a fuss there would have been no stopping her. He rushed them back into bed, tucking the covers around them and snuggling himself around her.

"Talk," he said, though he would rather make love to her.

Raven felt his shaft hard with need pressing against her and that he ignored his need to let her talk touched her heart.

"You gave me what I asked for, for me to trust you," she said.

"And do you trust me, wife?" he asked, her response far more important than he expected.

"I never thought I'd say this, but I do trust you," she assured him. And since you did as I asked, it's time for me to do as you asked, confide in you as I do with my men, in essence be as truthful with you as I am with them."

It pleased him that she would honor her word without him reminding her of it. "I see the way you talk and whisper with them and that is something I want us to share. It's part of trusting me and I trusting you."

"Then I will share something with you now that has troubled me" She paused a moment, thinking how the news she was about to share might affect their newly found closeness. She began cautiously. "Unfortunately, I haven't been able to reach out to those who may be able to help me discover the truth."

His brow furrowed. "What truth? Tell me, for you have me curious and perhaps we can solve the problem together."

That was what she had hoped for and it relieved her to hear it. "I think it would be wise of us to do so, for I think someone manipulates us."

His eyes narrowed, causing his brow to knit tight. "Tell me," he urged.

"You remarked that I was the one who initiated the proposal that we wed, but I was told it was you who proposed it and that the King looked favorably on it."

He shook his head. "I never gave thought to such a proposal."

"Either did I," Raven confessed. "But when presented with it, all I could think about was my brothers finally being free, since I feared it would take at least two more years of my thieving to get the money to free them both. And I worried they might not last that long."

The news troubled him and he didn't think twice about sharing a secret of his own. "I'm going to tell you something, something that I was warned never to share with anyone. But with this news, I feel it is imperative I share it with you. However, you must give me your word that you will never share it with anyone. It stays between us."

Raven's stomach turned with worry, sensing the manipulation she feared had far reaching tentacles. "You have my word."

"Your brothers were never part of my mercenary group."

Raven's mouth dropped open in shock and it took her a moment to speak. "I don't understand." She shook her head. "It is common knowledge you have a large band of mercenaries."

"I do, but your brothers and other men from your clan didn't join with mine. I don't force men to join my group. Loyalty is never gained by force."

Her brow knit tight with question. "Then who did they fight for?"

"Your King David, though it was not made known. As far as anyone was told, it was my mercenaries who fought."

She stared at him in complete shock.

Wolf continued explaining. "When my king heard of my plans to regain land here that rightfully belonged to me, he made it clear that there were things he wanted me to do since he was in negotiations, though more dispute, with King David over land, including several isles, your King insisted belonged to Scotland. The dispute was causing considerable trouble and my king thought it imperative that I install myself firmly in the area. When he discovered my grandmother's clan had once extended beyond Learmonth, he ordered me to lay claim to all of it.

"To use in negotiations against King David," she said, the reason becoming clearer.

"I can't say I argued against it. I was determined to regain the land that rightfully belonged to my grandmother's clan and my king's support made it that much easier."

"But how did my king wind up with my brothers and those men from the Clan MacKinnon?"

"Actually, King David got not only the men from your clan but all the ones captured from the other clans I claimed. It was part of a proposal struck between your king and mine. King David needed men to fight for him, few wanted to take up sword for him especially on foreign shores. I didn't object since I foolishly didn't want my sister marrying your brother. I had other plans for her which I'm glad didn't work out. Don't get me wrong, Raven. My king's plan only enforced mine and gave me opportunities that helped me succeed, so I made no objection to it."

Raven tried to comprehend all Wolf had said. "So the men who attacked my clan that day when my brother Royden lost his hand, they weren't your men?"

"Some of them were, but mostly they were the king's men. I insisted that one of my men be in charge of at least one group of men taken by the king's men. That way I would have someone who could keep me apprised of what went on. My king agreed. My man, Platt, kept me informed through the years and has returned home, since all the men from the various clans have been released. Thanks to you. Another stipulation you had wisely included in the proposal."

"That's how you knew Brynjar had captured Arran. Platt informed you."

He eyed her suspiciously, though he should have known better. "How did you know about Arran's capture?"

She smiled cunningly. "I know more than you think." Her brow suddenly creased in question wiping the smile from her face. "Why rescue Arran if he wasn't one of yours?"

"I'm beginning to realize you are a woman of vast knowledge," he said, reminding himself to keep it in mind. "As for your brother, your King would have left him with Brynjar and Arran would have died. Oria would have hated me even more than she did if I allowed that to happen. Besides, Brynjar believed Arran was one of my mercenaries and to not retrieve what belonged to me would have been seen as a surrender. And that is something I do not do."

Raven thought on all he had said and what she knew, trying to make sense of it. Two powerful men—kings—had thought nothing of playing with their lives as if they were pieces in a game they maneuvered for fun.

"Do you think it was one of the kings who manipulated us into marriage?" she asked.

"Kings do nothing without a purpose. The question is does our marriage benefit either or both of the kings, if not, they'd have no purpose to see us wed."

"If not them, then who?" Raven asked more curious than ever as to who had been responsible for bringing them together.

"A mystery to solve," Wolf said. "Even more so the decision behind it. Was it intended to bring peace or was it intended to cause more discord and possibly instigate more battles and cause more lives to be lost?"

Raven grabbed hold of his arm that lay over her waist. "Do you think Brynjar could have anything to do with it? He's made it obvious he wants me dead. Could that have been his plan. Force us into a marriage, kill me, and start a war between our clans?"

Wolf shook his head. "Anything is possible, though he would need to know a number of people here in Scotland to carry out such a plan and his contacts here are sorely limited."

"Evil men exist all over and I found that evil attracts evil. Perhaps Brynjar found someone here as evil as him and with the desire for power and chaos."

Wolf kissed her gently. "Then it is good we have foiled his plans. My people and your people will now see that we care for each other and intend to build a good life together. And, no doubt," —his hand went to rest on her stomach— "you will grow round with child soon enough, proving our intention."

Her hand drifted down to stroke his shaft. "Then you better get busy seeing that done."

"Keep touching me like that and my seed will wind up in your hand," he cautioned.

Her cunning smile returned. "A mighty warrior like you can't contain himself?"

His hand slipped between her legs. "How about we see who can contain themselves the longest?"

Raven chuckled before kissing her husband. "We both know I'd be defeated, but I am willing to give it a try."

"You are a brave woman, Raven, more brave than I ever imagined, and I am lucky to have you as my wife."

Her stomach fluttered and her heart felt a joy that she had thought long dead, and when he kissed her, both sensations increased tenfold and at that moment she was certain she caught a glimpse of love.

***

"I am not wearing this," Raven said, shaking the garment at her husband who had just entered their bedchamber.

"It will keep you warmer than your shirt and plaid," he argued.

"It's long length will restrict my movements. I won't wear it." She tossed the garment on the bed. Her hands went to her hips and she sent him an accusing look. "Was that what it was meant to do?"

It was a good thing his wife wore her shirt because if she was naked he'd rush her to their bed and enter her swiftly, he had such a need for her, a need that ached endlessly at him. The more they made love, which they had done throughout the day yesterday, the snowstorm keeping them inside, the more he desired her. They were definitely going to have many bairns.

"You know me better than that," he challenged. "My only thought was to see you kept warm."

Her husband had touched her heart far too often since yesterday and to her dismay she believed love was beginning to poke at her. Or was it fear that she would allow herself to love only to lose him and suffer loss once again?

"As much as I don't want to admit it," she said with a twinkle in her eyes. "You're right. Come over here to me and I'll apologize properly."

Wolf laughed. "If I come over there, wife, we won't be leaving this room for hours."

"I'm not eager to go out in the cold or tramp through the high snow."

"Pathways have been cleared with more to come," he assured, trying more to persuade himself than her.

"How does that stop me from being cold?" she challenged.

He held up his hand and she thought he meant to silence her, then he turned and left the room and she understood he wanted her to remain there. She had no intentions of going anywhere except back to bed with her husband and not to sleep.

She grew impatient while reminders of how he had made her feel last night growing her more and more aroused. Finally, the door opened and her husband entered with a bundle of furs, leather, and a dark wool shirt in his arms.

"These will keep you warm," he said and dropped them on the bed." He pulled the dark wool shirt from the pile and held it out to her. "Put this on, it's a heavier wool and will keep you warm."

Raven could tell he needed a little enticement and she walked over to him slowly.

Wolf stretched his arm out, practically shoving the shirt in his wife's face, not wanting her to get too close, not trusting what he might do.

"There are things I must see to," he said, wondering if he was reminding himself and not his wife.

"Aye, there is something imperative you must see to." She pushed his arm aside, grabbed him by the front of his shirt and dropped down on the bed, bringing him down on top of her. "Me. You need to see to me." She kissed him gently, then settled her lips near his ear and whispered, "I ache for you."

He muttered something beneath his breath and Raven smiled, familiar with the foreign word Northmen used, though not in front of their women.

"Make haste, husband," she said and wrapped her legs around him.

And he did what he had wanted to do ever since entering the room and seeing her standing in nothing more than her shirt, though haste wasn't on his mind.

"I want you naked," he said, his hands going to her shirt and pushing it up, and she obliged yanking it over her head and tossing it aside.

"You as well," she urged and dropped her legs off him to free him to do just that.

Wolf was fast, his shaft having grown too hard too fast. He leaned over her, letting his manhood linger teasingly between her legs while he rolled his tongue over one of her nipples then teased it with sharp, brief nips.

"Not fair," she said on a groan. "This was to be fast."

"I want more," he said and poked at her entrance with his manhood as he rose up over her, his muscled arms straight and taut at her sides as he hovered over her. He dropped his head not to steal a kiss but to invade her mouth with a passion that stole her breath.

Her mouth ached with pleasure, her nipples as well. Passion fired hot in her and she spread her legs in invitation. All she wanted was for him to plunge into her and make her scream with pleasure.

"Stop tormenting me," she warned, grabbing his forearms. "I was more than ready for you before you entered the room. Now see it done."

"Is that an order, wife?" he asked on a chuckle.

"It's a threat," she warned and locked her legs around him, his shaft slipping slightly into her. Feeling him there, knowing the pleasure that awaited, she met his dark eyes. "I need to feel you inside me."

It was the need in her gorgeous blue eyes he saw and the plea in her voice that he heard that had him enter her swiftly. Her groans of passion had him sinking deeper and deeper into her and he could feel her pleasure grow along with his. Her grip grew tighter on his arms as she thrust up against him and her moans grew as well.

She was as close as he was and he urged her on, wanting to join with her at that very moment when passion burst with a fury and pleasure rained down on them. He felt her body arch, her thrust filled with strength and he matched it slamming against her and they exploded together, both their roars ringing throughout the longhouse.

He collapsed on top of her after every last bit of pleasure drained away and her arms went around him, hugging him tight.

"You are the best husband," she said and kissed his cheek repeatedly.

He raised his head and she kissed his cheeks, his brow, and his bearded chin. "I'm glad I please you, wife."

"And you will please me often, right?" she asked and waited for him to answer as if it was the most important question she ever asked.

He kissed the tip of her nose. "As often as you like and then some."

She grinned with glee and hugged him tighter.

"I have duties to see to," he reminded.

"Since you saw to your most important duty, you can now go and see to the others," she commanded reluctantly and released him, her arms dropping to her sides.

Wolf bolted off the bed and reached down to yank her up into his arms. "Be careful, wife, my commands will want more from you."

She kissed his cheek. "I'm counting on it."

He released her hastily and stepped away from her. "Those words will echo in my head all day."

"Then be sure to do something about them. Now show me how to wear these garments."

Raven paid attention to how he wrapped the furs around her, from her shoulders to her legs and was impressed with the warmth that embraced her by the time he was done.

"It feels good," she said.

Wolf looked her over and smiled. "It looks natural on you and I'm proud to have you wear the garments of a Northman warrior."

Again he touched her heart, taking pride in her, something she never would have expected from him, but then he was nothing like the man she had assumed he would be.

"Time to brave the cold," he said, holding his hand out to her.

They would brave more than the cold, since she didn't have a doubt in her mind that people would see a difference in them, her men certainly would. But wasn't it for the better? Their getting along meant peace in the area, something someone may not have intended to happen.

The cold struck Raven as soon as she stepped outside, but she was pleased that her garments served as a good barrier against the sting of the cold and with Wolf's hand gripped firmly around hers, it kept it toasty warm.

The village was busy, men clearing pathways, women getting cook-fires going, and children running in play. The heavy snowfall had done nothing to dampen the villagers' spirits. It actually seemed to brighten them, perhaps reminding them of winter in their homeland.

When they reached the center of the village, Wolf stopped and turned to face her. "I have duties I must see to. Your men, all but Fyn, have returned to their cottages, if you wish to spend time with them. I will find you when I am done."

Raven sensed what he intended to do next, kiss her in front of everyone so they would see she accepted him as her husband. She decided to change that. She hurried and threw her arms around his neck and kissed him before he could kiss her.

His arms went around her, hugging her tight and like the mighty warrior he was, he took charge of the kiss, leaving Raven weak in the knees when it was over, not that she'd admit it. Nor did she need to, since he kept his arm around her waist longer than needed as if he knew his kiss had left her weak.

"I'm going to get back at you for that," she said softly and with a smile.

He faintly brushed his lips overs hers. "I'm counting on it."

His chuckle drifted behind him as he walked away and Raven's smile spread. She turned to go see her men when she noticed how many people were whispering, grinning, and nodding.

She knew exactly what they were thinking… the Beast had tamed his wife.

She continued on, chuckling to herself. They were about to learn how wrong they were.

Chapter Eighteen

Raven approached the cottages where her men resided to find Iver sitting alone outside in front of a fire pit, the heat from the flames melting the snow around it. He was lost in thought, his dark eyes focused on the flames. He might appear as if he paid no heed, but he was more than aware of her presence. She often thought his dark eyes could see without seeing, strange as that seemed.

She sat next to him on the narrow bench and stretched her hands out to the flames to warm them. "All alone?"

"Fyn and George are with the women in the keep and Brod is helping Ida, doing what I don't know." He shook his head.

She offered comfort with her words. "Things are changing, Iver, whether we want them to or not."

"I know, but I don't know if this change is for me," he said without taking his eyes off the flickering flames. "I enjoyed being on the road, going different places, hunting down information, and people." He turned to her. "I feel caged here."

"Then maybe it's time you went on a mission."

His dark eyes lit with excitement. "Tell me where and I'm off."

"I need to speak with Wolf about it since we've agreed to trust and be honest with each other in order to have a decent and bearable marriage as well as bringing peace to the area. To make sure that happens, there are some issues that need settling."

"Did you confide in Wolf about not being the one who initiated the marriage proposal?"

"I did and he was as surprised to hear it as I had been to learn about it. We want to find out who devised the proposal and made it happen," she said.

"The first message you received in regards to the proposal came from Stitchill Monastery. I should start there, and see what Abbott Thomas knows of the messenger," Iver said, anxious to be on his way.

"First we talk with Wolf and formulate a plan, then when all is set you can leave and hopefully discover something that will help us unravel this mystery."

"And we don't tell anyone," Iver warned.

"I trust all my men, Iver, but I agree with you on this. The less who know about it, the better for the time being," she agreed.

"I'm glad you think the same and I too trust our group, but not when women, we've just come to know, are involved. They say women's tongues wag endlessly, but men often don't mind their tongues around women. Men lose all common sense when a woman catches their fancy. And that's not going to happen to me." Iver turned his head to look at Raven. "Your husband approaches and he appears upset."

Raven turned to see that Iver was right, her husband wore a worried expression. "What's wrong?" she asked, standing when he got near.

"I assume you have crossed paths with Brother Noble in your adventures," Wolf said, stopping in front of the fire pit separating them and continuing when his wife nodded. "He took shelter here when the snow began to fall and now he's gone. He didn't sound well the last time I spoke with him and I'm not sure when he left here, and I'm concerned for his well-being. I'm going to take some men and search for him."

Iver sprung up off the bench. "I'll go. I'd probably find him faster than you could. I can also see that he gets back to Stitchill Monastery safely." He gave Raven an anxious look. "I could see to that matter we discussed."

Raven motioned for her husband to come closer and when he did, she kept her voice low. "I had plans to discuss this with you." She went on to tell him what she and Iver had just talked about.

"I agree," Wolf said when she finished. "Stitchill Monastery would be a good place to start. I always thought there was more to the monastery than prayers. And with Brother Noble being a messenger for the monastery, he might possess information he doesn't even realize is valuable."

"I'll leave now," Iver said.

Raven smiled at the gleam of excitement in Iver's dark eyes. It had been lacking since their arrival here. But she would not see him sent off in haste. "First, you'll make sure you are well prepared with food and warm garments and once I see that is done, I'll give you permission to take your leave."

Iver grinned. "I'm wise enough to adhere to the words of someone who has proven she knows better than me."

"Wise choice of words," Raven said with a chuckle. "Gather what you need while I have Ida prepare sufficient food for your journey."

"I'll have a moment with you, Iver," Wolf commanded and wasn't surprised to see the man look to Raven, seeking her approval.

She nodded and walked off.

"I take orders from Raven," Iver said, as if needing to remind the man.

"For the moment you do," Wolf said, letting the man know he allowed it for now but it wouldn't be forever. "I'm sure Raven warned you about being cautious while searching for the truth in this matter."

"I understand the delicacy of the situation."

Wolf wanted to make certain the man fully understood. "It is imperative we find out who formulated this plan and even more imperative that the person responsible doesn't know we're searching for him."

"For fear of what he might do," Iver said, his eyes on Wolf but also making sure no one was close enough to hear their whispers. "And worry not about Brother Noble. I'm certain I can find him and see him safely to the monastery."

"I rest easy knowing that, Iver. Safe journey." Wolf turned away.

"She deserves to be treated well."

Wolf didn't look back as he said, "On that we agree, Iver."

***

Raven thought to go to the keep and let Fyn and George know Iver had gone in search of Brother Noble but men were still working on clearing a path up the hill. She would wait until they were done. Brod also had to be told but when she looked for him, he was busy helping Ida disperse hot brews to the crews of men who worked diligently to create pathways through the snow. She decided to wait until later to speak with him.

Everyone was busy with their duties or chores and here she stood, after seeing Iver off, not knowing what to do with herself. Her days had always been full, few if any found her sitting around. And Iver's words of feeling caged, had her thinking that at times she felt the same herself. The few duties Wolf mentioned that was a wife's responsibility would bore her to death and were already being seen to by those more experienced and competent than her. The longhouse ran perfectly well without her dictate and would remain so without any interference from her. She'd much prefer to be involved with the security of the village and keeping everyone safe. And while the keep set high on a hill where the view stretched far and wide, there were some ground areas where the trees were so thick, a small group of warriors could slip through without being seen. Tree perches could be erected there, adding further protection to the village.

Raven decided to scout the outer edges of the village where tree perches might work well. She made her way along the cleared paths, planning to start at the spot where she felt her plan could work. Few if any people acknowledged her as she went along her way, an occasional smile being the only greeting she received. She had no one to blame but herself for that. She had made no true attempt to get to know any of her husband's tribe and having been at odds with him hadn't helped. With that changing, so should other things change, and she looked forward to the possibilities.

Some glares were sent her way, disapproving ones, and she wondered over them, then realized it had to be her garments that upset a few. She wasn't dressed as most wives… she was dressed as most warriors. She kept walking, ignoring the judgmental stares until a woman's pleading cry brought her to an abrupt stop.

"No, Ober, please don't—"

The frightened plea had Raven turning just as a large hand connected with a young woman's face. She would have collapsed from the vicious blow if the man hadn't had a strong grip on the woman's slim arm.

The woman pleaded again when the man raised his hand. "Please, no, Ober."

"Hit her again and I'll gut you," Raven cried out, stopping the man's hand in mid-air as she walked toward him.

Ober turned, his face filled with rage. "Mind your own."

"It is my own now with your leader marrying me and I'll not have any man taking a hand to any woman," Raven ordered, not showing a bit of fear as she came to stand right in front of him. "LET HER GO!"

Ober drew his head back as if recoiling from a slap in the face at her loud command. "She's my wife."

"Something you need to remember," Raven accused.

"And something that has nothing to do with you," Ober shot back.

"It certainly does when you raise your hand to a defenseless woman."

"She's my wife," Ober repeated as if that justified his actions.

"Let me make this clear for you, since you haven't the brains to understand it," Raven said, shaking a fist at Ober. "Any man who raises his hand to a woman in this village will be punished."

Ober laughed right in Raven's face. "Wolf will put you in your place soon enough."

Raven's hand shot out so fast, the man had no time to react, catching his cheek with a hard slap. His other cheek caught an even more vicious slap and left his cheek to redden with her handprint.

Ober released his wife with a shove that sent her stumbling while his hand rushed to his face. Rage stirred in his eyes as he felt the welt growing.

"Twice. You hit her twice from what I can see on her tender face." She turned to the stunned woman. "Did he hit you more than that?"

Ober yelled at his wife. "Keep your mouth shut."

Raven delivered another vicious blow to this cheek, so hard it stung her palm. "You answered for her. You raise a hand to her, I raise a hand to you." She jabbed him in the chest. "Do I make myself clear?"

Ober's face reddened with fury and he clenched his hands at his sides. Both were telltale signs that he fought to contain himself. If she wasn't Wolf's wife, he would have taken a hand to her. And oh how she wished he would. She wanted to give him what he richly deserved.

"You want to strike me, don't you?" Raven said, giving him another jab. "Now you know what it's like to feel helpless, not able to retaliate against someone causing you harm and fear."

"I don't fear you," Ober spat.

"You should," Raven warned with another jab.

"Wolf will have something to say about this," Ober threatened.

"You're right, I do have something to say."

Raven turned not only to see her husband standing there, but also Gorm, as well as several villagers. The fury in her husband's eyes made her wonder if it was meant for her. Had she overstepped her bounds? She didn't care. There was no way she would stand by and let a man beat on a helpless woman. Ober was three times the size of his wife.

"Are you all right, Dearyn?" Wolf asked.

"Aye, sir," Dearyn said, a tremble to her words.

"Tell him. Tell him why I hit you," Ober said.

Raven wanted to hit him again, forcing his wife to condone what he did.

"I was clumsy and spilled a hot brew on his hand," Dearyn said and Ober held his left hand out to show a red spot on the back as proof.

"You strike her three times for a burn that is barely visible?" Raven shook her head. "You're a coward."

Ober's knuckles turned white he gripped his fists so tight and he looked ready to charge at Raven. "I'm no coward and I am a good husband. Isn't that right, Dearyn?"

"Aye. Aye, Ober is a good husband," Dearyn said, her slim fingers twisting her apron in a knot.

Wolf spoke up loud and clear for everyone to hear. "You're three times your wife's size, Ober. DON'T hit her again."

Ober looked ready to argue.

"My word is final!" Wolf commanded. "If you strike her again, you will suffer three strikes for each one you give her. And I will gladly deliver each one myself."

Raven was pleased to see the fear suddenly replace the fury in Ober's eyes. Her husband must deliver a powerful punch if it caused fright in Ober.

"Get back to work!" Wolf called out and everyone scurried off except Gorm. "See an eye is kept on him for a few days." Gorm walked off and Wolf turned to his wife, folding his arms across his chest. "You place yourself in far too many dangerous situations."

"I'm your wife, Ober wouldn't dare strike me," Raven said confidently.

"You know that for sure? I've seen him strike men for less."

"His fear coupled with the respect I see that your men have for you wouldn't let him do such a foolish thing," she argued. "Besides, if he had raised his hand to me, he'd be minus a hand right now."

"You do realize you now have a husband more than capable of defending you?"

"I don't question that," she said as if it was never a thought. "What I do question is, will he defend me regardless of the situation?"

"You mean whether I agree with you or not?"

Her hands went to rest on her hips. "That's exactly what I mean."

Raven didn't even have time to gasp, her husband moved so fast, hooking his arm around her waist and yanking her against him.

"We'll always have our differences, *kona*, but that doesn't mean I won't defend you." His kiss stopped any response or protest she intended. He hastily stepped away from her after ending the kiss.

"You don't start what you can't finish," she challenged, his possessive kiss leaving her wanting more.

"I'll finish it—later. There's work to be done." He turned, needing distance from his wife or he'd rush her into the longhouse and into their bed for the remainder of the day. "And not another word, wife, or I will make you wait even longer."

Her laughter had him turning around and she approached him and whispered, "With what you've taught me, I believe I would be able to please myself."

Wolf brought his face so close to hers that their noses almost touched. "Only if I can watch."

Raven's eyes shot wide and she stepped back.

"I look forward to it, wife." Wolf chuckled and walked off.

Damn if he didn't get her on that one. She walked away shaking her head.

The path to the keep had yet to be finished, but it was enough for her to make her way up it to the keep. She found Fyn and George at the top, working to clear the abundant snow that had accumulated in front of the keep.

"Nightmares disturbed Tait's sleep last night. He finally sleeps comfortably and Greta is keeping watch over him," Fyn said.

"Eria keeps her company," George added. "Is there something you need from us?"

"No, I wanted to let you know that Iver was sent to look for Brother Noble and see him safely to the monastery."

"I'm sure he'll have no trouble finding the leper and seeing him home," Fyn said.

George nodded in agreement. "Iver needed a mission. He can stay put for only so long."

Fyn grinned. "If he found a good woman, he'd stay put."

"He might be too set in his ways for a woman," George said.

Fyn looked to the keep. "I thought that once and to my surprise I was proved wrong."

Even with the many furs she wore, the cold managed to shiver her.

"Go inside and get warm," George said, seeing the shiver that hurried over her. "There is hot cider to warm your innards and honey oat cakes to enjoy."

Raven smiled and rubbed her hands together. "That sounds much too inviting to refuse."

Fyn opened the door for her. "We'll join you as soon as we finish this section."

"Take your time," Raven said and entered the keep.

Fragrant and familiar scents assaulted her when she entered the Great Hall. Pine branches graced the top of the mantel, their strong scent drifting throughout the room along with the delicious aroma of hot apple cider.

She quickly made her way to one of the few tables in the small room and, of course, one closest to the fireplace. She filled a tankard from the crock on the table and cupped her hands around it to let the heat seep into her cold hands.

"You have no gloves?"

Raven shook her head as Detta approached the table.

"Did you lose them?" Detta asked, placing a plate of fresh honey oat cakes in front of Raven.

"I traded them," Raven said and reached for one of the warm honey oak cakes.

"I hope it was a fair trade."

Raven confirmed with a nod, her mouth too full to speak, recalling the young lass who needed them more than her.

"You don't remember your visit here when you were young, do you?" Detta asked.

Raven took a swallow of cider before responding. "I have a vague remembrance of being here once, but how would you know of it? You weren't here that far back."

"Burnell often spoke of your visit with fondness and laughter." Detta smiled. "I believe he told me that you were barely five years old and there was no stopping your determination to explore and climb whatever caught your fancy."

"Which meant I probably climbed whatever was necessary for me to get where I wanted to explore," Raven said, recalling her da's repeated warnings of punishment if she didn't pay heed to his word.

"Burnell often remarked how fearless you were, letting nothing stop you, not even several falls that left you with bruises. He thought you a brave and remarkable lass."

Raven laughed. "My da would dispute that."

"Burnell said you were a chore to your da that day."

Memories had Raven smiling. "That would be most days back then."

"You made a lasting impression on Burnell and he very much enjoyed your one and only visit here."

"I imagine my actions embarrassed my da and was the reason he never brought me here again."

"Sometimes it takes only one look to know a person." Detta's words softened as she continued, "It's often that way with love. You look upon someone and you know deep in your heart he is the one for you."

"You know that from experience?" Raven asked.

"I do," she said with a soft whisper as if lost in loving memories. Her eyes flickered and the softness that had been there disappeared. "I will tell Lord Wolf that you are in need of gloves."

"Not necessary, Detta, I have a pair right here for her."

Raven hadn't heard her husband enter the room, she'd been too lost in the past and the memories Detta had stirred in her. She planned on visiting her da as soon as the snow allowed and asking him about her visit here. There was something she felt she should remember but she couldn't quite grasp it.

"Lady Raven traded her gloves and says it was a fair trade," Detta said as if she didn't quite believe Raven.

Wolf dropped the gloves on the table and removed his cloak, Detta reaching out to take it from him. He joined his wife, sitting beside her. "And what did you receive in this fair trade?"

Raven grinned wide. "A hug!"

Wolf's brow creased in annoyance. "A hug from who?"

"A hug from a young lass whose hands were bitter cold and needed the gloves more than I did, but refused to take them without trading something. I told her I missed my friends' hugs, hadn't had one in five years, and asked if she would trade a tight hug with me for the gloves. She gladly obliged." Raven turned a smile on Detta. "A fair trade, would you say?"

"A generous trade, my lady," Detta said.

Raven thought she caught a glimmer of tears in the old woman's eyes.

"I'll fetch more hot cider," Detta said and hastily hurried away.

"You have a good heart, wife," Wolf said and went to kiss her.

She pulled back away from him, eyeing him skeptically. "You didn't come here to just bring me gloves. You made it clear you had duties to see to, so why come find me?"

Wolf shook his head. "You are far too observant, wife."

"You should keep that in mind, since it will save us time when there is news you wish to tell me but hesitate to do so," she admonished. "Now tell me, what's happened?"

"I will tell you if you promise me you will warm yourself with more hot cider before we leave here."

"Gloves, hot cider, you want me warm against the cold. Where do we go?"

He turned a glare on her and she understood. "All right. I promise to warm myself with more cider." She hurriedly added. "And I do appreciate the gloves. Now please don't keep me waiting."

"We go into the woods. Another body has been found."

Chapter Nineteen

"Iver found him and returned to alert me. I sent him on, worried for Brother Noble's safety," Wolf explained as they walked through the woods, a dozen or more of his warriors spread out around them.

"It's one of Brynjar's men?" Raven asked.

"I can't say for sure, though his garments are those of a Northman," Wolf confirmed.

They said no more until they reached the spot where Iver had come across the body.

"With no visible wounds, I assume he got caught in the storm and froze to death," Raven said, staring down at the man. Sadly, she had come across more than one person through the years with bad luck enough to be caught in a snowstorm and freeze to death.

"I'd say that was his fate," Wolf agreed and watched how his wife drifted off in thought. He waited a bit before asking, "What thoughts simmer in your head?"

"I feel that we miss something. Why does Brynjar risk the death of so many men just to see me dead? What does it matter if he waits? Winter is a time of hibernation. Everything stills from the cold and emptiness of the season. Why rush the task? What does a few months matter?" She shook her head. "What makes him so impatient to see it done?"

"I have bested him many times, perhaps his patience for revenge has come to an end," Wolf suggested.

"We're missing something, I know we are," Raven insisted.

"I'd listen to her," Fyn said, standing not far from them along with George, and Brod walked over to join them.

"Raven has excellent instincts," George said.

"We can all attest to that," Brod agreed. "She saved us many a time when we thought all was clear and we were safe to thieve travelers along the road, only to find warriors lurked near that would have meant the death of us."

"Then what do you think goes on with Brynjar?" Wolf asked his wife.

"There is a reason he rushes to see this done," Raven said. "But how would he benefit from my death? What if it isn't truly my death he seeks?"

"What do you mean?" Brod asked.

Raven wasn't sure herself but continued to reason. "What if he seeks to see me dead to hide his true intentions for being here?"

"Wolf's death?" George asked.

"Something I'm sure he covets," Wolf said.

"I don't believe so," Raven said. "Wolf's death would give him no satisfaction. My death could disrupt the relative peace our marriage has brought between clans. And could very well bring war to the area, causing Wolf endless strife and suffering, something Brynjar would relish."

Wolf admired his wife's quick mind. She reasoned faster than most and could project other possible scenarios they might face. She truly was a warrior.

"It's his impatience that has me questioning his reason," she said, frustrated she failed to see what it might be.

"More men will come," Wolf said, looking to each of her men.

"We'll protect her," Fyn said and George and Brod agreed with forceful nods.

Raven ignored them, studying the dead man. "Why didn't he seek shelter?" she asked of no one in particular.

"I wondered the same," Wolf said. "Northmen know how to survive in a snowstorm."

"He could have been a captive," George suggested.

"Perhaps Sten would recognize him," Raven said.

Though they thought the same often, Wolf still found it surprising when her words mirrored his thoughts. Or was it surprising that it continued and grew even stronger that amazed him?

"His body will be brought to the village and we'll see what Sten has to say," Wolf said and gave a quick look to the sky. "We need to return. The dark clouds warn of more possible snow."

"At least more snow will keep the culprits at bay," Brod said.

"It didn't keep this one at bay," Raven said, glancing down at the frozen dead man.

***

Sten hugged himself against the cold, though he wore a warm cloak, and stared at the dead man on the table in the small shed. After a few moments, he shook his head. "I've never seen him before."

"You never came across him in any of Brynjar's camps?" Wolf asked.

Sten shook his head again. "No, never. He is a stranger to me. I've never come across him at any of Brynjar's camps I've been to."

Wolf waved at Lars to return the man to the keep.

"What if he's not one of Brynjar's men?" Raven asked, staring down at the dead man who if she ventured to guess was maybe five or six years older than her. A man of fair looks, not that tall and slim. "He looks more a farmer or craftsman than a warrior."

"He does," Wolf agreed. "But then Brynjar doesn't care about one's trade. His captives fight for him or they die."

"I never thought of a man in more need of dying than Brynjar."

"Many would agree with you," Wolf said, "but like most evil men, he has powerful friends, who more than likely fear him."

"They know he craves their power and will think nothing of taking it from them." She shook her head and glanced down at the dead man again. "So is this man one of Brynjar's men or is he nothing more than a traveler the snowstorm claimed?"

"A question we may never get an answer to," Wolf said, annoyed at the thought.

"Perhaps we should have Greta take a look at this man," Raven suggested. "She may spot something we missed about his death."

"A good thought," Wolf said. "I'll have Fyn bring her here. In the meantime, I need to go see if the trackers were able to find anything that might help us." Wolf kissed her gently. "Don't do anything foolish, Raven."

She laughed lightly. "I've done the most foolish thing I've ever done and it has turned out surprisingly well."

"And what's that?" he asked, though he had his suspicions.

She draped her arms around his neck and relished the feel of his arm circling her waist to hold her firm. "I wed you." She kissed him, her passion taking them both by surprise and forcing Wolf to end the heated kiss.

He rested his brow against hers, calming his breathing and trying to douse the fire she had ignited in him.

"Sooner than later," she whispered softly near his ear.

"Much sooner," he agreed and suddenly was looking forward to the cold winter ahead, intending to spend a good portion of it in bed with his wife.

"I'll wait here for Greta," Raven said. Wolf gave her a nod and hurried off.

Making love with her husband had changed everything. She shook her head. That may have been the breaking point, but it hadn't been the only thing to change things between them. It had been a series of small things, some good, some not, that allowed them to see each other truthfully and finally allowed them to trust each other. Though, it was her husband believing her word that she'd never been with a man that made the biggest difference to her. For some reason, it had opened her heart to hope and the possibility that there might be a chance for a sliver of love between them.

Dare she give that thought or even want it from a man who was once her enemy? Was she being a fool?

She shook her head. This wasn't the time for such thoughts. She forced herself to concentrate on the dead man to see if there was anything she missed. No weapons had been found with him and a quick glance had seen none on him. That was until she took a closer look and caught sight of the hilt of a knife barely peeking out from one of his boots. It was tucked down too far to catch sight of it without a closer look. She thought of slipping it out, but it would be better to wait until he thawed some to retrieve it. Any symbols engraved on it might help identify the man.

Raven turned as the door opened and Greta entered.

"Lord Wolf summoned me, my lady," Greta said.

Someday she was going to get people to call her by her name and not some fancy title that didn't belong to her. For now, she ignored it.

"Aye, Greta, but first, how is Tait?"

"Other than some nightmares he does well, but that is thanks to Fyn. He's teaching him what to do to protect himself and he's fashioning a wooden knife so he can teach Tait how to use it wisely." She smiled. "I am grateful he cares for both me and my son. He is a good man."

"Fyn is a good man and he would make a fine husband to you and a good da to Tait."

Greta blushed. "I feel safe with him."

"And well you should," Raven said, truly pleased for Fyn and Greta. "I'm sure Fyn told you that a man was found frozen to death in the woods or so we've surmised. Lord Wolf and I would like you to examine him the best you can and see if you can tell us if perhaps we missed something where is death is concerned."

"I'll do my best, my lady," Greta said and approached the table, Raven moving aside.

Raven was surprised to see Greta's hand rush to cover her mouth and tears rush to pool in her eyes. "Do you know this man, Greta?"

She shook her head, her hand falling slowly away from her mouth. "No, I didn't expect one so young. He is one of Brynjar's men?"

"We can't be sure. He could be a traveler whose bad luck it was to be caught in the snowstorm. Though his Northmen garments define his origin."

"I will take my time and look him over. If there is something you need to do, my lady, I can come find you when I'm done," Greta said.

Raven was eager to find out if her husband had learned anything from the trackers. "I won't be long."

"No need to rush, my lady," Greta assured her, her eyes already intent on the dead man.

Raven slipped out of the shed to find Brod waiting there.

"Fyn is with Tait and George is with Eria, trying to calm her after she heard the news. She fears Brynjar is here to take her back home and wed her. She's dreadfully frightened he'll find a way to abduct her."

"That is a possibility, I suppose," Raven said.

"Yet you doubt it," Brod said as they walked off.

"I tell you there is something we are missing," she insisted, annoyed she couldn't piece together what it was that nagged at her.

"It will come with time," Brod encouraged.

"But will it come too late?" Raven stopped abruptly and swerved around. "I don't need you following me, Hagen. My men take good care looking after me."

Hagen scratched his bushy, graying beard. "Maybe once, but with Clive gone and now Iver gone on a mission for Wolf, that leaves three of your men who are more taken up with the women that caught their fancy, than watching over you."

Brod went to argue and stopped. "He's right. we haven't been as vigilant as usual. Iver accused the same recently and I was too annoyed to see he spoke the truth."

"You admit it now and that's what matters," Hagen said. "Leif and I keep a good eye on her."

"An unnecessary eye," Raven argued.

"I do as Wolf tells me," Hagen said. "And Wolf does what is right. He protects his wife."

"He's got you there," Brod said with a chuckle.

Raven walked away from them both, shaking her head.

Brod kept his eye on her as he spoke. "You know she can lose you anytime she wants."

"So I've been told, so it might be good to have a few more eyes on her," Hagen said.

"I'll tell the others and we'll talk with you later."

"Wolf will be glad we work together," Hagen said and hurried off after Raven.

***

Raven ducked into the longhouse for a hot brew after spending an hour with her husband and Gorm. Nothing more had been found in the surrounding area where the dead man had been discovered, but then the snow hadn't helped in the search. There could be clues buried beneath some of the mounds of snow but until it melted, they had nothing. However, it had given her time to discuss her ideas about some tree perches and she was pleased that her husband and Gorm had been receptive to her ideas. Gorm even appeared enthusiastic about it and Wolf had told her to work with Gorm on it.

She was pouring herself another hot cider when Greta entered the common room. "Join me," she offered, the young woman appearing pale.

Greta gripped the tankard Raven handed her.

"You're upset. Did you find something that disturbed you?"

"No," Greta said and took a sip of cider before continuing, "I know that death is part of life, but some deaths trouble me more than others. It appears you were right. The dead man froze to death and it wasn't necessary."

"What do you mean?"

"His garments tell us he's a Northmen and Northmen know how to survive in a snowstorm. I can only assume that this man thought he could reach his destination before the snow and cold captured him. It could mean that he knew he'd be welcome here."

Raven said her thoughts aloud. "So he was friend not foe or he wanted us to believe that or" —she paused in thought— "he had an urgent message for Wolf and fought the snowstorm to make it here."

"Then he was a brave soul," Greta said, tears shining in her eyes.

Fyn entered, a dusting of snow covering him. "George is with Tait and Eria. I've come to escort Greta back to the keep before the weather worsens." He rushed to her side when he saw the tears in her eyes that had yet to fall and took her in his arms. "What's wrong?"

She buried her face against his chest, shaking her head.

"I think everything has been a bit much for her," Raven said. "You should get her to the keep and let her rest."

Greta eased away from Fyn and shook her head again. "No, I am good, lack of sleep last night and worries over my son's nightmares, that's all. I'm the healer and need to be strong even when I don't feel strong."

"You have my strength to lean on," Fyn said, worry in his eyes for her.

"I so appreciate that, Fyn. And right now I can use some of it since I need to tend some people in the village before I return to the keep."

"I'll go with you," Fyn said, then cringed as he looked to Raven. "I'm supposed to meet with the others and Hagen and Leif as well."

"Are you now?' Raven asked with a quirk of her brow.

Fyn realized his mistake, letting her know what they were up to.

"Go with Greta, she needs you more than the others. I'll send Ida to them with a message."

Fyn went to speak.

She saw how torn he was, loving the woman in his arms yet feeling as if he abandoned the woman who had once saved his life.

"Go, Fyn, with my blessing," she said as if releasing him from any responsibility for her. He hesitated. "Hurry, before the snow turns bad and Greta is unable to get back to her son."

"Aye, we must hurry, Fyn," Greta said.

Fyn sent her a smile before rushing off with Greta, and Raven smiled as well, knowing he realized she had mentioned her son on purpose to get them both moving.

Her smile grew at the thought of the men who had become her family growing, of them all becoming part of a bigger family, and the happiness it would bring them. Her smile faltered. That was if Brynjar didn't steal it from them. She had enough of family being taken from her, she wouldn't let it happen again.

She grabbed her cloak and left the longhouse. She wanted to retrieve the knife she had seen in the dead man's boot. It might reveal something about him. Could he have been a messenger with an important message for Wolf that had him anxious to take a chance in the snowstorm? But who sent him? Or had he been a foe who had come to plant himself in Wolf's tribe? But then why would he rush to get here?

Raven hoped the knife would reveal enough to answer some of her questions.

She kept a quick pace, the falling snow turning heavy. There was no guard outside the door and one wasn't necessary. After all, the man was dead. She entered the small shed and saw that Greta had covered the body with a blanket. A thoughtful gesture from a kindhearted woman.

A quick toss of the blanket at the boot where she remembered seeing the knife had her scrunching her brow. She threw back the blanket up to his knees and examined both boots.

The knife was gone.

Chapter Twenty

Raven went in search of Greta to find out if she had seen a knife in the dead man's boot. Of course, by the time she tracked her down, she and Fyn were already heading to the keep. And by the time she reached the bottom of the hill that took her up to the keep, they were halfway to the top.

She thought of waiting and speaking with Greta tomorrow. It wasn't urgent that she find out today, but she knew it would nag at her if she didn't. With a hefty sigh of resignation, she started up the hill. Snow was covering the path that had been cleared, but some spots had iced over and were slippery. It was probably the reason Fyn held Greta firmly to his side.

The thought of climbing the entire path had her taking a chance the couple would hear her shout and stop and wait for her to reach them. "FYN!"

He turned as did Greta and they stopped.

Raven tried to hurry her steps, not wanting to keep them waiting in the cold and she almost went down twice, her boot catching icy spots. She was relieved when she finally reached them.

"I won't keep you," she said, huddling close to them. "Greta, when you examined the dead man, did you happen to notice a knife tucked in his left boot?"

"I did," Greta said. "But I thought it best not to disturb it, at least until he thawed some."

Fyn was quick to ask, "Is there a problem, Raven?"

"The knife is gone," she said, the significance of its disappearance unnerving.

"If someone here took it…" Fyn didn't finish, the thought too disturbing.

Raven said what Fyn didn't. "Someone here knew him and knew what that knife could confirm."

Fyn finished the rest. "That he was one of Brynjar's warriors, which means someone in the tribe is faithful to Brynjar."

"I need to inform Wolf," she said. "Stay warm and alert, and we'll talk tomorrow."

"Be careful going down, there's ice in spots," Fyn cautioned.

"I hit a few coming up," she turned away and left Fyn and Greta to make their way up the rest of the way while she began to make her way down.

She slipped a couple of times but managed to remain on her feet. Though, she came to an abrupt halt when she saw someone approaching her. She couldn't make out who it was through the heavily swirling snow and cautiously remained where she was. Relief swept over her when her husband got close enough to see it was him and to hear his shout.

"RAVEN!"

She smiled and, eager to reach him, she hurried forward far too fast and hit a spot of ice that not only took her off her feet but sent her rolling down the hill with such force that it ripped her fur cloak off her and a few of the fur wrappings.

Wolf stilled for a sheer moment when he saw his wife slip, then roll rapidly toward him. He sprung forward, throwing himself at her. Her momentum was so strong it took him off his feet before he could stop her, but he managed to wrap himself around her when he went down to try to protect her as much as possible as they rolled with speed down the hill.

They slammed into a snow drift, snow almost burying them.

Wolf felt his wife shiver in his arms and he got the both of them on their feet.

Snow stuck to Raven's lashes, blurring her sight, and she spit it from her mouth as well. The snow had buried itself deep in every part of her and along with it the bone-chilling cold.

Wolf yanked his fur cloak off and wrapped it around his wife, her body shaking badly, then he scooped her up in his arms and rushed her as fast as possible to the longhouse and straight to their bedchamber.

She hugged herself tight when he placed her on her feet, her shivering worsening. "I'm so cold."

"Your garments are damp from the snow," he said, his hands working quickly to strip her naked.

When he was done he rushed her up into his arms again and hurried her into the bed, piling blankets and furs on top of her, but it did little to stop her trembling. He stripped himself fast and slipped beneath the blankets to take her in his arms, but his body was as chilled as hers and only worsened her shivers. He hurried out of bed, grabbed one of the furs off it, and spread it on the floor in front of the hearth.

Raven protested when her husband, yanked back the blankets, scooped her up in his arms, and carried her over to the hearth to lay her on the fur.

"Cover me," she pleaded, hugging herself against the cold.

He came down on top of her, shoving her arms away from her breasts and covering her with his body.

"I'm going to warm you," he said, his knee slipping between her legs to spread them apart.

A harsh chill raced through her, shivering her senseless.

He cursed beneath his breath as he hurried off her and pulled her to her feet. "You need the heat of the fire." He turned her to face the hearth, his arm going around her waist.

The heat of the flames raced over her body, chasing the chill from her skin, but not the bone-deep chill that was consuming her.

Though her skin warmed, he could feel the cold that seeped to the surface. He pressed his face next to hers. "Brace your hands on the mantel." As soon as she did he tugged at her waist. "Bring your feet back and spread them."

She did as he said, realizing his intentions and the image it brought to mind excited her and raced a shot of heat through her.

"I like when you obey me without question," he whispered against her ear.

"Don't get used to it," she said and gasped when his hand slipped between her legs and his fingers slipped inside her.

"Wet and ready," he whispered.

"Always… for you." She fought back a groan and lost.

"I'm going to pleasure you until you're so hot, you might just burst into flames."

"Promises. Promises," she said and moaned loudly when his thumb began to tease her pulsing nub, sending an exquisite burst of pleasure and heat through her and caused gooseflesh to rush over her entire body.

Wolf pressed his body against hers as he teased her senseless, her moans a seductive song to his ears and the way she pushed back against him, seeking the satisfaction of his shaft hardened him even more.

His desire soared out of control rapidly and he could feel hers did the same, but it was a chill settling in her backside that decided it.

His hand suddenly fell away from her and she released her disappointment with a groan.

He turned her around quickly, his arm slipping under her backside as he hoisted her up and ordered, "Wrap your legs around me."

Raven's arms went around his neck as her legs locked around his waist. His hands gripped her bottom to adjust her against him so his shaft could slip easily into her. And he did with an intentional slowness. Pure pleasure invaded his senses as her sheath welcomed him with a tight hug and he had to stop himself from roaring aloud. Once he was settled comfortably inside her, he placed one arm beneath her bottom, holding her firm, then reached out his with his other arm to plant his hand firmly against the mantle.

"Hold on," he ordered and she did.

She cried out with sheer joy as he moved inside her with powerful thrusts and she tried to match their strengths, but it was impossible. All she could do was hold on tight to him as his shaft plunged repeatedly into her. Heat flooded her along with intense pleasure. Many talked about the strength of the Beast and at this moment she felt its full force.

Her climax came upon her suddenly, forcing her to cry out in shock and pleasure, and to tighten her grip on him.

His hand dropped off the mantle and joined his other one at her bottom, squeezing the taut flesh tight and keeping tight hold on her as he rammed into her again and again. He let out a roar as his climax hit him with a fury and his seed spewed out planting itself deep inside her.

His forceful thrusts and loud roar sent a ripple of pleasure shooting through Raven again and spent from the sheer pleasure of it all, her head dropped to rest on his shoulder.

Once Wolf gathered his senses about him, he walked to the bed, keeping a firm hold on her and enjoying the feel of her warm flesh against his. He had chased the cold from her and that pleased him in a most satisfying way. He went down with her on the bed, his shaft still inside her as he rested over her.

After a few moments, she pressed her lips near his ear and said, "I think my bottom got burned."

He chuckled and slipped out of her slowly and onto his side. He turned her over and gently ran his hand over her backside. "Warm and lovely not only to touch but to look at as well, but no burns."

She rolled over and kissed him. "You definitely kept your promise… the fire you set in me felt as if it scorched more than my bottom."

"It's a good thing it actually didn't, since I intend to scorch you often."

She laughed softly as she reached for the blanket to pull over them, then wrapped herself around him to keep from losing the delicious heat that consumed her body.

He settled himself around her, stroking her arm and down along her hip to make sure she stayed warm. After a few minutes, he asked, "What were you doing at the keep?"

"I needed to speak with Greta," she said and continued to explain. "I discovered the dead man had a knife tucked in his boot, but with how frozen he was I didn't want to remove it yet. I returned to retrieve it later and it was gone. I asked Greta if she had seen the knife and she confirmed she had, which meant—"

"Someone else removed it," Wolf said, annoyed at what that could mean. "I saw no point in having a guard watch over a dead man."

"I thought the same and it worries me that whoever did remove the knife did so to hide something."

"That someone in the tribe didn't want anyone to know the dead man's identity," Wolf said, a spark of anger to his words.

"That could mean the dead man was one of Brynjar's men and someone here in the tribe has a connection to Brynjar."

His wife said what he didn't want to admit.

"And might be faithful to him."

"Which means he spies on us." That didn't sit well at all with Wolf. "I find it difficult to believe anyone in my tribe would betray me."

"Are you suggesting it could be someone from the Clan Learmonth?" She gave a brief thought to it. "That doesn't make sense. How would anyone from the clan be familiar with Brynjar?" He didn't respond and she saw in the way he stared off that his mind had wandered. "What are you thinking?"

"Something I don't want to think?"

"Tell me," she urged, curious.

"What if Brother Noble is not who he seems to be?"

"I can't believe that," she said, dismissing it as nonsense. "He is known by many."

"How do you explain his sudden disappearance right after it snowed?" he argued.

"He probably had an important message to deliver to the monastery."

"And take a chance in the snow?" Wolf shook his head.

"So what are you saying? That he was to meet the dead man and discovered he was brought here and slipped in the village without being seen to steal the knife?" Raven chuckled. "Now that's a tall tale, which will easily be settled when Iver returns."

Her husband scowled at her.

She placed her hand on his cheek. "Please, Wolf, maybe Brother Noble isn't who he seems, but you must promise me that if he should show himself before Iver returns you won't take a chance to prove what you think, for if he truly is a leper…" She shook her head and closed her eyes for a moment. "I don't want to lose you. Who would keep me warm?"

"No one but me," he snapped, the thought of anyone touching her but him sending a fiery anger through him.

"I couldn't bear the thought of anyone else touching me, so please promise me you won't place yourself in such danger." She didn't care if she sounded as if she pleaded with him. She had to know he wouldn't take the chance and unmask Brother Noble.

"If Brother Noble shows himself before Iver returns, won't we have our answer?" he argued.

She pulled out of his arms and turned away from him. "You're a stubborn fool."

Wolf turned and wrapped himself around his wife, his leg going over hers and his arm beneath her breasts, cupping one in his hand. His lips went to nibble at her ear and she tried to move away but he held her firm.

"I won't make you worry, wife. I will wait until Iver returns with news," he whispered near her ear, and he felt her relax against him.

"I appreciate that," she said and pressed back against him, relishing his warmth, the comfort of his arm so snug around her, the strength of his leg locked over hers as if he intended never to let her go, and she loved the intimacy of his hand cupping her breast. They had found a comfort with each other she had never expected and never thought she'd cherish.

"Now that your worries are appeased, tell me why Hagen and Leif did not follow you to the keep." He felt her soft chuckle.

"Your men and my men work together to protect me. Fyn was to join them but Greta needed him and I told him I would send Ida to let them know he wouldn't be able to join them."

"You had Ida tell them you were in need of him, didn't you?"

"You know me well, husband," she said, another chuckle interrupted by a yawn.

"Ease my worries as I ease yours," he said. "Let your men and my men watch over you."

"Only if it is not constant. I feel caged when I am constantly watched," she said, her hand going to rest against his arm beneath her breasts.

"That can be arranged," he assured her, feeling her body ready for sleep.

"You are a good husband," she whispered, her eyes closing.

"And you a good wife," he said. *And I believe I've lost my heart to you.*

He wasn't sure where that thought came from but he wouldn't deny it. He couldn't. It was too strong of a feeling in him and one he found he favored. He also favored the thought that he could actually love his wife, once his foe but no more. Raven wasn't anything like he thought she'd be and she was exactly what he wanted in a wife, something he never truly knew until he met her.

He had thought by agreeing to wed her, he had condemned himself to a life of misery and constant battle. Instead, he had found something he thought he never would.

He'd found love.

Chapter Twenty-one

Raven sat at the table cuddled close to her husband in the common room. It wasn't only his warmth she sought but also the comfort it brought her when close to him. She had given it much thought since the snowstorm four days ago. She hadn't wanted to admit it, but more and more she was feeling as if she'd come home. She had expected that feeling to embrace her on the day she had returned home to her family but, to her disappointment, it hadn't. While she'd certainly been relieved and happy to see her family, she hadn't felt the immense joy she had anticipated.

"Warm enough?" Wolf asked, keeping his wife tucked close in the crook of his arm.

"Aye, you've kept me well heated," she said with a chuckle.

"I intend to heat you even more today," he said, his hand sneaking to playfully squeeze her breast.

The door to the common room opened and a cold wind rushed in with Lars.

Wolf reluctantly dropped his hand off his wife, but kept her snug against him.

"The cold lingers but at least the snow leaves us be," Lars said, joining them at the table and quickly filling a tankard with hot cider, his large hands wrapping around it to chase his chill. "A rider was spotted heading this way. He should be here soon since he wasn't far off when I left the keep."

"He rides alone?" Wolf asked.

"From what can be seen, it appears so," Lars said.

"I wouldn't be surprised if it was one of your brothers, checking to see if I caused you harm," Wolf half joked, looking to his wife.

"My brothers wouldn't be foolish enough to brave a ride here when so much snow still covers the ground. Besides, Clive probably told them all was well here." Raven may have sounded confident, but if her husband's thought proved true, then something was definitely amiss.

The door opened just as she finished and the wind rushed a man in, his dark cloak concealing most of him. After shutting the door, he tossed back his hood.

"Arran, where is your common sense riding here when snow makes travel dangerous?" she admonished with a welcoming smile while her gut twisted with worry.

"Making sure my little sister isn't getting into any more trouble," he said, approaching the table and casting a suspicious eye on Lars.

"Arran, meet a loyal and trusted friend, Lars," Wolf said, seeing the questionable look in Arran's eyes.

Arran nodded at the man and Lars returned it with a huge grin. "Sit and warm your innards with a hot brew."

Raven watched her brother do just that and by the time he got done filling a tankard, without sending a teasing jab her way, she knew something was wrong. "What do you hesitate to tell me? Is it Da? Is he not well? Oria?" Her husband's body grew as taut as a bow string upon hearing his sister's name.

"All are well," Arran quickly assured her.

She leaned across the table, her eyes directly on her brother. "I see worry in your eyes."

Arran looked ready to respond, when his glance suddenly shifted to Wolf. "Brynjar is here in Scotland."

"How? When? And how did you learn of this?" Wolf demanded, annoyed Arran learned of it before he did. He paid people generously to keep him updated on such things.

"It's all thanks to you," Arran said, a spark of anger to his words. "I made acquaintances on foreign soil when fighting for you, and once free I began to trade with them. One such acquaintance, having no like for Brynjar, spotted him and sent word to me."

Raven wished she could tell her brother the truth, that it had been the King he fought for and not Wolf. One day she would.

"Where is he?" Wolf asked, resting his hand on his wife's back, needing to make sure he kept her close.

"He was last seen on his ship, but he could be anywhere by now," Arran said. "My sister is not safe. I have come to take her home with me."

Wolf's words rang with warning. "My wife isn't going anywhere."

"If you want to keep her safe, you'll let her return home with me," Arran argued.

"I am home, Arran," Raven said and leaned back against her husband, his arm going around her and capturing her tight, making it clear he wouldn't let her go.

Wolf didn't allow the joy her words brought him to show. He felt the same, that he'd finally come home and it was because of her. He wasn't about to let her go or leave her safety to someone else.

"My wife has nothing to fear. She is not only well aware that I will keep her safe, but she also knows that I am well aware that she is more than capable of protecting herself," Wolf said with pride.

Raven turned a huge smile on him. "I'm glad you've finally admitted that." Her smile softened when she turned to look at her brother. "You need to realize that, Arran."

"I've spoken to Clive—"

Raven interrupted, eager to ask, "Are he and Bethany doing well,"

"They are, but Angus isn't," Arran said and shook away the distraction. "Clive told Royden and me much about you. It tore at my heart to hear what you were made to endure, though I can't deny that you've come out stronger for it. But Brynjar is pure evil, I know, I suffered at his hands."

"I'm sorry you suffered like that and I'm grateful to Wolf and Royden for rescuing you, but I won't live in fear of this man. And I have no doubt that my husband will make certain Brynjar's reign of terror comes to an end."

Arran sneered. "I want that pleasure."

"We can share it," Wolf offered, understanding his need for revenge.

"Your word on that?" Arran asked.

"I would agree, but it will depend on the circumstances, which may leave either one of us no choice."

Arran nodded. "That's true, though I would like to be the one who delivers the last blow. I owe it to him not only for what he did to me and countless other prisoners, but for what he intended to do to my wife and now my sister."

"Hopefully that can be arranged," Wolf said and went on to explain what they had pieced together so far concerning Brynjar.

"So he has men passing information to him and if one fails to do so another shows up, which means it is never-ending," Arran said. "Even if you catch one of them, there's a good chance he won't know anything that will help. Brynjar often sends out prisoners with only one task to accomplish and they are given no other information or instructions, except if the person fails to carry out the task, his punishment is death and not an easy one."

"With Arran once having been a captive of Brynjar's, maybe he would recognize the dead man," Lars suggested.

Arran's scowl went straight to his sister. "Another attempt on your life?"

"We're not sure since this one froze to death before he reached us," Raven said.

"Let me take a look," Arran offered.

Lars joined them as they walked to the shed that housed the dead man. The village was alive with activity. Women busy chatting with each other after days confined to their homes, while children engaged in endless snowball fights, and men sat around campfires talking while others whittled away at pieces of wood.

Raven smiled when she saw Eria pointing to one of the many intricately carved posts throughout the village. George was mastering the Norse symbols and language as well as gaining favor with Eria. She spotted Fyn having a snowball fight with Tait, the little lad's cheeks blossoming red and peals of laughter spilling out of him. Greta looked on, her smile one of pure happiness. Life was good here and the thought startled her.

Raven trailed into the shed after the men to see Arran shaking his head, though he remained silent and continued staring at the dead man. It was almost as if by staring at him he'd will himself to recognize him.

"He is a stranger to me," Arran finally said. "He had nothing on him that might help identify him as belonging to a particular tribe since his garments are those of a Northman?"

"A knife that has since disappeared," Raven said.

"Someone took it?" Arran asked and his sister confirmed with a nod, then his eyes darted to Wolf.

Wolf acknowledged his thought without Arran speaking. "We are well aware Brynjar could have planted one of his people among us."

"What are you doing about it?" Arran demanded, worried for his sister.

"Your sister is never alone. Her men and two of my best warriors follow her at all times. Gorm is compiling a list of those who are relatively new to the tribe and volunteered to move from our homeland to here. I'm not concerned with the clan members already here. They would have no connection with Brynjar. I don't believe they were even aware of his existence before we arrived and even if they were, there was no way they'd have contact with him."

Arran wasn't happy to hear that. "So this dead man remains a missing piece to a puzzle."

"For now," Raven said, "but pieces usually fall into place after a while."

"Let's hope so," Arran said.

"Maybe Arran saw Sten when he was a captive of Brynjar and would know if Sten's tale is true or false," Lars suggested.

"A good point," Wolf said. "Bring Sten to the longhouse."

Lars left and the three stepped out of the shed.

"I need to speak with Gorm. I will join you and your brother back at the longhouse," Wolf said and gave Raven a quick kiss before walking off.

"He gives us time to talk," Raven said, pleased her husband had done so.

"You favor him," Arran said, having seen it for himself and recalling the advice Purity had given him before he left.

You may have reason to hate Wolf, but you have more reason not to if you love your sister.

Raven wasn't ready to admit to anyone, especially Arran, that she actually had feelings for Wolf, deeper feelings than she ever would have thought possible. "We have found common ground that makes our situation more than tolerable."

"Afraid to tell me the truth?" Arran accused.

She kicked at a patch of snow and shook her head. "I'm not sure, Arran."

"Are you afraid to tell me or are you afraid of the truth?"

"I suppose a bit of both," she reluctantly admitted.

He took her hand and squeezed it gently. "Never be afraid of telling me anything, Raven. I may tease you endlessly but I love you with all my heart and would protect you with my life. I hated that you gave, in a sense, your life so that Royden and I could be free. It would be a relief to know that you and Wolf care enough for each other to have a good life together."

"You think he cares for me?" she asked anxiously.

"I don't care for the man, but I must admit that he looks at you far differently from when he first arrived at the Clan MacKinnon. And he touches you with a tenderness that I never expected to see, though I am glad for it. I will worry less knowing that you're not trapped in an uncaring and unkind marriage."

She never thought she would have any reason to say, "Wolf truly treats me well."

Arran laughed. "Good, then I don't have to kill him."

Raven punched him in the arm.

He lowered his voice. "I would if necessary."

Raven squeezed his hand this time. "I know, which is why I agreed to this marriage. I knew you and Royden would keep me safe if it proved necessary."

Arran came to an abrupt stop, shocked by the realization of her remark.

"I knew I could depend on you both, though I'm grateful it isn't necessary," she said with a gentle smile.

"You are an amazing woman," he said. "You protected us, knowing we'd protect you if it became necessary."

"I knew you'd keep that promise you all made that day in Da's solar and I made it right along with you, though you didn't know I did. It didn't matter that I was young. I was willing, just like all of you were, to protect family, to protect those I love."

"And you do that now with Wolf?" Arran asked.

"Aye," she said without hesitation.

They continued walking.

"You do realize what you just admitted to me, right?" Arran asked as they neared the door to the longhouse.

Raven scrunched her brow. "What are you talking about?"

"You said you protect family, those you love, and I asked if you did that now with Wolf and you didn't hesitate in saying, aye. That means… you love Wolf."

Raven turned her head to shake it, to deny what her brother had said, and stopped. Her husband stood not far from them and from the questioning way he looked at her, she knew he had heard them.

She was relieved that Lars approached with Sten at that moment, but she knew this wasn't the end of it. Wolf would ask her about it when they were alone and she wasn't sure what she would say to him.

"Inside, you're shivering," Wolf ordered and slipped his arm around her when he reached her and hurried her inside.

Arran followed with a smile on his face, eager to tell Royden that their sister was doing more than well.

Wolf slipped off his wife's cloak and placed one that had been warming by the fire around her before she took a seat at the table. He ordered Ida to bring more hot brew and once he and Arran were seated, Lars approached them with Sten.

Before Arran could say anything, Sten spoke up. "I saw you there. You are the brave one everyone talks about, the one Brynjar hates. The one who escaped him, then stole from him the woman who was to be his wife. He took his wrath out on many when he returned home a failure."

"I don't recall you," Arran said.

"You wouldn't. You didn't see me. I was one of many who were forced to watch you and the other prisoners get whipped," Sten said and shuddered at the horrible memory. "You were strong and brave and Brynjar hated that you didn't fear him like everyone did. He intended to have his revenge against you. He planned to kill you and take your wife."

That news unnerved Arran and he had the urge to rush home to Purity. He was glad he insisted she stay with Royden and Oria while he came here. He thought to stay the night if necessary, but not now. He'd head back soon.

Sten shook his head. "Suddenly, it all changed. Brynjar was intent on going after Wolf."

Wolf explained to Arran. "Brynjar intended to force the woman, Eria, I had planned to wed into marriage. To see her kept safe, her family sent her here to me."

Arran nodded. "Brynjar followed and being you took Eria from him, he intends to take Raven from you and get Eria for himself."

"I don't know about that," Raven said.

"Why not? It's obvious," Arran argued.

"That's just it. It's too obvious," Raven said.

"She's right," Sten said. "Brynjar deflects with something he cares little about while he's actually going after something much more important to him." He looked to Arran. "He wanted to marry the woman you wed, but cared nothing for her. It was the land he would get by marrying her that was important to him."

"He wanted to make sure I didn't have control of it," Wolf said.

"You don't," Arran reminded.

"You would go against me? Against family? My sister is wed to your brother and I am wed to your sister. We are family," Wolf said with a quirk of his brow that challenged Arran to deny it.

Arran muttered several oaths before saying, "Not by choice."

Raven ignored her husband and brother's bickering. She was too engrossed in what Sten had said. "If my death is meant to deflect from his real reason for being here, then what does he want that is so important to him?"

Sten shook his head having no answer. No one did.

Chapter Twenty-two

Raven found the silence, since entering their bedchamber several minutes ago, between her and Wolf unnerving. They never lacked in conversation except when making love and even then they exchanged a word or two. It was obvious what was on his mind… that he had all but heard her admit she was in love with him.

She wasn't ready to discuss it yet, so she purposely diverted any talk of it by saying, "We need to find out why Brynjar is here."

Wolf shed his garments as he spoke. "As I've said before, it wouldn't be to see me dead. My death wouldn't give Brynjar enough satisfaction, at least not presently."

"I would say he was here for Eria, but there have been no attempts to abduct her."

"He believes your death would bring turmoil, which he might foolishly think would make it easier for him to snatch Eria. Her father rules over several tribes in his region. With Eria being the only child, her husband would have a good chance of inheriting the position."

"The problem is that Brynjar is so unpredictable," she said, trying to ignore the passion that was burning slowly and steadily inside her as she watched her husband disrobe.

"It's what puts fear in people. No one ever knows what he will do. He can't be trusted, not ever. He lies with every word and cares for nothing. Your brother defined him perfectly—he is pure evil."

"What made him that way?" she asked as her husband discarded the last of his garments.

Wolf approached his wife with slow, languid steps. "His father was a brutal man and more than likely instilled that same brutality in his son. My father and his father clashed several times, my father not only having more power than him, but having a strong friendship with the King."

"So there has always been hostility between your families," Raven said and began to shed her garments, thinking making love with her husband was another good way to distract him from discussing anything else.

"It got worse when Brynjar's father died and he took control of his tribe." Wolf helped his wife shed her garments, eager to hold her naked in his arms. "Some say he grew impatient to take command and sent his father to an early death. Brynjar's sister and brother also met early deaths."

"His mother?' Raven asked, glad for her husband's gentle touch after hearing such horror.

"She died shortly after Brynjar was born, though many believe she took her own life. Two more wives followed, one giving him another son and the other a daughter. After those wives died, far too soon,

Brynjar's father simply took whatever woman he wanted."

"Brynjar is left with no one and has had no success in finding a wife," Raven said.

"A wife who would prove beneficial to him," Wolf reminded, tossing the last of her garments aside and took his wife in his arms. "Enough talk of a man who doesn't deserve disturbing our precious time together."

Raven's arms went around her husband's neck. "There is a more important matter for us to see to."

Wolf's lips touched hers ever so lightly, sending a shiver through her.

"That there is, wife." His kiss was much stronger, a promise of what was to come. He ended it with another faint brush of his lips across hers, and his dark eyes held hers in as much of an embrace as his arms did. "Will you admit to me what you admitted to your brother?"

She should have known he'd have his say and she went to step away from him, but his arms held her tight. He would not be denied an answer.

Defiance sparked in her brilliant blue eyes and she shot back. "Will you tell me you love me?"

He swung her up in his arms and planted his face close to hers. "*Ek elska þik.*"

"You truly do love me?" she asked, not expecting the words from him.

He smiled. "I thought you understood my language. Now I know for sure."

Raven poked him in the chest. "You tricked me."

His smile faded and he rested his brow to hers. "I did, but I didn't lie about loving you. I don't know how it happened or when I fell in love with you, and I don't care. All I know is that you somehow stole my heart and it would break if I ever lost you. *Ek elska þik, kona.*"

A burst of joy raced through her and she grabbed his face in her hands. "*Ek elska þik*, husband. Like you, I don't know when I came to love you and I was confused at first, unsure, and truthfully concerned—"

"That I wouldn't feel the same?"

Raven nodded and was shocked to feel tears trickle from her eyes. "I haven't cried…"

Wolf finished for her. "Happy tears in a long while."

"I don't think I've ever cried happy tears," she admitted.

He kissed her. "Then I'm glad it was our love that brought you happy tears."

"You truly do love me?" she asked as if she didn't quite believe it.

"There isn't a doubt in my mind that I love you, Raven. We are one, you and me, joined forever together. You're my heart, my soul, you're everything to me."

His loving words astonished her. That she loved him astonished her. "Never would I have believed this possible. I thought you a savage, my enemy for so many years, and now… my heart would shatter if I lost you." She sniffled back her tears. "So you will take care to keep yourself safe."

"Is that an order, wife?" he asked with a teasing smile.

"It's a plea," she said softly.

"And I will do my best to see it so," he whispered and kissed her.

Raven had no use for further talk. Her only interest was making love with her husband. Somehow it was different now—now that she knew he loved her. She held on to his neck when he placed her on the bed. It didn't matter, he followed her down. He felt as she did. He didn't want to let go.

She cherished the tenderness of his touch and the way his lips traced where his hands had been. Though he had touched her in a familiar way before tonight, it somehow felt different. Or was it that she felt different? It wasn't only passion that stirred in her, it was love and it made more of a difference than she had expected.

"Please don't stop," she urged when his hands and lips stilled. He looked at her with an intensity in his dark eyes that made her shiver. "You feel it, don't you?"

Wolf nodded. "I've never felt it before."

"I haven't either," she confessed. "I never knew it could be so amazing, but then I've never been in love before you."

"Nor I before you," he admitted. "We belong to each other, you and me, forever and always."

"That's fine with me," she agreed and sighed when his hands and lips continued to explore her.

Wolf didn't intend to rush this special time. He wanted to give her a memory that would last forever, one that would live long in her mind and heart, and his as well. And he hoped his seed would take root tonight so that their child would be conceived with love.

Raven wanted to linger in their lovemaking forever, wanted to let the passion seep deep inside her along with his shaft. She hurried his hands away and pushed him on his back to mount him, fumbling to slip him inside her.

Wolf's hands went to her waist and he lifted and maneuvered her so he could easily enter her. His hands went to her breasts as she rode him and she loved the feel of his strong hands squeezing her breasts and the way his thumbs played across her nipples. Her head fell back as pleasurable moans spilled from her lips.

He would never get enough of this woman—he loved—who stirred him to life with one look, one touch. He couldn't keep his hands off her and he loved that she welcomed his every touch. He slipped his hands down along to rest at her slim waist. He could let her remain riding him, but the ache to take command was too strong. His hands tightened at her waist and with one swift flip he had her on her back, barely disturbing his shaft inside her.

It wasn't long after their movements turned demanding that he knew neither of them would last. He leaned down and swiped her lips with a rough kiss. "Together, wife."

"Aye, husband," she confirmed and gripped his upper arms, meeting his every pounding demand.

Raven cried out at the exact moment her husband let loose with a roar, and it was several minutes before their senses calmed and Wolf collapsed on top of her and rolled onto his back, taking her with him to rest on top of him. He kept his arms locked around her as their hearts pounded and their breaths labored.

"That was magnificent," she said after a few moments."

"Thank you," Wolf said and chuckled when she poked him in the side with her elbow.

"Need I remind you that you were not in it alone," she scolded teasingly.

His hands cupped her face and he kissed her. "You're always magnificent, wife, and even more so since you finally admit you love me."

She laughed and he captured her mouth in another quick kiss before she could argue with him. Then his arm went around her as he eased them both to their side and quickly reached down to untangle the blankets and pull them up over them.

"I'll let you have that one," she said, snuggling against him once he settled beside her and she yawned as she slipped her leg between his two. "I'm too tired to point out you told me you loved me first."

He laughed and pressed a kiss to the top of her head and he wasn't surprised when only a few moments later she was sound asleep. He soon followed into a peaceful and much satisfied slumber.

***

Wolf didn't know what woke him, though it could have been the crackle and pop from the fire in the hearth until he realized what it was… his wife wasn't beside him. He turned on his side ready to jump out of bed when he saw her. She paced before the hearth in her shirt. Her dark hair was half pinned to her head and the other half fell haphazardly around her face and neck. She looked deep in thought and that proved true when she didn't even notice when he got out of bed and approached her.

"Raven," he said softly to catch her attention, afraid he'd alarm her if he touched her, she appeared so deep in thought. When she didn't respond, his tone turned demanding. "Raven!"

She jumped and stared at him, shaking her head. "I'm missing something, something I saw and yet didn't quite understand. It's there right in front of me, but I can't see it."

His arm found its way around her and he eased her against him. "Leave it be and it will come to you."

She shook her head again. "It's important. It will make things clear."

"The more you fight it, the more it will elude you." He walked her to the bed.

"It's not just one thing. I know it's not. There are pieces and if I can put them together, I will know what I'm seeing," she insisted and raised her arms as he slipped her shirt off.

"Sleep and perhaps a dream will show you the way," he suggested and turned back the blanket for her to slip under.

"True—a dream—a dream just might show me the way." She eagerly snuggled under the blanket, returning to his arms once he joined her.

Wolf ignored the arousal that stirred his shaft. His wife was too anxious with what she had on her mind and he'd not bother her with his sudden need when she needed the benefit sleep would bring her. He settled around her, hoping sleep would claim him quickly.

Unfortunately, it wasn't long before she turned restless, tossing and turning.

He kept his eyes closed, lying still, hoping his calm might settle her, until he felt a tap to his cheek and he opened his eyes to see her face planted close to his.

"I need to sleep and dream," she said as if he had the answer to her problem. "A fast one, then you can go back to sleep."

"Are you asking me to make love to you?"

"You don't have to fuss, just a good pounding that will wear me out and let me sleep," she explained, making it sound a simple request. Her hand hurried to take a strong hold of his shaft. "I felt you stir against me, so it shouldn't be a chore for you."

"Making love to you is never a chore, but if you want it fast, then I suggest you tease him hard," he said with a nod toward her hand beneath the blanket.

"I can do that," she said.

She did much too good of a job and it wasn't long before Wolf couldn't take much more, he yanked her to her hands and knees on the bed. "Grab the board, I'm going to give you what you want."

She was glad she did since he kept his word and it wasn't long before they both climaxed together once again. And it wasn't long after that, that they fell asleep, both completely spent.

***

"I don't need to be watched over," Raven argued the next morning, after stepping outside.

Wolf turned a generous smile on her. "Your brother, Arran, would disagree."

She slipped out of his arms, annoyed his smile alone could flutter her stomach, but he caught her around the waist before she could get far and eased her back into his embrace.

"My men and yours will stick close with you whether you like it or not. I'm not finished," he warned when she went to protest. "Take pity on me, wife, and do as I say, since I love you far too much to lose you."

The flutters in her stomach multiplied and she jabbed him in the chest. "That's not fair."

"Fair or not, wife, it is true, and," he said his voice taking on a note of command, "I expect you to spare my poor heart and not purposely lose the men who follow you, since your men made it very clear that you could escape the guards anytime you wanted to."

"I need to talk with my men," she mumbled.

"Your men worry about you as much as I do. You are well-loved and protected by those who care for you. Keep that in mind.

"I will not cause any problems today," she said in peaceful surrender.

A small chuckle slipped out with his smile. "I'll believe that when you're in my arms in bed tonight."

She kissed his cheek and whispered, "If you change that to you'll believe that when *you're inside me* in bed tonight, then I will make sure no trouble finds me today." She went to flee his arms and he yanked her back against him.

"I will definitely see to that and I look forward to a worry free day." A quick kiss to her cheek and Wolf left her side.

"Change is in the air."

Raven turned to see Detta standing not far from her. "How so?" she asked, walking over to the woman.

"You and Lord Wolf appear to be getting along and anger no longer lingers in your eyes." Detta took a step and faltered.

Raven was quick to steady her with a firm hand. "You shouldn't be outside with so much snow on the ground and you shouldn't walk the hill to the keep. Ice hides in spots beneath the snow."

"Lars helped me make my way and will do the same when I am ready to return."

"What brings you out of the keep?" Raven asked.

"Curiosity?"

"Over the dead man?"

Detta's eyes shot wide. "How did you know?"

"With Greta still residing in the keep with her son, I assume she told you about the dead man, hence your curiosity."

Detta bobbed her head. "Your mind is sharp, my lady."

"I believe yours is far sharper."

"I am nothing more than a humble servant," Detta said, bobbing her head again.

Raven didn't believe that for a minute. There was more to her than a humble servant and she was going to figure out what it was sooner rather than later. She didn't believe that Detta was connected with Brynjar.

Too many, including Wolf, treated her as if they had known her for years.

"It is good you're curious about the dead man," Raven said. "You might recognize him. Come, I'll take you to the shed where he lies."

Raven thought the old woman might refuse her when she hooked her arm tighter with hers. But she didn't. She nodded and went along with her, Raven keeping her steps slow and careful.

Detta remarked on how well the clan was doing since Wolf became the new lord, pointing out the many improvements he'd made and how content the people seemed. Raven listened, asking only a few questions to show her interest. What truly captured her interest was the way the old woman spoke with pride about Wolf. Had Detta helped raise him as Bethany did her? Did she have some special place in his heart as Bethany did for her? Could that be why he sent Detta here to live and report to him what she learned? Did he have complete trust in her?

Raven released her arm as soon as they entered the shed.

Detta looked down at the men and wrinkled her brow.

"Do you recognize him?" Raven asked, the quizzical look on the old woman's face making it seem that she had.

"I can't say I do," Detta said, "but there is something familiar about him, as if I've seen him before now."

"Could he have stopped here on his travels?" Raven suggested.

The wrinkles in Detta's brow turned deeper. "I suppose it's possible, but I can't truly recall if that is it. Hopefully, it will come to me in time."

"Unfortunately, time isn't our friend at the moment."

Detta faltered again when they went to leave and Raven caught her again, holding her steady.

"My leg, an old injury, and the cold weather doesn't help it," Detta explained.

"Let me get you to the longhouse. You can rest and have a hot brew." Raven didn't give her a chance to reject the offer. With a firm arm around her, she led her out of the shed.

She was near the longhouse when she caught sight of her husband and Lars talking and when his eyes spotted her, a quick look of concern crossed his face, but he wasn't looking at her, his dark eyes were on Detta.

Her husband and Lars started walking their way, though Raven kept walking to the longhouse, feeling the old woman's steps weaken beside her.

The shout echoed in the cold air. "ATTACK!"

Arrows followed, flying through the air, and several were headed straight for Raven and Detta.

Chapter Twenty-three

Raven took Detta to the ground out of instinct, easing her impact with the strength of her arm.

"Raven!"

She turned hearing George's shout, he had been assigned to follow her along with Hagen, and her hand shot out to grab the wooden shield that George tossed toward her and landed near her side. She raised it just in time, shielding herself and Detta, though an arrow came dangerously close to her leg. Not knowing how much time she had before another round of arrows hit, she all but lifted Detta off the ground and rushed her into the longhouse. She shut the door on the startled woman and turned to join the battle, only to find herself colliding with her husband.

She braced herself, sensing from the worry in his stormy eyes that he was about to send her into the longhouse.

"You have no sword," he said.

She could have kissed him. "George will see I get one."

He didn't say another word, he turned and she followed him, taking a sword from George as he hurried to her.

"No more arrows fly and no warriors engage," she said, keeping an intent eye around her as they hurried through the village.

"A small troop that my warriors probably already contain," Wolf said and quickened his step, which she easily matched.

Shouts led them in the right direction. They came to a stop just beyond the village border to the south, where anyone who approached could easily be seen by the guards posted at the top of the keep.

Lars approached Wolf. "The fight was over before I arrived here. Your warriors had things well in hand, and thanks to Brod's curiosity and quick action they never got off another round of arrows."

A glance at the scene told it all. Four men lay dead, arrows riddling their bodies. Their garments indicated they were mere travelers familiar with this land, their arrows and bows told a different story.

Wolf summoned Brod with a firm command and the man hurried to him. "What happened?"

"I saw that your men let them pass after asking if they could get food and drink here and with nothing to think them other than travelers, they were granted permission. I decided to follow them without them seeing me after noticing the way the one man kept adjusting the sack slung across his back. It's a habit some men have when carrying a cache of arrows. I called out to them and that's when they whipped out their hidden bows and arrows, and I roared out the alert.

I stopped one, while the other three launched a round of arrows. Your men prevented them from launching anymore." Brod shook his head. "They had to have known they wouldn't survive this mission."

"I am indebted to you, Brod," Wolf said.

"Not at all. This is my home and I will see it kept safe," Brod said, casting a glance to Raven and he was pleased to see her smile at him.

"That is good to know, Brod," Wolf said, pleased the man considered the tribe his home. It meant he would put down roots and be family.

"Men are already combing the woods to see if any other warriors linger nearby," Gorm said. "Word was received from the keep when the small group was first spotted, but as Brod said there was nothing to think them anything more than travelers. I will see that a more thorough search is conducted of any strangers who wish to enter the village."

"Brynjar sends a strong message," Lars said.

"And an obvious one," Wolf said. "He doesn't intend to stop until he gets what he wants and he is willing to sacrifice endless men to achieve his goal."

"Don't even think of meeting with Brynjar anywhere but here surrounded by your warriors," Raven warned as they left the group and made their way back to the longhouse. "His actions prove he has no intentions of negotiating."

"Brynjar never truly negotiates. He uses it as a ploy, so you have no worry of me doing that." An urge to feel her close had him reaching out to take a strong hold of her hand.

Raven responded, clutching his hand in return. "You can't still think this is all to see me dead?"

"No, there is definitely more to his intentions, though he plays the game as he usually does. He instills fear in people, making them wonder and worry of what's to come next, who's to suffer next, or who's to die next. Fear can make people do foolish things and that's what Brynjar counts on."

Raven laughed. "Then he has failed miserably since his men have been the only ones to die and the captive you took is willing to cooperate."

"A humorous conclusion," he said though didn't smile, "that once he realizes is bound to cause great anger."

A thought she had considered but hadn't voiced. She did, however, speak of another concern. "The snowstorm didn't seem to slow his men down."

"When the snow melts, I wouldn't be surprised to find numerous bodies frozen dead from the cold. As you've seen for yourself, Brynjar's warriors' lives mean nothing to him. They live and die to serve him. He paces his men, sending the weakest or least dependable in first. Men like Sten and Toke. He limits how many he sends to accomplish a task, sending the more talented and reliable warriors later so by the time he arrives his target is worn down or left with little to defend. There is one thing your brother Arran realized that I believe Brynjar once again has failed to consider—"

"He's on foreign soil," Raven finished. "Not knowing the land and its people can prove disastrous."

"You know this—"

"From experience and from what Charles taught me," she finished again. "Even when on your own soil, people, customs, languages are different in various areas of the country. To learn other tongues, at least some words, could prove beneficial."

Wolf stopped, his glance curious. "What other tongues do you know?"

She shrugged as if it didn't matter any longer that he knew. "George taught me Latin and French. Brod is well-versed, knowing Latin and French as well, but he taught me your language and some Germanic."

"You know more tongues than me. You'll have to teach me," he said, giving her hand a light tug to continue walking. "Don't let anyone know how many different tongues you speak."

"I would say you do that because you are jealous, but since I know you so well, I know that's not the reason."

He turned a smile on her. "I assumed you would understand."

"You want it kept a secret thinking someday it might prove beneficial when dealing with someone who doesn't know I understand their language." She grinned. "A secret weapon of sorts."

Seeing her husband's smile vanish when his eyes left hers briefly had her following where he looked. Detta stood in the doorway of the longhouse, with her arms pressed tightly against her chest, and he hurried Raven along to reach the woman.

"Are you hurt?' Wolf asked, releasing Raven's hand and going to Detta.

"No, and it's all thanks to Raven," Detta said with a nod toward her. "I suffered no injury at all, but I am concerned for others."

Wolf hurried to reassure her. "We suffered no casualties or injures, not so the men who thought to harm us."

Raven watched the caring exchange with interest. Her husband had been unable to contain his worry for the old woman. She also had taken more notice of late how Detta looked at Wolf with more than caring eyes. There was also the way Gorm treated her, as if she was more than a mere servant. And in all the time Raven had been here, she hadn't once seen Detta serve anyone.

It struck her then and the thought seemed more than plausible. It actually made sense and explained a few things. She decided the only way to confirm it was to test her sudden thought.

She approached her husband and Detta. "Let's go inside and have a hot brew, then you can explain, husband, why you haven't told me that Detta is your grandmother."

Detta smiled and hooked her arm around Wolf's. "I warned you she would figure it out."

Wolf waited until they were seated at one of the tables before he asked, "How long have you known?"

"I've been suspicious of her since we met, but truthfully, the thought only struck me after seeing how worried you were for her." Raven looked from her husband to Detta. "If I had looked more closely, I would have seen the resemblance."

"He gets his fine features from his grandfather," Detta said with a loving glance at Wolf. "And also his concern and rage when someone he loves is harmed." She turned to Raven, her words a challenge to her to deny them. "Wolf is a good, honorable man."

Raven had no trouble responding, "I'm learning that and more about him, but I'm more curious as to how so many could keep your secret?"

"They understood the importance of holding their tongues until told otherwise," Detta said.

Raven thought of her friend. "And was it just as important you not say anything to Oria, your granddaughter, in the five years she lived here?"

Sorrow filled Detta's eyes. "A regrettable but necessary situation, which I plan to rectify when she visits next, though I am grateful for the time I got to spend with her. She is a brave woman and has a kind heart and soul."

Anger sparked in Raven. "Your intent to reclaim your land caused my family to suffer loss, heartache, and almost destroyed them, including Oria."

"Land and titles are constantly being manipulated, given and taken, in the name of power or greed, or to benefit those already in power. My mother's family occupied this land and surrounding land, including the area you claim as home, for over a hundred years and her mother before her and her mother before her and so on. It has been passed down through women, strong women who made sure the land remained ours. It was my fault the land was lost. I fell in love with a Northman. My father disavowed me when he discovered I was carrying a Northman's bairn. He made sure my heirs would never get what was rightfully theirs by rewarding pieces of my family's land to other clans in return for favors and benefits or simply for what wealth they could surrender until only Learmonth was left for any heir of mine to claim. I had to sneak into my home when my mother laid dying. I promised her then that I would see our land returned to us. I couldn't fail her. I couldn't lose what so many women before me sacrificed and fought to keep."

Raven thought of her own promise to her brothers and the things she had done to keep it. How could she blame Detta for keeping her promise when she had done the same?

"You know as well as I do that only the strong survive the harsh dictates of this land and those who rule it," Detta said. "I was proud to see my granddaughter, Oria, do what endless women in my family have done before her, fight to survive, and unlike other women in my family who had no choice, Oria kept hope and love alive for the man promised to her, the man she loved. She reclaimed what rightfully belonged to her without ever knowing it."

"You must have been pleased when she wed Burnell," Raven said.

"Not at all." Detta shook her head. "That wasn't part of the plan, though the man she claims as her father showed how much he loved his daughter by marrying her to Burnell to keep her safe. I wasn't happy that Burnell saw it done before I could stop it. Both men protected her well." After a short pause, she continued to explain. "Burnell was a distant cousin of mine on my father's side. He was never a strong man. When his two marriages bore him no heirs, I approached him and reminded him that Wolf was the true heir to Learmonth."

"So you left him little choice," Raven said.

"I left him to right a wrong," Detta corrected. "I am truly sorry for what happened to your brothers and father and others in your clan. It was never meant to go that way. Needless bloodshed was never intended."

She believed the woman, though she might not have if Wolf hadn't told her that Scotland's King had gotten involved in his plan, insisting men be taken to fight for him. In return, he voiced no opposition to Wolf's plans.

"It took you five years to return to your home, your family, and your friends," Detta said. "It took me over fifty years to see my home and land returned to my family. We're both home now and I hope peace can exist between us all."

Raven stood. "I'll think about it." She turned and walked out of the common room.

"Let her be for now," Detta cautioned, seeing the concern on her grandson's pinched face. "She needs some time to digest it all."

Wolf would have preferred to go to his wife, but his grandmother was right. Raven needed time alone to think. He'd be better off waiting until tonight when they were alone in their bedchamber to discuss this with her.

"I see love in your eyes for your wife," Detta said, placing a gentle hand on her grandson's arm. "And I am more than pleased that I see love in her eyes for you as well. You make a good pair, both stubborn and brave. She is a good wife for you. You will do well together."

"Something I never anticipated," Wolf admitted.

Detta's aging eyes softened with memories. "I didn't care much for your grandfather when I first met him."

"You never mentioned that."

"It was trivial to what came soon after, a love that still wraps me in its warmth and strength to this day. A love I'll always be grateful to have found."

"I never thought I'd be grateful to have Raven as my wife, but now," —he shook his head— "I don't know what I'd do without her in my life. It's as if she's become an essential part of me, that without her…" He shook his head again. "I don't want to think about life without her."

"You don't have to. You belong to each other now and your love will grow along with a family, and peace among families will grow as well. All will finally be good."

His grandmother's strong, confident words had always reassured him through the years and he was always glad to hear them. This time, however, there was one thing that cast a doubt on her forecast.

"Brynjar," Wolf said in a whisper and his grandmother shivered beside him.

***

Wolf stood at the top of the hill looking down over the village. He was proud of what he had established here and he hoped in time to see it all grow along with the many children he and Raven would have. The thought brought a smile to his face. His grandmother was right. Life was going to be good and Raven had a lot to do with that.

Having deposited his grandmother safely in the keep, it was time to find his wife. Halfway down the hill, he spotted Iver and he hurried his steps, glad to see he had returned and eager to hear what he had learned. Raven would want to hear it as well and he glanced around hoping to spot her.

Iver hurried his steps to Wolf when he neared the bottom of the hill. "You need to speak with Brother Noble. He returned here with me, but has little time to spare. He's on a mission for Abbott Thomas. He waits for you where you usually meet."

Wolf nodded. "Find Raven and wait in the common room for me."

Iver bobbed his head and took off.

Wolf called out when he reached the wooded area where he usually met the leper. "Brother Noble."

A raspy cough sounded before the familiar brown-robed figure stepped partially out from behind a large pine tree.

"You are well?" Wolf asked.

"As well as can be expected," the leper said, though his rough cough stated otherwise.

"These missions are too much for you," Wolf cautioned.

"The end will come soon enough and I will know peace at last."

Wolf didn't want to think of losing the man who had become a trusted friend to him, but he supposed death was welcoming to one who suffered greatly. "I am here for you, if you need anything, my friend."

"You are appreciated, Wolf, but I have little time and must be off soon. Some information has come to light that you should know about. King David and the Earls of Orkney vassals to your King have continued their bitter disputes over the Orkney Isles, leaving them little time to care what happened between you and Raven."

"Are you saying they had nothing to do with forcing a marriage between me and Raven?" His remark implausible to his own ears.

"I am, though they were quick to agree to it, each thinking it could benefit them in some way now or in the future. King David made no complaint about releasing the prisoners he had demanded from you, his foreign exploits not going well and costing far more than he expected."

Wolf rubbed at his beard, his brow pinching tightly. "That would mean someone manipulated both kings into agreeing to the marriage." He shook his head. "But who would have such power to present such a proposal?"

"Or courage," Brother Noble suggested.

"Or who would benefit from such a union?" Wolf shook his head again. "Raven would be the only one to benefit, since our union freed her brothers and others from not only her clan but other clans as well. But she denies she had any part of the proposal."

"Do you believe her?' the leper asked.

Wolf gave no thought to his response, he needed none. He knew his wife. "I do. She has no reason to lie about it."

"She's been truthful with you?"

"We both have. I trust her explicitly," Wolf said, not a shred of doubt in his voice.

"Then you are blessed with a good union."

"I am blessed with a woman who is brave enough to love her foe," Wolf said, thinking on his own words.

"Perhaps she is brave enough to forgive her foe and to recognize that there is always more to situations than what can be seen."

"Raven is brave," Wolf agreed. "She is also a wise woman and foolish as well, stubborn and strong, and beyond beautiful." The last of his words drifted off in a whisper on the cold wind.

"Your heart is filled with love for your wife."

Wolf grinned. "It overflows with it."

"She feels as strongly?"

"She has shown how strongly she loves by what she did for her brothers and to reunite her family, but for how strong her love is for me, I can't truly say. I think it is strong, I wish it so, and sometimes, when we come together as one, I believe I can feel it's depth and strength. One day perhaps I'll know for sure, but what does it matter when my love is strong enough for us both." A ragged cough had Wolf take a step forward. "Are you all right?"

"Stay back," Brother Noble warned. "I am fine and it is time for me to go. You do well, my son. I am happy for you and, if I do not see you again, I want you to know that I am truly grateful for your friendship and the time we got to spend together."

"You are a trusted friend, Brother Noble."

"Always remember that, Wolf," the leper said and disappeared from view.

Wolf remained where he was for a few minutes, thinking how he would miss talking with the leper. They had had good conversations since he had come to know him, intelligent, thoughtful, and informative conversations. He would miss the man very much.

He turned and made his way back to the village, eager to see his wife and hear what Iver had to say. He was delayed several times by people stopping him with concerns, some he could rectify right away and others that would take time while other people, mostly those from the Clan Learmonth, simply needed reassurance. His tribe needed no such reassurance.

Gorm caused him more delay, but it was necessary, letting him know all that had been done and that nothing of any consequence had been found, though searches continued.

He was glad when he finally entered the common room, but not happy at what he found.

His wife wasn't there, but her men were and they looked concerned.

Chapter Twenty-four

Wolf and Raven's men combed the area by the men's cottages where Raven had last been seen, but nothing was found.

"Maybe she went into the woods," Lars suggested, having joined the men while several warriors searched throughout the village for her.

Wolf shook his head. "She gave me her word she wouldn't go into the woods alone."

"And she would keep her word—" Fyn's sudden pause had everyone staring at him. "Unless she spotted something suspicious and had no time to alert anyone."

"I'll see if I can find any tracks," Iver said and took off not waiting for permission.

Wolf thought what had to be on all their minds… someone had taken her. But Raven would not go quietly, unless she had been silenced. He fought against the anger that was building in him. He didn't need it exploding. He had to keep his head clear, his mind focused.

"Who was to follow her today?" Wolf asked.

Her men looked from one to the other.

"It got a bit mixed today," Fyn said.

Wolf's hand fisted, itching to punch someone. "Or was it that my wife requested to be left alone?"

"With being here in the village and so many about, we didn't think there was anything to worry about," Fyn admitted.

"Why would you?" Lars asked as if the question was foolish. "From what I've seen of Raven, she can protect herself."

Gorm hurried toward them. "No one has seen her so far and she's not at the keep."

Wolf's worry grew as time seemed to rush by with no signs of her. "We don't stop looking even when it grows dark," he ordered.

"I'll see torches are prepared and ready for use," Gorm said and left them.

Wolf was at a loss, something he wasn't used to. He couldn't go charging off in any direction when he had no idea where she might be. Until something could be found as to where she might have gone, he could do nothing but wait. He wasn't good at that and he didn't like feeling helpless. The last time he felt that way was when he was young and his sister had been abducted, and she hadn't been found until twenty plus years later. He would not see that happen with Raven.

"TRACKS! I found tracks," Iver called out.

Wolf ran and followed behind Iver and what they found a few feet ahead stilled them all.

There near a tree lay Brother Noble collapsed in the snow.

Iver went to rush toward him.

Wolf grabbed his arm, yanking him back. "No, you can't touch him."

"BROTHER NOBLE! BROTHER NOBLE!" Iver called out frantically.

Fyn stepped forward as well and joined Iver in calling out to the leper.

"He's dead," George said in a worried whisper.

"BROTHER NOBLE!" Iver called out again and the leper stirred. "Brother Noble, it's Iver, are you hurt?"

The leper struggled to sit up, then finally managed to get himself braced against the tree.

"Have you seen Raven?" Wolf shouted.

The leper struggled to speak, his voice raspier than usual. "I saw a cloaked figure before darkness claimed me, in that direction." He lifted his arm with effort and pointed.

"I'll stay with the leper to make sure he's all right," George said.

"See if you can get him to the cottage where he last stayed so he can rest," Wolf said and hurried past the others to follow behind Iver, who had taken the lead.

Iver stopped and pointed to the ground. "Blood."

Fear rushed up to choke Wolf. Was it his wife's blood? Had she come this way? He hoped not.

They followed the drops of blood until they finally vanished. Footprints led them in another direction. Time seemed to rush by, though it passed more slowly than felt. When Wolf found his wife, he intended to keep her by his side until this thing with Brynjar was done. He refused to give thought that she wouldn't be found. She was too skilled of a warrior not to survive.

Wolf determined they would only continue so far, dusk growing near. They would have to return to the village and gather torches to continue the search.

He was about to call a return to the village when they came upon a cropping of rocks and at the foot of the largest rock laid a crumpled body, a cloak concealing much of the person.

Iver stopped and stared, his face pale as if afraid to proceed and find it was Raven.

Wolf had no such qualms, he hurried to the fallen body and dropped down beside it. He almost roared to the heavens, but kept control of his relief as he called out, "It's not Raven."

At first glance one would surmise that the man had slipped off the rock and died, but that was not what happened. On closer inspection, a knife was found protruding from his chest.

"Another of Brynjar's men?" Fyn asked, coming up beside Wolf.

"I can only assume," Wolf said and pulled the knife out of the man.

The man's eyes burst open and he drew a quick breath.

"A woman. Did you see a woman?" Wolf demanded before life could drain completely out of the man.

He gagged as he struggled to speak. "He knows."

Wolf roared out his rage so strongly it echoed through the woods and was returned by the woeful howl of wolves.

Fyn spoke after Wolf stood. "Dusk draws near. We need to get torches to continue the search."

"He knows," Wolf repeated the dead man's words, a fiery anger in his dark eyes.

"Does he speak of Brynjar, and what would he know?" Fyn asked.

Lars shook his head. "He could refer to anyone."

Iver pointed to the dead man. "It must be important that he used his last breath to tell us."

One of Wolf's warriors rushed out of the woods, his shouts interrupting any further discussion. "She's been found. Lady Raven has been found."

Wolf listened to his warrior explain as they made haste back to the village. His wife had been found making her way to the village, a gash to her head. She was presently at the longhouse, Greta tending her. He kept a quick pace, needing to feel his wife in his arms as fast as possible.

He stopped once inside the longhouse and stared at his wife sitting calmly at a table, Greta clearing the tabletop of the bloody cloths and bucket. Raven met his eyes and smiled and his heart nearly stopped, the relief that she was there safe overwhelming him. He hurried to her and yanked her off the bench into a fierce hug.

With her arms locked in the hug, she was unable to return it and though it said much, she preferred to have her arms around him as well—and also be able to breathe.

"You steal the breath from me, husband," she said with some difficultly and he loosened his hold on her, though didn't release her.

She was able to get her arms up and around his neck and was startled when he drew his head back as she went to kiss him.

"How did you get that gash on your head?" he demanded, his eyes focused on it. Before she could answer he turned to Greta, who was nearly to the door. "Greta, she will heal well?"

Greta turned quickly and nodded. "Lady Raven does well. The wound is not deep and bled little. The thick coat of honey should help it heal nicely."

"You will look in on her later," he ordered.

Greta nodded and took her leave, Fyn following her out, along with her other men and Lars, leaving the couple alone.

"Tell me what happened?" Wolf demanded and annoyance sparked in his dark eyes when she shook her head.

"Not until you kiss me."

His annoyance fled as his lips landed on hers in a powerful kiss, lingering in it, letting himself feel the depths of it and know this was real. She was there with him, safe in his arms. He followed it with several short kisses, needing the taste of her to linger on his lips. Finally, though reluctantly, he eased his face away from hers and with one arm around her lowered them to sit on the bench.

"Tell me what happened," he said, filling two tankards with ale and placing one in front of her.

"I heard the leper was here and it's been some time since I've spoken with him, so I went to look for him."

"Alone," he accused.

She ignored him and continued, offering somewhat of an explanation. "I knew he'd be close to the village, seeking shelter or food. There was no reason for me to think it unsafe. After all, you have many warriors still combing the woods since the attack earlier. I was barely in the woods when something struck me. I was hit hard and I had little time to take shelter. Unfortunately, I passed out behind a cropping of rocks which is why your men never spotted me when searching. As soon as I came to and gathered my wits about me, I made my way into the village, ordered word be sent to you, and sought Greta's help."

His eyes had been on her wound the whole time she spoke. "That is no wound from a missed arrow. A rock perhaps, but why throw a rock at you?"

"It puzzles me as well," she said and gripped his forearm as if needing to feel his strength. "George told me what happened to Brother Noble. He rests in the cottage you provided for him and is grateful for your care. Do you know what happened to him?"

Wolf thought on it a moment. "Since he is a leper, no one would get close to him, so I would think the same happened to him that happened to you. He was hit with something that knocked him out."

"Why though?" she asked, contemplating her own question.

"A warning perhaps, since if it was meant to harm then you would both be dead."

"Warn us from what?"

"We came across what we thought was another dead man, but when I pulled the knife out of him, he had enough breath left in him to say… 'He knows.' I assume he meant Brynjar."

"It sounds like a warning for someone. Could it mean he knows Eria is here?"

"I wish I knew. The puzzle accumulates more pieces when the ones we have already collected have yet to link."

"If Brynjar was responsible for his death, then he had to have done something to displease the man," Raven said.

"Brynjar punishes those who fail him," Wolf reminded.

Raven was eager to share a thought with him. "Could the archers have been a diversion? Could the man have been tasked with doing someone harm during the attack and chose not to carry out the deed? His punishment for failure—death?"

"Why not at least try?" Wolf questioned. "If it was freedom in death he sought, he could have easily gotten that by trying to carry out his task. He had to have known he'd be followed and swift punishment measured if he didn't succeed."

"Maybe he wasn't part of Brynjar's crew at all. Maybe we see it wrong."

Wolf gave it a moment of thought. "Yet who else could he be referring to when he said he knows? Brynjar is the most likely person."

"I suppose," she admitted reluctantly.

"You still feel we're missing something."

Raven nodded. "The most important piece to the puzzle. The one that connects all the other pieces. It's right here in front of us. I know it is."

"Whatever it is, it must hold great value to Brynjar to send men after men to see the task done."

Her eyes went wide. "Then why come here himself?"

"To finish it, to see firsthand what chaos he has caused, what pain he believes he's made me and others suffer."

"But he hasn't been successful, so why come here until his mission has proven at least somewhat fruitful?" It was a question more to herself, and she continued, "Did you have the man who spoke to you brought back to the village? I'd like to see him."

"Why?"

She shrugged. "Maybe I'd recognize him."

"He's being brought back to join the dead archers." He held up his hand when his wife went to protest. "I'll have him put in the shed with the dead man we have yet to identify."

She smiled, pleased.

Her smile was like a bright ray of sunshine to his soul. It chased away any darkness that lingered there and replaced it with joy. He reached out, his hand gripping the back of her neck and his eyes focused intently on hers.

"Will I constantly have to warn you never to frighten me like that again?" he whispered harshly, just the thought of the pain of losing her feeling like a vicious blow to his gut.

"I wish I could promise you otherwise, Wolf, but I am who I am, and that will never change. What I can promise you is something that I never thought possible." She kissed his lips gently. "I promise I will never stop loving you. Even after I take my last breath, know that I still and always will love you."

"I'll hold you to that promise, wife, and I promise you the same as well." His lips barely touched hers when the door burst open.

Gorm hurried in. "The sentinels in the keep spotted a troop headed this way—Northmen. They should arrive in a day or more."

Raven was pleased to hear Wolf order, "Send word to Royden and Arran."

"I'll see everyone prepared for battle," Gorm said.

"No," Wolf said. "If Brynjar has anyone among us, word will be sent to him. Or if he has men secluded in areas we have yet to find or obscured from the keep's sentinels, they will see and alert him. It is time to use the warriors I have positioned for just this moment. Get them in place and have them ready. Hagen will lead them."

Gorm nodded.

"Has the body of the man in the woods been brought back?" Wolf asked.

"He has," Gorm confirmed.

"Place him in the shed with the other dead man," Wolf ordered. "Warn the sentinels to remain extra alert as well as the villagers. With Brynjar close there may be those who wish to gain his favor and fulfill any task that others have failed at, or mistakenly believe they would gain their freedom as Brynjar often falsely promises."

"Lady Raven's men wait outside. They plan to remain with her wherever she goes."

"Send them in," Raven said.

Gorm opened the door and summoned them in.

Raven didn't wait, she spoke up as soon as they gathered in front of the table. "Brynjar heads this way with a troop of warriors. Wolf has things in hand, which Gorm will explain to you. Fyn, you will stay close to Greta and Tait. George you will keep watch over Eria. Iver see that Brother Noble is informed of the situation and have him remain where he is until it is done. You and Brod shall keep close to me when I'm not with my husband." She turned to Wolf. "Does that work for you, husband."

"It does, though I may need Iver's tracking skills at some point."

"I am ready whenever you need me," Iver said with a nod.

"Do you think Brynjar comes for Eria?" George asked, wearing his worry for everyone to see.

"I don't believe it's his main reason for being here," Wolf said. "Though I also don't believe he'd leave her behind, since he would see it as failure. I'll see that warriors are assigned along with you to watch over Eria."

"Brynjar's troop is no match against us," Lars boasted.

"Brynjar has captured villages with far less men," Wolf said. "He is sly and plans well, and he keeps his tongue to himself. He creates chaos before he even attacks and his victims fall easily when the final blow comes."

"That won't happen here," Lars said with a strong resolve as he turned to the others. "Come, we'll prepare for our unwanted guest."

The men followed him out, their tongues wagging more rapidly than a bunch of women.

"They begin to work well together," Wolf said as the door closed behind the men.

"They would since they are all good, skilled warriors."

Wolf's eyes settled on her wound.

"You're not going to leave my side for the remainder of the day, are you?" she asked, though knew the answer.

"That smile of yours tells me you don't mind," he said, his smile matching hers.

"I miss you at times," she admitted.

A playful scowl scrunched his handsome features. "Only at times?" She jabbed him in the chest and he grabbed her hand, bringing it to his lips to kiss. "I miss you whenever we're apart, even if it is only for a short time. It sometimes annoys me at how necessary you've become to my life."

She looked about to laugh. "It's good that I can still annoy you—in a good way."

He kept hold of her hand. "We need to talk later—"

"About your grandmother?"

"She means a lot to me."

"Worry not. We both may be stubborn women, but we're not foolish women. Besides, we both love you and we'll only make you suffer so much," she said unable to stop from chuckling.

"You forget I'm called the Beast," he said and with a low growl settled his mouth at her neck to nip and nibble.

She playfully shoved him away, his nips and nibbles far too tempting. "You can unleash the Beast tonight in bed. Right now I want to go see that dead man."

"You prefer a dead man over me?" he asked as if wounded.

"Let me think on that," she said scrunching her brow.

"I'm going to make you pay for that." His dark eyes narrowed as passion shot like lightning through them.

She leaned closer, her warm breath briefly fanning his face as she whispered a single word. "Promise?" She hurried off the bench, fearful his response would have her rushing him off to their bedchamber.

It was his turn to chuckle. "Don't trust yourself?"

"Not in the least. My body drips in readiness for you."

"Damn it, wife," he said, bolting off the bench.

"Frist the dea—"

Wolf swing her up in his arms and carried her to their bedchamber. "I decide what comes first and that would be us." She looked about to argue and he held his tongue, since he intended to have his way no matter what she said.

"Your need is great so I won't deny you," she said, her arms going around his neck.

He laughed. "My need?"

"Aye, we'll see your need satisfied before anything else."

"How generous of you, wife."

"We'll be quick now and take our time later," she said.

"Are you implying this quick one won't satisfy you?"

"Are you implying you won't want me later?" she countered.

He stepped into their bedchamber and when she reached past him to shut the door, he stole a forceful kiss, then whispered, "I always want you, Raven."

"And I you," she murmured.

He hurried to the bed, dropping her down on her feet, ready to strip her naked when she paled and looked ready to topple over. He swung her back up in his arms and sat on the bed, cradling her in his lap.

"What's wrong?" he asked.

"I am lightheaded and my stomach churns," she said, resting her head on his shoulder.

He silently cursed himself. He had given no thought to her wound. "You need rest not a poke. Your wound has done more damage than you think."

He was probably right, but she wouldn't admit it. "I am fine."

"You will be after you rest," he said and stood, then placed her on the bed.

"I don't need rest," she protested as he went to slip off her boots. She tried bolting up but grew dizzy when she did and collapsed back on the pillow.

"This is no time to be stubborn," he warned. "If you don't rest now, what will happen if you grow worse?" If anything, he knew his wife was good at seeing reason as she did now, her eyes closing in thought.

"I suppose a short rest could prove beneficial," she said. "But first you must promise me something."

"That depends on what you ask," he said, thinking she'd insist they make love first.

She knew what he had assumed. "I'm not going to force you to make love with me." The grin on his face told her enough, but it was nice to hear him confirm it.

"Never will you ever have to force me to make love to you." He kissed her gently. "So what is this promise you want from me?"

"Before someone else has a chance, I want you to go and see if the dead man has a knife in his boot and bring it to me so I can see if it is similar to the other one I saw and was stolen."

"You think them connected?" he asked.

"I'm not sure, but if he carries a similar knife then it proves they are connected, and I don't think that connection is Brynjar. And you'll come back right away and let me know?"

He eased her anxiousness. "I will return immediately to report one way or the other."

"I wait impatiently."

"Of course you do." He kissed her cheek and left the room, hurrying to carry out her request before she got out of bed and saw to the task herself.

Though nightfall was nearly upon them, the village was busy with activity. Wolf held no doubt that they would be prepared for whatever Brynjar intended just as they had been when the attack came on the village and was stopped before any lives were lost or damage done. But what was his intention? He scowled without realizing it, people staying clear of him as he headed to the shelter that housed the two dead men.

Wolf hurried into the shelter and went straight to the recent dead man's boots and stood and stared for a moment. A hilt of a knife was tucked in one of them and he carefully slipped it out. His steps were rushed as he headed back to the keep, many casting curious eyes at him, and he not noticing. He was eager to find out if the knife was similar to the one his wife had seen in the other dead man's boot.

Wolf wasn't surprised to find Raven sitting up in bed or that her hands eagerly reached out to him when she spotted the knife he held.

She barely had it in her hands when she said, "The top is identical to the one I saw in the first dead man's boot. With the first one having been stolen, that means that someone here knows these two men or at least what they're doing here."

His hand went out to take the knife back just as hers reached out to return it to him.

"We think alike, wife," he said and took the knife from her. "I'll put the knife back and we'll see who attempts to take it."

Chapter Twenty-five

"I did not think you a coward," Raven said to her husband when he entered the common room the next morning. He smiled, which annoyed her even more.

Wolf leaned down and kissed his wife's cheek. "And good morning to you, wife."

"You purposely left our bed this morning before I woke to avoid making love with me," she accused.

He took firm hold of her chin. "You had a restless night last night, waking on and off. I left because you finally fell into a much needed sound sleep." He leaned close, her lips not far from his. "And I will see you fully healed before we make love since you can be quite demanding." He kissed her quick before she could protest. Not that it mattered since he knew as soon as her lips were free of his, she would protest. And she did, though not the way he expected.

"Of course I'm demanding. I love you and when we join, I feel that love more intensely and simply can't get enough of it."

He kissed her again, purposely lingering and stirring their passions, which were already too close to the surface.

"You kiss when a monster is close to your doorstep?"

The familiar voice echoed in Raven's head.

Wolf shook his head. "I forgot to tell you that your brother Arran arrived a short time ago."

"Alone?' Raven asked as Arran approached them, wishing he had brought Purity with him but knowing he wouldn't dare chance her safety.

"You don't think I'd be foolish enough to bring Purity with me, do you?" Arran asked as he swung his leg over the bench to join them at the table.

Raven grinned. "You snuck away from her, didn't you?"

"She gave me no choice," Arran confessed, his fine features growing taut with anger. "I need to see this done. I need to see Brynjar dead."

"Royden watches over Purity and Oria?" Raven asked, concern for her friends fading her grin.

"He was eager to join me, but one of us had to remain and see our wives and clans kept safe." Arran turned to Wolf. "The warriors you keep at mine and Royden's home are much appreciated. Our clans feel safer with their presence."

"We are family, are we not? And family protects family," Wolf said.

"Never would I have thought us family, but it cannot be denied. We are family and we fight as one," Arran said. "I did bring one family member with me." A slight smile lightened his solemn expression.

Raven eagerly asked, "Who?"

"Clive."

Raven jumped up off the bench. "Where is he?"

"I left him with your men," Arran said. "Brod waits outside for you."

Raven shot narrowed eyes at her husband.

"You're not going anywhere alone until this matter is settled to my satisfaction," Wolf reminded.

"I never thought I would take your husband's side, but I agree with him. I was told about what happened to you yesterday. Someone continues to see you harmed and your husband takes precautions to protect you as he should. Don't make it more difficult for him," Arran scolded.

Raven normally would have retaliated with a sharp remark, reminding her brother she was no longer a young lass he could dictate to, but that he took an allied stand with Wolf had her holding her tongue—more like biting it. Wolf was right. They were all family now and that was more important than anything.

Arran laughed. "It's killing you to hold your tongue, isn't it?"

"You're an arse," Raven said and swiped a fur cloak off the pile by the door and didn't bother to look back at either her husband or her brother before walking out the door.

"You know she's going to make you pay for that, don't you?" Wolf said, smiling.

Arran laughed. "She can try."

Wolf rested his arms on the table, leaning forward. "Tell me how many times did she outwit you when she was young?"

Arran scowled. "More times than I care to remember."

***

Raven hugged Clive tight and whispered, "Tell me you're not here to stay."

Clive grinned as he stepped back. "Bethany and I plan to wed."

Raven hugged him again. "I'm so happy for you."

He gave a nod toward Fyn, holding Tait in his arms as he talked with Greta. "I predict another one of us will wed soon as well."

"Tait loves Fyn. He follows him around everywhere, and it's easy to see that Greta loves Fyn as well. They make a fine family and I'm happy for them."

Clive gave another nod, toward George this time. "And George? How does it go for him with Eria?"

"She's much like him, interested in everything, wanting to learn everything she can. They make a fine pair." Raven looked to Brod talking with Iver. "Brod talks often with Ida and I see interest in her eyes for him as well."

"Iver?" Clive asked in a worrisome tone.

"He misses the adventures we had. He was happy to go on a mission for me and Wolf. He returned with Brother Noble."

"How does Brother Noble do?" Clive asked, worry deepening the wrinkles at the corner of his eyes.

"His missions are at an end. He will return to the monastery very soon and live out his remaining days there."

"It's for the best," Clive said with a nod. "He's placed himself in danger more than need be." He cleared his throat. "I thought you quite mad when you agreed to this union with the Beast, but it turned out to be the best thing for all of us."

"I wonder if the one who is responsible for it was hoping it would be just that, best for all."

"Have you any clue as to who it might be?" Clive asked.

"We know who it wasn't," Raven said. "Our king and Wolf's king continue to squabble and have no time to care what happens between him and me."

"But you were led to believe otherwise as was Wolf. Who would have the boldness to do such a thing?" Clive asked.

"I don't know, but I plan to find out no matter how long it takes me."

***

Raven stood just inside the door of the room where Oria had slept for the five years they'd all been separated. It was more a cell than a room. She didn't know how Oria had managed, though she had told Raven there were many nights she had slept in the Great Hall by the hearth to keep warm.

After Arran and Wolf came to fetch Clive to go speak with Gorm and make them aware of what plans Wolf had made, she had made her way to the keep. Brod had accompanied her and she had left him in the Great Hall to talk with Ida.

Raven had recalled Oria telling her about the window in the room and how looking out it, you could see farther than from any other place in the keep. She had wanted to see for herself. Now that she was here, it troubled her to see that Oria had been confined to this small space each night. Raven had been used to the sky as her roof more often than not and would have gone mad in such a confined space.

"What are you doing here?"

Raven jumped and swerved around to face her husband. "You startled me." Her brow having gone wide. "Did you follow me?"

"I did," he admitted and stepped toward her.

She instinctively stepped back, the room so small, she didn't think there would be enough space for them both. His overpowering presence took up far too much space. "You were to talk with Clive and Arran."

"Gorm has that well in hand and you had me curious as to why you came here when it wouldn't hurt you to rest some."

"I've had more than enough rest and I recalled something Oria had told me about this room, which I wished to see for myself." She went to the window, drawing back the tapestry, and realizing she would have to go up on her toes to see out, grabbed the lone chair and moved it under the window. Her husband's hands were at her waist when she went to climb up on it and he swung her up to stand on it.

Wolf's arm went around her waist to keep a good hold on her once she stood steady on the chair, then he moved to take a look out the window along with her. Though his wife was far from short, he possessed the extra height needed to see out the window without a problem, and he knew what she would see.

"Are they your men?" she asked, seeing the sizeable troop camped in the distance, the area open for all to see from this height, though not from below.

"They are," he confirmed. "I brought a large contingent with me, though not all will remain. Some will return home."

"They've built shelters. It looks like a small village."

"Enough shelters for warmth, but permanent building will start in the spring. Crofts will be established as well as a small village."

"They keep you informed as to who enters that area."

"They do and their presence provides added protection for the clan," he said. "There has been no sighting of any of Brynjar's warriors in that area."

"He must know you came with such a large troop of warriors," Raven said, continuing to stare out the window.

"I would imagine he does."

"Yet he comes here anyway," Raven said, shaking her head, since it made no sense to her.

She looked down at her husband and was caught off guard by the intensity of his dark eyes. Passion flared in them but so did love so vibrant that it overwhelmed her.

With his hands snug at her waist, he swung her off the chair and laid her down on the narrow bed. He waited a brief moment, staring down at her, and she worried over his decision since obviously his desire warred with his concern for her wound.

She hurried to challenge, "Don't start something you can't finish, husband."

His dark eyes smoldered with such passion that she shivered in anticipation.

He stepped to the end of the bed, slipped his hands under her backside to pull her bottom down near the edge, knelt on the bed, and brought her legs up to rest against his shoulders. His hands returned to her backside to lift her just enough to make it easy for him to enter her.

There was no time for enticements, his need was too great as was hers, since a day rarely went by that they didn't make love. Sometimes slow. Sometimes fast. Always satisfying.

He slipped into her and her wetness welcomed him as she closed around him snugly. He dropped his head back, reveling in the pleasure that rushed through him, then he began to move inside her with haste.

It would be a quick joining, a needy joining, but always a loving one and that thought fired his blood even more.

Raven struggled not to moan too loudly, fearful she would bring unwanted visitors to the open door. She muffled her desire as best she could, her hands clenching at the blanket beneath her as passion mounted rapidly in her. She would come quickly, though she would have preferred not to, but he felt so good deep inside her that pleasure quickened with his every thrust.

He squeezed her bottom as he pounded against her and she tightened around him, forcing a groan from his lips.

"Wolf," she begged in a whisper.

"Let go, Raven. Let go," he urged and let himself do the same.

The intensity of his climax almost stole his strength, but he held firm, wanting them both to enjoy every last bit of pleasure that poured out of them.

He wanted badly to drop down beside her when it was done, take her in his arms as he usually did when they finished making love, but there was no room, the bed too narrow. He went to pull out of her.

"No," she said in a labored breath and reached her arms out to him.

He dropped down on her, unable to resist her welcoming embrace. Her arms wrapped tightly around his back as far as they could go and he relished their loving warmth.

"I love you," she whispered and kissed near his ear.

His warm breath fanned her cheek as he raised his head and said, "More—I love you so much more."

Her smile bordered on a gentle laugh. "I won't argue with you, since your words touch my heart."

"A heart that belongs to me and me alone," he said as if it were a command.

"And your heart belongs to me alone," she countered.

"Always." he kissed her slow and easy, then reluctantly slipped off her and the bed. He reached his hand out to her. "It will grow dark soon. We should return to the longhouse unless you prefer to spend the night here."

"No," Raven was quick to respond, hurrying off the bed. "I'm ready to return home."

That Raven had embraced the longhouse as home filled him with a sense of peace. His hands went to her waist and he hurried her off the bed and through the open door, then took her hand to walk to the stairs.

"We should stop and see if anyone has dared to steal the knife from the dead man," Raven said.

"It grows dark," he reminded. "The theft would be more likely to take place at night under the cover of darkness. We can wait until morning. The guards will let me know if anyone enters throughout the night."

"Are you sure no one will spot them?"

"The guards won't be seen but our culprit will," he assured her.

"Still, it would be wise to see if the knife is still there and limit the time to when it may have been stolen."

Wolf nodded and they were soon out of the keep and taking careful steps down the hill, patches of ice almost causing Raven to slip a couple of times if Wolf hadn't kept firm hold of her.

Torches lit a path through the village and Wolf grabbed one of the smaller torches before they entered the shed.

Raven went straight to the dead man's boots and turned wide eyes on Wolf. "It's gone. The knife is gone."

Raven remained in the shed while her husband stepped outside to summon the guards who had been watching it. She hoped only one person had entered, then there would be no question as to who it had been.

Wolf entered with three of his warriors and they stood at the one end of the table while Wolf joined his wife at the other end.

"Tell me of anyone who entered the shed after I left it," Wolf ordered.

"Lady Raven's brother was the last person," the one warrior said.

Arran wasn't even a possibility and she eagerly waited to hear who else had visited the shed.

"Lars was here," another warrior said.

The third warrior added what he knew. "The healer, Greta, was here."

"And Eria as well," the warrior who first spoke said.

"Were Greta and Eria here together?" Wolf asked.

"No, they came separately," the one warrior confirmed.

"Who was here the longest?' Raven asked.

The three warriors cast a quick glance at one another and their baffled expression was answer enough, though one spoke for them all. "None stayed that long so it is difficult to say."

"Your duty is done here. Go home and stay warm," Wolf ordered and the men smiled their appreciation and hurried out.

"Now we question them," Raven said, "except my brother. He wouldn't have anything to do with this. Besides, he wasn't here when the first man was found."

"Lars has been a trusted friend for years. I can't see it being him," Wolf said, though there was a question of doubt in his eyes.

"What troubles you?"

"I thought another man a trusted friend."

"The one who tried to kill Purity," Raven said.

Wolf nodded not surprised she knew. Purity probably told her, though Raven had an uncanny way of finding things out.

"I doubt it's Lars. Anyone can see how loyal he is to you, to the tribe. But it would be wise to ask all of them, even my brother, why they were there."

***

Eria stood in front of the table, wringing her hands. "Have I done something wrong, Wolf?" she shook her head. "I mean, my lord."

"We're friends, Eria." At least he hoped they were. "You can call me Wolf as you've always done."

She folded her hands in front of her, her worry eased some. "I'm glad. Our friendship means much to me."

"Sit and have a hot brew?" Wolf offered.

Eria cast a hasty glance to the door. "George waits for me. We will sup with Fyn and Greta at the keep, Detta as well."

"Then I won't keep you. Tell me why you went to the shed where the dead men rest."

"Greta suggested it. She thought I might recognize one of the men since many say the two are Northman."

"Wise of her," Wolf said.

"And did you recognize either of them?" Raven asked, sitting beside her husband pressed close to him, enjoying his warmth.

"I'm afraid I didn't." Eria's brow knitted.

"Anything you may have noticed would be of help," Raven said.

"I thought there was something familiar about the one dead man, but I can't figure out what it is," Eria said, it obviously troubling her.

"If you think of it, let me know," Wolf said.

Tears quickly glistened in Eria's eyes. "I am forever grateful to you for protecting me, but then you always did. You truly are a good friend, Wolf."

"I will always keep you safe, Eria, though I believe there is another man who would gladly take on the task."

Eria's cheeks blossomed red.

"Go and enjoy supper with your friends," Wolf said. "Please send Greta in. I won't keep her long."

Eria hurried out and Greta entered a moment later.

Greta stood in front of the table as worried as Eria had been. "How may I be of help, my lord?"

"Tell me why you went to see dead men."

"To see if I could recognize the second dead man," she said and hesitated as if she stopped herself from saying more.

"What else, Greta?" Wolf urged, a warning that he would have an answer.

"It will sound strange, but being a healer I am curious when someone dies. I want to see the wounds and try to discover whatever I can about them."

"You're a wise healer," Raven said. "Tell me, did you notice if the second man had a knife tucked in his boot?"

Greta shook her head. "I'm sorry, but I had no reason to look at his boots."

"Anything else catch your interest about the two men?" Wolf asked.

"No," she said, a sadness drifting over her. "Only that I wish I could have saved them."

"That's all, Greta. Go and enjoy your night," Wolf said.

"Can I send Arran and Lars in?" She smiled. "They complain of deep hunger."

"Send them in," Wolf said.

Arran and Lars both dug into the food on the table as soon as they sat.

"Are you going to tell us what goes on?" Arran asked and tore a chunk of bread off one of many loaves of bread in the middle of the table.

"Why did you go to see the dead man?" Wolf asked him.

Arran shrugged. "When I learned there was another dead man, I got curious. I thought by chance I might recognize him. If he had been a captive of Brynjar I may have run into him."

"Did you?" Raven asked, though knew if he had he would have shared the news immediately.

"No. He, like the other man, wasn't familiar to me."

"I went to have a better look myself," Lars said. "I thought that maybe there would be something familiar about them if I saw them together." He shook his head. "There wasn't."

"So you still don't know if they were sent by Brynjar or why they were coming here," Arran said. "But it matters little now. We'll know tomorrow with

Brynjar's arrival what his intentions are. I say we kill him and his men quick and be done with it."

Lars wiped his wet mouth on his sleeve, nodding. "I agree. Gut him and save us from the devil."

Talk went on, though Brynjar wasn't mentioned again. Arran entertained them with tales of Raven when she was young. And she countered with her brother's escapades with women. Lars added tales about Wolf when he was young and much laughter was shared through it all.

When Wolf and Raven were finally in their bedchamber, Wolf asked his wife what he'd been waiting to ask her all evening. "So we have three suspects, excluding Arran since he wasn't here when it all happened, and all gave reasonable explanations."

"It's obvious," Raven said with a shrug. "One of them is lying."

Chapter Twenty-six

"I sent Iver on a last minute mission," Wolf said the next morning as he dressed. "He actually suggested it. I meant to tell you yesterday but with everything that had gone on, I forgot."

Raven donned her shirt and plaid. The furs and leather kept her warm but they were also cumbersome at times and with a possible battle on the horizon she didn't want to be weighted down. "That's all right. He talked with me about it first. His suggestion certainly held merit. I'm glad you agreed to it."

"I should have known he would speak to you first. Will he ever trust me?" Wolf asked, a bit disappointed but not surprised Iver went to Raven first.

"I think he already does, but he is accustomed to coming to me with things and he knows that I share them with you before any decision is made."

"I have to admit, Iver was wise in suggesting that he track Brynjar's troop even though I have warriors already keeping watch on them. Iver made it clear it was easy for one to slip off unnoticed, meaning something more could be planned that we don't see."

"Iver often sees things others don't. If anything is amiss, he will spot it," Raven said with confidence in her friend. She walked over to her husband and draped her arms over his shoulders to lock her fingers at the back of his neck. "We don't know what today holds for us. So I will tell you now in case I don't get to say it again—words I never ever thought I'd say to you but now say them most willingly, truthfully, and from my heart. "I love you, Wolf, and I always will. Nothing will ever change that."

His arm hooked her waist to tug her close, needing the feel of her snug against him. "Ours is a most unusual union, love not expecting to grow from it, not even friendship. I am grateful we found both. I love you beyond reason and you *will not*—I repeat you *will not*—place yourself in harm's way today. Brynjar battles without honor. He often has others make it easier for him to deliver the final blow. I will not lose you. You will let me battle if necessary and you will keep yourself safe."

Raven went to speak.

"I will hear no objection. I understand you have the scars of battle to prove you capable, but those were mere skirmishes compared to what you would face against Brynjar. You have fought and protected your men well, but it is my turn to protect you and you will let me do that today. If not, you will leave me to worry and it could cost me my life. So promise me you will take no unnecessary chances. You will let me and Arran deal with Brynjar."

She settled her brilliant blue eyes on his dark ones. "If your life is in danger I will not hesitate to help you, otherwise I will take no unnecessary chances." A slight scrunch of his brow told her that he wasn't too sure of that. "You have my word." Her smile surfaced as his scrunch vanished and they kissed.

Arran looked up from the table in the common room when they entered. "You will keep yourself safe, Raven, and take no part of any fight."

"How sweet of you to worry about me, Arran, but you don't get to tell me what to do anymore," she said with a pleasant smile.

"But your husband does," Arran said and turned to Wolf.

"Raven gave me her word. There is nothing to worry about," Wolf assured him.

"I don't believe that for a minute," Arran argued.

"Then believe this," Raven said when she saw worry heavy in her brother's eyes and the wrinkles at the corner of his eyes that seemed to have deepened overnight. "I will not rob you of the pleasure of killing Brynjar, nor will I make it difficult for you to do so."

"I appreciate that, Raven, and I am pleased to know that Wolf will protect you with his life." Arran looked once again to the man.

"That I will," Wolf confirmed.

Raven chuckled. "Don't be upset if it comes down to me having to save the both of you."

Neither man laughed.

Gorm entered the common room, a light dusting of snow on his head and shoulders. "It begins to snow, but all is in place and ready."

"Then there is nothing for us to do but wait," Wolf said.

Arran shook his head. "The most difficult part."

Talk lagged among them as they ate, though little was eaten. Raven felt somewhat vulnerable not knowing the reason for Brynjar's arrival. She had made sure she never let her men go into anything without knowing what they were going into. She had never allowed random attacks on travelers. The men would learn who traveled the roads and why and what they carried on them. Only then would they lay in wait and seize the opportunity, leaving less chance of a surprise attack or losing any of her men. Nothing was known of why Brynjar was here, leaving them all vulnerable.

When word came that Brynjar was not far off, cloaks were quickly donned and Raven stepped outside with her husband and brother.

Arran took her arm to hold her back when Wolf continued to Gorm. "I need your word."

"You don't have to ask, Arran. If anything should happen to you, I will see Purity and your bairn well cared for and protected as will Royden," she said, well aware of what he would ask of her.

"And you will convince Purity to find a good man to wed so she will not be alone," he said to Raven's surprise. His dark eyes warned when she laughed.

"Don't waste your thoughts on that. There is no way Purity would ever love or wed again. She has loved you and only you for as long as she has known you." Her smile softened and she laid a gentle hand on her brother's arm. "I understand now how and why she feels that way, for I would feel the same if I lost Wolf, and I would never force her to go against her heart. It would be quite impossible for her to do." She jabbed him in the arm. "So you have no choice—you can't die today."

"Either can you," Arran warned.

"If death claimed me, he'd want nothing to do with me and spit me right back," she said with a laugh that brought a smile to Arran's face.

"And I wouldn't blame him."

They both laughed and went to join Wolf.

Snow fell gently around them and Raven couldn't keep a grin from her face when she saw Wolf's warriors all but surrounded Brynjar's troop, not giving them room to attack, as they led them to the longhouse. Brynjar rode in the front, his hood draped low on his face. She had never seen the man, but she had heard stories of the many scars on his face that had destroyed his once good features.

Brynjar's troop slowed and let their leader move forward on his own. He had barely dismounted when Wolf was upon him.

"Where is Brynjar?" Wolf demanded.

The man pushed his hood back and there wasn't a scar on his face. "He had a task to see to. I am here to collect his intended, Eria."

"No, you're not," Wolf accused. "You're here to divert our attention from the true reason for Brynjar being here."

Arran stepped alongside Wolf, recognizing the man. "Where is he, Rouard?"

The bulky man shrugged. "I ask no questions. I do what Brynjar commands. Give me Eria and I will be on my way."

"Eria isn't going anywhere with you and Brynjar knew that when he sent you here," Wolf said, a stinging anger to his tone.

"We've had a long, tiresome journey. The men need rest and food. We will rest today and talk more tomorrow." Rouard nodded as if it were settled. "We will make camp on the outskirts of the village." He turned away and ordered his men to turn around, that they would make camp and eat. They all eagerly complied, many of them appearing worn out and definitely hungry.

"I will send drink and food to your camp," Wolf said.

Rouard didn't hide his surprise. "That is generous of you. I will speak with you tomorrow."

Arran waited until the group was a distance away, Wolf's men continuing to surround them, before he voiced his annoyance. "He lies and you let him."

"His presence here is nothing more than a ruse. Whatever Brynjar has planned, he will see it done today. And tomorrow before dawn, Rouard and his men will be gone as long as Brynjar has succeeded. If not, they will attack," Wolf said.

"We have to find Brynjar before nightfall," Arran said and shook his head. "But how? He could be anywhere."

"I think there is someone who knows where he went," Wolf said with a smile to Raven.

"Who is he? Where do we find him?" Arran asked anxiously.

"He'll find you," Raven said.

***

It wasn't long before one of Wolf's trackers arrived with a message from Iver and plans were formed. Raven stood behind the longhouse where the men gathered so none could be seen. She wished she was going with them, but she and others would remain behind to keep watch on the clan. With Wolf's warriors surrounding Brynjar's camp and ale plentiful to keep them busy, she didn't fear any problems with the men.

Wolf came to stand in front of her, looking like the Northman warrior, swathed in furs, leather, and weapons, that had come to claim her the day she had returned home. He had put a fright in her that day, but not today. Today she saw him as the mighty warrior the Beast, ready to devour anything in his path.

"Make sure and stay here, wife," Wolf ordered.

"I will stay here," she assured him. "And you will give me your word that you will do your best to return home safe to me."

He kissed her and whispered, "It's difficult to kill a Beast."

She grinned. "I had no trouble taming one."

"We'll see about that later tonight," he challenged and kissed her again. He turned away from her and her words stopped him.

"Come back to me or I will make it my mission in life to kill the one who took you from me."

He turned and grabbed her arm. "You will do no such thing. You could be with child right now. You will keep that in mind and do nothing that would put you or our bairn in danger." He didn't wait for her to respond, he walked away and didn't look back.

Raven remained where she stood, stunned by the intensity of his words and the way his dark eyes had flared with angry worry. The man truly did love her. She watched with a heavy heart as her husband, brother, and four warriors made their way into the nearby woods.

Iver's message had been clear. Two of Brynjar's warriors had left the camp and Brynjar joined them a short time later. One warrior went ahead of Brynjar and one trailed behind him. They were headed toward the village from a different direction. Iver told them where they should go to stop them from reaching the village.

Raven understood why her husband didn't take a troop of warriors with him. He planned on a surprise and quick attack that would see Brynjar and his two warriors dead before they could lift a weapon. This would finally be done and Brynjar would threaten them no more.

She joined Clive, who waited at the back corner of the longhouse for her.

"It is good that this will be done and over," he said as he walked with her around to the front.

Raven nodded and squared her shoulders. "I need to keep busy or I will worry endlessly. Where are the men?" She held up her hand. "George is at the keep with Eria and also Detta where he was ordered to remain. What of Brod?"

"He's drinking with Brynjar's men to see if he can find out anything." Clive shook his head. "I don't know how he does it, but he works his way in with strangers without them even realizing it. Fyn is with Greta, watching over her and Tait."

"Where's Lars?"

"He's with Gorm making sure all goes well," Clive said.

"And you're to look after me?"

"Your life has been threatened," he reminded.

"No more than a ruse to distract from Brynjar's true intention."

"Clive, can you help a minute?" Lars called out, waving him over toward one of the storage sheds throughout the village.

"Come with me," Clive said reluctant to leave her.

"Go, I'm good. The village is well protected and I can well protect myself," she urged. "Besides I wouldn't mind some time to wander alone with my thoughts."

"Stay where you can be seen," he said like a parent worried for his child.

"I will, now go," she ordered with a smile and he left with a shake of his head.

Raven felt as if a burden had been lifted off her. She hadn't realized how much it had made her feel a prisoner to have someone constantly following her. She was glad for the reprieve.

She smiled at the bairns who ran about in play oblivious to the possibility of battle that loomed around them. Their parents weren't. Weapons sat conveniently at hand by cottages and hung from belts. Shields were everywhere, ready to be grabbed at a moment's notice and caches of arrows waited alongside bows. The village was well prepared, though Raven doubted they would need to fight. The troop guarding Brynjar's men would be stopped before one warrior could enter the village.

Raven didn't believe that Rouard had any intention of attacking the village. He appeared more ready to wait than to battle, which meant he expected Brynjar to be successful at his mission. But why would Brynjar leave his men and head toward the village without them? It couldn't be her who he was after. He would know Wolf would see her well protected. So what did Brynjar want?

She shook her head annoyed she couldn't find an answer and her eyes caught on the shed that housed the two dead men. For some reason, she felt they held if not the answer, then at least an important piece to the puzzling mystery.

Raven entered the shed, hoping to find something that would help her. It was the first man they had found frozen to death that caught her interest. She stood over him staring. There was something familiar about his face, but try as she might she couldn't recall him. She had met many people through the years, though they mostly were brief meetings, so faces didn't remain long in her memory. Why then was it that his face seemed so familiar?

She shook her head and turned away to leave, then turned back for one last look.

It struck her then. She saw it clearly. She knew where she had seen him.

Chapter Twenty-seven

"Where's Clive?" Fyn asked looking about. "You're not to be by yourself."

"He's helping Lars and I believe I'm safer here than ever before with everyone prepared for battle," Raven said and smiled when little Tait squealed with delight when his snowball hit Fyn in the leg.

Fyn grinned and leaned down to scoop up a handful of snow. "Now you're going to get it." He shot Raven a questioning look as he formed the snowball.

"Go. I'm here to speak with Greta," Raven urged.

"She's in the cottage," Fyn said and turned to throw the snowball only to get hit in the leg with another one. "Now I'm going to get you." He laughed as he ran after a laughing Tait.

Raven gave a hasty knock on the wood door before opening it.

"Raven, come in," Greta greeted. "Are you in need of healing?"

Raven shut the door and stared at Greta a moment.

Greta grew uneasy, her hands gripping her apron.

Raven kept her tone gentle. "You took the knives, didn't you, Greta?"

Greta's hand remained tight on her apron. "What do you mean?"

"The missing knives from the dead men," Raven said, though knew full well that Greta had understood what she asked. "You took them. You know the two men or you know at least one of them. You need to tell me, Greta. I need to know if my husband is in more danger than he realizes."

Greta all but collapsed on the chair near the hearth.

"The dead man who froze to death. He's your brother, isn't he?" Raven said, stepping closer to her. "I finally saw what I'd been missing. It was his eyes— your eyes."

A tear rolled down Greta's cheek. "Aye, Knud was my brother. I feared someone here would realize it eventually. Gard, the other man, was a good friend of my brother's. I took their knives so I could return them to their families and let them know of their heroic deed so tales would be told about them and they would live on."

"Your brother must have had an important message for you if he braved a snowstorm to reach you. And I can only assume that Gard followed in case your brother failed his mission."

Greta nodded slowly, another tear slipping from the corner of her eye. "That is probably what happened. They have been close friends since they were young."

"What was so important that they both braved death to reach you?" It was a question Raven believed she already had the answer to.

Greta's hand went to the scar on her face. "Brynjar struck our village just before dusk one day. The gods were with my brother and Gard. The two were away trading. Brynjar took me and a few other women captive along with some men. I will never speak of what he did to me," —her hand went to the scar again— "He told me I wasn't worth keeping, but so I would never forget him, he left me with this scar. A few other scars as well and in places a husband only has a right to see and would be reminded of each time he…" She turned her head away in shame.

"I'm so sorry, Greta," Raven said, aching to run her sword through the evil man. "You can rest assured Fyn is not the type of man who would let that trouble him."

"I have discovered that and I'm grateful to have found him." She closed her eyes a moment as if gathering strength, then continued, "My brother and Gard found me where Brynjar had left me. It had been a couple of days. I didn't want to live but Knud refused to let me die. Unfortunately, not all in the village were happy with my return. They feared Brynjar would return for me and…" She fought back the tears pooling in her eyes but they overflowed anyway and rolled slowly down her cheeks. "I needed a safe place. A place where no one would know my secret. A place Brynjar would never dare attack. I sought refuge with the Beast."

Raven needed Greta to confirm what she surmised, but before she could a horrific roar from outside had both women jumping up and running out of the cottage.

***

"He changed course away from the village?" Wolf asked as he tried to make sense of it.

Iver nodded. "He has stopped by the river and looks as if he waits. I assume he waits to hear from the warrior who went ahead of him. Or he waits for another and the one ahead of him makes sure no one lingers about."

"He can't mean to cross that river," Arran said. "The melting snow swells it and causes it to rush wildly this time of year. Could he be meeting someone from your tribe?"

"Anything is possible, but I have yet to uncover anyone unfaithful in my tribe," Wolf said, annoyed that it was even a possibility that someone may have betrayed him.

"What could he wait for?" Arran asked.

Iver shrugged. "Information?"

The three men shook their heads.

"None of his actions thus far make sense and yet he is up to something and I have no doubt it will bring harm to someone," Wolf said.

***

Raven rushed toward Fyn when he stumbled toward them, blood running down his face from a wound to his head.

"He's gone. Taken. Tait," Fyn managed to say.

Greta screamed and Fyn reached out and wrapped her in his arms.

Raven let loose with a roar that would have her men rushing to her. Clive was there in no time along with Lars and Gorm. It wasn't long before Brod was there, but she had a message rushed to George to remain where he was and that he was to let no one enter the keep until he heard from her.

Fyn urged Greta to tend his wound so that he could join the search for Tait.

Raven thought otherwise. "You need to stay here and protect Greta. She has much to tell you."

Fyn looked to Greta but her eyes were on Raven. "I beg you, please bring my son back to me and please make sure there is no chance of him ever being taken from me again."

"You have my word," Raven said and joined Clive and Brod, who were huddled in talk with Lars and Gorm.

A plan was formed quickly, men were gathered just as hastily, and Raven stood by and watched as the men set off.

"It is good you obey your husband and remain behind," Gorm said, standing beside her and watching the group of men disappear into the woods.

"You should go and keep extra watch on Brynjar's men," Raven advised. "I go to wait in the longhouse."

Gorm looked to Clive. "You will stay with her."

"I won't leave her side," Clive confirmed.

Raven watched along with Clive, Gorm hurry off, comfortable that Clive would look after Raven.

"You know what I intend to do," Raven said.

"Aye," Clive said with a nod, "and I'm right by your side."

***

Wolf and Arran scrunched behind bushes along with Iver and watched Brynjar pace not far from the river's edge.

"He's impatient," Arran whispered.

"He waits for his warrior to bring someone to him," Wolf said, his stomach knotting. Had he truly been after Raven all this time? Had he made it seem obvious so that they would think otherwise? Had his plan been all along to take Raven? Had he been foolish to dismiss it? Had he placed his wife in danger?

"I see your fear for Raven," Iver whispered. "If he sent a warrior to capture her, then wait and watch for she will deliver his body to Brynjar with a smile."

"She has not the strength," Arran argued.

Iver grinned. "She has what is needed—no fear and skill."

"I can attest to her fearlessness," Arran admitted. "I watched her get into the damnedest things when she was young and the consequences didn't discourage her in the least."

The knots in Wolf's stomach grew worse and a low growl rumbled from his lips.

Iver shook his head. "The Beast may be powerful, his attacks vicious, but the Raven flies free and waits patiently before attacking her prey and leaving them helpless."

A whimpering cry caught their attention and they watched as Brynjar's warrior appeared, Tait tucked under his arm.

"Give him over," Brynjar ordered and the man was quick to obey.

Tait's skinny little arms and legs thrashed out, making the exchange difficult, but a quick slap to Tait's face had him gasp and go still long enough for Brynjar to take hold of him by the back of his shirt, his small wool cloak having been lost in his struggle along the way.

"Anyone see you?" Brynjar demanded.

"No. it was easy. He was right where I had often seen him, with the tall fellow called Fyn. I left him bleeding in the snow. It will take time to find him and for them to gather and search."

"Good. We will be gone by then and not easily found," Brynjar said with gleeful satisfaction.

Wolf didn't waste a minute, he lunged forward past the bushes and trees. Anger raged in his dark eyes and his words rolled out on a growl. "Not likely. Hand the lad over. He belongs to my tribe."

Brynjar turned to his warrior. "Get him!"

The warrior rushed forward but came to an abrupt halt when Arran and Iver made themselves known, coming forward to flank Wolf.

"Let the lad go," Wolf ordered.

"He belongs to me. I have every right to take him," Brynjar said.

It hit Wolf then, what they'd been missing. What Brynjar would risk so much to get. "He's your son."

Brynjar laughed. "It took you this long to realize it?"

"It took you this long to learn of it?" Wolf countered.

Brynjar snarled. "I learned months ago. Why do you think I demanded to wed that sniveling, weak Eria?

I knew she'd seek safety with you, giving me the perfect excuse to come here after her. And to torment you with attempts on your wife's life. I didn't care if they succeeded or not. It was pure pleasure just knowing the chaos it would cause you. When all the while, you had no idea what truly brought me here." He shook Tait. "He's my son and he goes with me."

Tait raised his little chin and cried out. "Fyn is my da."

Brynjar's hand went up in the air to strike the lad.

"Touch him and I'll see you lose that hand and let you suffer for days before you die," Wolf threatened, his hand gripping the hilt of his sword.

Brynjar went to laugh and it vanished in an instant when Clive and Lars emerged from the woods to join Wolf while a line of his warriors formed behind them.

Wolf was relieved to see his wife wasn't with them.

"Release the lad and I'll see you have a swift death," Wolf said and heard a snarling protest from Arran.

Brynjar looked around, his own warrior having put distance between them. "I have a right to my son."

"You have a right to die for all you've done and all those you've made suffer," Arran said.

"It's thanks to you, Arran, I learned I had a son. I left men behind after your wife's father failed to deliver what he promised. I sent them to keep watch on Wolf. They came and went from his village, travelers stopping by for food and shelter. One of my men spotted Greta and remembered her and one look at Tait was enough to know he was my son. As soon as I found out I made plans to get him."

"Fyn, my da," Tait said, tears streaming down his cheeks.

Brynjar shook him. "I'm your da and I decide your fate. And where is Fyn? Is he here to save you?"

"You hurt him," Tait said, his little chin shooting up, though it quivered. "My mum will heal him."

"Hand the lad over," Wolf warned.

Brynjar backed up closer to the river. The water rushed by in an angry flow, grabbing what it could along the way and devouring it beneath the surface and when the captured debris surfaced it got sucked down again.

"Let him go!" Arran ordered, frightened for the small lad. He didn't know what he'd do if it was his bairn Brynjar held and he intended to make sure the evil man never got a chance to cause him such horrific fear.

"You'll step away and let me go or the lad will not live to see another day," Brynjar warned.

"You don't want to do that, my son," the raspy voice said.

All eyes turned to see the leper emerge from the woods and step toward Brynjar.

"Stay away from me, leper," Brynjar warned, backing away from him.

"Let the lad go, my son," the leper said calmly. "It does no good to harm the innocent bairn."

"I decide my son's fate," Brynjar yelled.

"Only God can decide his fate, just as he will decide yours," the leper said, the rasp in his voice heavy.

"Wolf the Mighty Beast thinks he will decide my fate," Brynjar said with a laugh. "I chose how to live and I will choose how to die. And I will choose who dies with me." His eyes went to Arran. "I will make sure to take you with me for all the trouble you've caused me."

Arran scowled, though a slight smile lingered on his lips. "Do you hear that, Brynjar? The devil is calling to you and I'm more than happy to send you to him."

"No devil," Tait cried.

"You're already with him, son," Brynjar said and raced to the water's edge and held Tait out over the rushing water by the back of his shirt. "If I can't have my son, no one can have him."

"Don't," Wolf warned, knowing he would never reach the lad in time. He was too far away. The water would gobble him up and sweep him away, and he'd be lost to them. "Let Tait go and you'll be free to leave."

"You think me foolish enough to trust you. You'd see me dead and if not you another would see it done." Brynjar snarled, the scars on his face giving him a distorted look. "Besides, it's a good day to die."

He flung Tait in the air and the lad spiraled out over the river, his fearful cries stabbing at everyone. The leper didn't hesitate. He ran toward the river ripping his cloak off and shock had mouths dropping open and eyes nearly bursting from their heads to see… Raven.

She dove in and the rushing water swallowed her up.

Chapter Twenty-eight

Wolf gave Arran a quick look and Arran drew his sword and ran with him. Wolf shed his furs and weapons as he went, the only thing on his mind—saving his wife and Tait. But first he had to get past Brynjar.

Brynjar had his sword drawn and was running toward them, his eyes filled with rage. He raised his sword, ready to strike Wolf but met Arran's sword. Wolf ran past them and dove into the river, praying he wasn't too late.

"Ready to die?" Arran asked, shoving Brynjar away.

"As I said, it's a good day to die—but not alone." Brynjar charged at Arran,

Arran deflected his blow easily and stepped away from him. "Do you know what I learned while you held me captive?"

"I don't care," Brynjar spat.

"You should. I watched you fight your warriors, kill those who displeased you or nearly beat you, and I learned how you fight. I waited for this day to come,"

Arran said, pointing his sword at Brynjar. "I'm not going to let you have an easy death. I'm going to make sure that it's slow and painful, make you suffer as you have made others suffer."

"Aren't you worried about your sister, Wolf, and the bairn?"

"Wolf will save them and he will expect me to give you what you deserve," Arran said.

Brynjar laughed and drew a knife from his belt, waving it in one hand and gripping his sword firmly in the other. "You should have listened to what I said. I chose how I lived and now I choose how I die."

Brynjar rushed the knife to his throat, but Arran was quicker. His sword came down on his hand taking the knife and several fingers with it.

Brynjar roared with rage and pain.

"You're right. It is a good day to die and I'm going to choose how you die," Arran said and raised his sword.

***

Wolf swam some of the coldest lakes and rushing waters in his homeland, his grandfather having taught him how to survive them. He managed to keep his head above water with sheer brutal strength. It wasn't long before he caught sight of his wife and to his surprise, she had Tait tucked high up in her arm.

He thought he heard someone yell her name. When he was able, he cast a quick look to the shore and saw Fyn running along the water's edge, Greta following after him.

"RAVEN!" Fyn's voice boomed through the air.

Wolf was glad to see that his wife heard Fyn, her head turning his way. He also saw Fyn pointing up ahead and then he took off running. He realized what the man intended when he saw him climb out on a toppled tree limb that extended over the water.

Fyn intended to grab them. Wolf wished he could reach them before then. He could help snag them, giving Fyn enough time to grab firm hold, but he didn't think he'd make it.

He saw his wife's intentions as she got near the branch and wanted to scream at her. She hoisted Tait up high so Fyn could grab the lad and when he snatched him from her hands, she disappeared beneath the rushing water.

Wolf was grateful Fyn rushed Tait into Greta's arms and started running down along the water's edge. He was trying to find another spot to snag Raven. It had to be soon. The rough water tumbling her about was exhausting her and if he or Fyn didn't reach her soon, she'd go under never to surface again.

The thought had him pumping his arms until they felt on fire. Fyn got his attention, waving and pointing and he saw what he pointed at. A cropping of tangled branches jutted out from the water's edge. It could snarl them once caught in them and possibly cause them harm, but he had to take the chance. He had no other choice.

Fyn waited there, marking the spot and ready to help them.

Wolf wasn't far from Raven and he could tell from her slow movements that her strength was waning, but she didn't give up. She kept fighting to survive. He was nearly on top of her, a hand's length away. He reached out anxious to grab her, keep hold of her and never let her go. The tips of his fingers grazed her arm and before he could take hold of her, she went under, the water sucking her down. He didn't hesitate, he went under after her.

He managed to grab her arm as the water tumbled them about and he gripped it so tight he feared he would break it. But it didn't matter. Now that he had hold of her, he'd never let her go. He surfaced, dragging her along with him, getting his arm around her waist so he could free his other hand. He had seconds, barely seconds to spare. They were nearly on top of the tangled branches. He pushed hard against the water and swung out his hand to grab one of the bent branches and got caught in a small whirlpool that twirled him around, sending him directly into the mouth of the snarled branches ready to devour them both. He felt a hand grab his arm and bring him to an abrupt halt with only moments to spare.

He looked to see Fyn, keeping a strong hold of his arm, and Clive stood behind him.

***

Raven shivered even though she wore several wool garments and was covered in furs and she sat right beside the fire pit, the heat toasting her warm. The scowl that quickly surfaced on her husband's face told her that he had seen her shiver and she knew what he would do. Sure enough, he grabbed another fur from a pile near the table where he stood and walked over to her.

"You should be in bed," he scolded, wrapping the fur around her.

"Not without you to keep me warm," she whispered. "So hurry and get done so I shiver no more."

Detta approached them before Wolf could respond and handed a tankard she held to Raven. "A good hot brew will help warm you—for now."

Raven smiled at the twinkle in the old woman's eyes before she walked off.

"Make sure you drink it," he ordered and gave her a quick kiss before he returned to where he had been standing.

He had kissed her endlessly since rescuing her as if he needed to assure himself she was safe and well. She'd been amazed that he had had the strength to carry her all the way back to the longhouse. He had suffered the brutal rushing river and its cold just as she had and yet it hadn't hampered his strength as it had her. He had refused all help from those willing to carry her. He would allow no one to take her from him.

It had been sheer stubbornness that kept him going and—love.

Once in their bedchamber, he again, refused all help to tend her. He had stripped her bare, wrapped her in a blanket, and sat her before the hearth, then rid himself of his wet garments. He wrapped a blanket around his waist, dropped another blanket beside the chair before he lifted her in his arms and set her in his lap after he sat. He snatched up the blanket he had dropped and wrapped it around them both. And there they had sat in silence snuggled close together.

Passion may have tickled at them, but it wasn't what either wanted at the moment. They simply wanted to hold on to each other, know the ordeal was done, know that all was safe, know that death had failed to claim them today.

Now she sat and watched her husband as he brought the whole ordeal to a close.

Greta came to stand in front of him and Fyn joined her, taking her hand as he stood by her side. She moved closer to him and he let go of her hand to wrap his arm around her waist.

"Fyn stands for the woman he loves," Arran said, joining Raven on the bench.

"Fyn is a good man," Raven said, proud of him and she, as well as her brother, turned quiet as Wolf spoke.

"How is Tait?" Wolf asked.

"He does well, sir," Greta said. "Eria and George are with him now. He tells everyone that the evil man lied and that Fyn is his da."

Fyn spoke up. "And he is right. I am his da now and always. Tait is my son, Greta will be my wife, and I will protect them both with my life."

"That is honorable of you, Fyn," Wolf praised. "But I will hear from Greta why she never told me the truth about Tait."

Greta paled. "I feared for my son's life. Brynjar was an evil and hated man. No one would have accepted Tait if they knew Brynjar fathered him. They would believe him evil as well."

"She's right about that," Arran whispered.

As sad and unfair as it was, Raven agreed with a nod. There would be those who would want to see the lad dead.

"My son would be hunted and killed for nothing more than having an evil father. I couldn't let that happen. I had to protect my son. My brother felt the same, which was why he told me to seek shelter with you. He told me that you were a great warrior who kept his people safe."

"Why didn't you tell me it was your brother we found frozen to death or that you also knew the other man who died?" Wolf asked.

"Fear," Greta said. "Pure fear. My brother would have only come here for one reason—to warn me that Brynjar knew of his son. I prayed that Brynjar would meet your sword before anything was learned about Tait. Before the tribe demanded that Tait and I be turned over to Brynjar." Tears started rolling down her cheeks. "I never meant for harm to come to anyone. I only wanted to protect my son and give him a chance to grow into the good man I knew he would one day be."

Wolf scowled. "You believe I would have given Tait to Brynjar?"

"I've seen what Brynjar causes people to do. Toke had a chance of freedom here with you. But I think he must have been one of the men Brynjar captured from a nearby village a day or so after attacking my village and he remembered seeing Brynjar—" She stopped not able to say what had been done to her. "He must have realized Tait was Brynjar's son and thought if he could bring Tait to him that Brynjar would free him. His fear of Brynjar was greater than his trust in you. Seeing that only made me fear more for my son's life." She wiped at her tears. "I am truly sorry for any harm I have brought you, but I am not sorry for protecting my son."

"I would have done the same in her situation," Raven said.

Fyn turned a smile on her for speaking up for Greta.

"No, you wouldn't have," Wolf argued. "You would have foolishly attempted to kill Brynjar."

"I wouldn't have attempted it. I would have succeeded at killing him," Raven corrected. "Though I must say my brother did a fine job of seeing that Brynjar's death was not an easy nor a painless one."

A cheer went up in the room, though quieted when Wolf's face turned menacing.

Raven knew her husband well enough to know he planned no harsh punishment for Greta's deceit, but he couldn't allow it to go entirely unpunished. Greta has also proved valuable to the tribe, her healing skills much sought after and Tait was adored by all, his sweet nature much like his mother's.

"I cannot let this go unpunished," Wolf commanded.

Greta grabbed Fyn's arm and Fyn looked ready to argue, but wisely held his tongue.

"Fyn," Wolf said with a nod to him, "will follow you wherever you go and report your actions back to me until I feel certain you are no threat to the tribe."

"Aye, my lord," Fyn said. "I will watch and tell you of her every move."

Raven smiled and Arran chuckled.

"Your husband is a wise man," Arran whispered. "He makes it seem that Greta is being punished while seeing she is protected against anyone who thinks to harm her or Tait."

"Wolf is a better man than I first believed," Raven whispered.

"Even though he held Royden and me captive for five years?" Arran asked, still angry at what had been done to him and his brother.

"You need to talk to Wolf about that," Raven advised, feeling it better that her husband tell Arran the truth.

"And why would I want to do that?" Arran asked, annoyed.

"Because it wasn't Wolf who held you and Royden captive—it was our king."

Arran stared at her, speechless.

"Wolf can offer more detail than I can, though I think it would be better if he told you and Royden together. Perhaps then the three of you can make sense of it."

Arran leaned closer to Raven and kept his voice to a whisper. "And tell me, dear sister, did you pose as the leper just today, or have you been posing as Brother Noble all along?"

Raven smiled sweetly. "All along, dear brother."

Arran looked ready to strangle her. "So Purity and I were never truly wed the first time thanks to you."

"But you thought you were and that was all that mattered and I told Abbott Thomas he better hurry and wed you properly."

"Abbott Thomas knew you were the leper?" Arran asked, shocked.

"That's a discussion for another time," Raven said. Her brother's smug grin warned her that she was not going to like his response.

"The discussion I wish I could hear is when you tell your husband that you've been the leper all along."

***

Raven stood by the hearth in her nightshift, a shawl draped around her shoulders. "Rouard gave you no problem?"

Wolf shook his head as he undressed. "He seemed more relieved as did many of the warriors with him. He leaves in the morning for home. There is much he must see to, many who need to be freed."

"All is settled then," she said, avoiding his eyes.

"Mostly," he said, shedding the last of his garments and walking over to her. "You are feeling well after your ordeal."

"I have more aches than usual and a chill that refuses to leave me, but otherwise I do well," she assured him seeing the worry in his dark eyes.

He cupped her face and ran his thumb gently over her lips. "I feared losing you."

She rubbed her cheek against his hand. "I had no doubt you would rescue me."

"I never expected to rescue the leper."

Raven scrunched her eyes shut for a brief moment, then took a step back. His arm went quick around her waist not letting her go far.

"I've waited until we were alone to ask you this—"

She didn't wait to answer the question she knew he would ask. "Aye, I've been Brother Noble all along."

His eyes shot open wide. "All along?"

Her eyes turned as wide as his. "Isn't that what you thought?"

He stepped back. "No. When you revealed yourself, I assumed you posed as Brother Noble to distract Brynjar." He shook his head. "Do you mean to tell me that you've been posing as a leper all this time?"

"I thought you would realize that when I revealed myself."

Anger flared in his eyes. "Why would I when we agreed to be honest with each other?"

She cringed. "I thought it better you didn't know."

His eyes went wide again and an oath flew from his mouth. "You were there in front of me all along. I revealed much to you." He stepped back rubbing his face. "You tricked me."

"I admit I did," she confessed, "but you have to admit it was wise on my part."

He glared at her and shook his head. "The things I've told you."

"Were wonderful to hear and made me realize you were a far different man than I had first thought. And when you confessed your love it made all the difference."

He was struck by a thought. "The wound on your head,"—he shook his head— "it was Brother Noble who was struck." He shook his head again. "That's why your men got so upset and shouted out to the leper. They knew it was you."

She hurried to explain, a slight cringe to her face. "I assumed, though I never saw him, whoever was after Gard didn't want a leper interfering and when he spotted me, a rock was the best weapon of choice."

Wolf groaned, turned his back on her, and continued to shake his head.

Raven approached him and laid a gentle hand on his back. "Please let me explain about Brother Noble."

He turned, anger still sparking in his eyes and crossed his arms over his chest.

His annoyed stance and silence told her he would listen and so she spoke. "I needed a way to discover things while keeping my identity unknown and staying safe. Charles came up with the idea of assuming the role of a leper, better still a cleric who was a leper. I took the name we knew Charles as… Noble. And he was a noble man, helping many. The disguise helped me gather much information and even visit with those I missed. I never set out to meet you. Our meeting was pure accident, but I did take advantage of it. I also will admit that I enjoyed talking with you. I think in a way it helped me decide to agree to wed you. I thought that if anything, there might be a slim chance we could establish a friendship."

"I enjoyed talking with you as well," Wolf admitted. "There was wisdom to the leper's words—your word."

"And there was a thoughtfulness to your words that at first I refused to see but could not deny once we were wed." She reached out to him, though she didn't touch him. She waited for him to reach out to her as well. "I did what I had to do to protect those I love, just as Greta did, just as you do, just as we now do together."

His hand shot out and grabbed the back of her neck to yank her up against him. "You better never pose as the leper again."

She scrunched her face. "You never know when Brother Noble might be needed."

"Raven, so help me, I'll give you a good beating if you ever do that again," he threatened.

She laughed. "Don't be foolish. You'd never raise your hand to me. You love me too much."

He muttered several oaths. "You are impossible, *kona*."

"I have been truthful with you from the beginning, husband. I am who I am and I make no excuse about it. You love me for who I am, or you don't. The choice is yours to make freely. I made mine freely. I love you for who you are, Beast and all, even when your annoying I love you."

"When I'm annoying?" he asked, his hand slipping off the back of her neck to rest around her waist.

"Aye, you can be annoying at times, but I manage to deal with it."

"And how do you deal with it?"

She chuckled. "I ignore you and do as I please."

"That is all the time."

"See how well I deal with you," she said, her chuckle growing.

She brought a smile to his face. "You're lucky you stole my heart."

"You mean you're lucky I *gave* you my heart." He went to argue and she silenced him with a faint kiss. "And I'm lucky you *gave* me your heart."

Wolf grinned, scooped her up in his arms, and walked to the bed. "And now I'm going to show us how lucky we both are."

Her arms coiled around his neck and she kissed him again, though not faintly this time. "You can show me how lucky we are tonight, tomorrow morning, perhaps mid-day and, of course, at night—"

"And for all the days to come," he said as he went down on the bed with her.

Epilogue

Eleven months later

"The pain is not so bad," Raven said.

Oria and Purity laughed.

"Your labor just started," Oria warned.

"And do you forget attending my daughter's birth and Oria's son's birth?" Purity asked with a raised brow.

Raven cringed, though not from pain, from memory. "I tried to forget that."

"But look at the beautiful bairns a short time of pain brought you," Wren said, folding cloths on a nearby table.

"Wren is right," Greta said. "The pain is forgotten once you hold your bairn in your arms."

"The pain faded when I looked upon Duncan's sweet face and he rested his small cheek next to mine," Oria said.

"I felt the same when I held my tiny Margaret," Purity said.

Raven laughed. "I took such joy in seeing Arran so fearful of holding his daughter. And tiny or not she cried louder than Duncan when born."

Purity laughed as well. "He thanks the heavens every day that we named her after your mother since she seems as sweet and kind as her. He worried she might be as stubborn as you."

Raven went to laugh but grabbed her stomach as a pain hit her just as her husband entered the room.

He hurried to her side. "You're in pain."

"Of course I'm in pain. I'm having your bairn," she snapped. "What brings you here? I told you I will do this with the help of my friends."

"I thought you'd want to know that Iver has returned and—"

Raven threw the blankets off her and struggled to get out of bed while her husband tried to keep her in the bed.

"Let me go. I've waited too long to hear word on this," she said and grabbed her husband's arm to gain leverage to hoist herself up and on her feet.

"You should remain in bed," Purity urged.

"You all told me it's early in my labor. I have time and I will speak to Iver," Raven insisted and went to grab her shawl off the end of the bed.

Wren snatched it up and draped it around her shoulders. "Let her be done with it so she can return to bed and birth the bairn."

Wolf shook his head, knowing it would be senseless to argue with his wife.

"What is she doing out of bed?" Parlan demanded when his daughter entered the common room.

Arran cradled his daughter in his arm and laughed. "I'm glad she's your problem now, Wolf."

Royden shook his head, his son smiling as he bounced him on his knee. "I agree with Arran."

Raven looked at her husband, a sharp warning in her blue eyes. "Pick me up and carry me back to bed and you'll be sorry."

Arran laughed. "I never thought I'd feel sorry for you, Wolf."

The door opened and Detta entered holding on to Faline's arm, a light snow covering their cloaks.

Faline hadn't been here long with the tribe, but she was only too glad to help Detta with whatever she needed. She was Sten's wife and had arrived about six months ago with their son. She had been so grateful to find Sten alive and safe she had immediately sworn loyalty to Wolf. She was even more grateful when Sten had shown her the cottage he had been given and how thankful and relieved he was to have been forgiven and accepted into Wolf's tribe… forever a loyal servant to the Beast.

Faline took Detta's cloak she handed her and hung it on a peg before joining Ida to help her serve.

"Why are you out of bed?" Detta demanded, heading toward Royden.

"Because I want to be," Raven shot back and cringed not meaning to be abrupt with Wolf's grandmother. They had become friends, talking often, and finding shared interest—like the stubbornness that her husband insisted they both shared.

Detta smiled. "She's a strong one and the baby will be as well. Now hand over my great-grandson, I haven't held him in in ages?" She reached out to Royden who reluctantly handed his son over to her."

"It's a good thing Oria has such a forgiving heart. If it were me, I'd make you suffer a while longer for not telling her who you were when she lived it," Royden said.

Detta grinned at her great-grandson smiling and tugging at her braid. "Oria is too kind for her own good, which is why I'm glad she has a strong and wise husband to protect her. Though, I am thankful she is so forgiving."

The door swung open again and Iver hurried in, shaking a dusting of snow off himself before approaching Raven. Though, it didn't matter. She hurried, as best she could, over to him.

"What did you find out?" Raven asked and grabbed her side as another pain hit her. She didn't understand why it had come so close to the other one. She had time yet.

Wolf saw her cringe and slipped his arm around her. "You need to go back to bed."

She shook her head unable to speak through the pain. Her breath was labored when she finally spoke, looking to Iver. "Tell me."

Iver hesitated and looked past her.

She turned to see where his glance settled… Detta.

"I should have told you and Wolf," Detta said and returned her great-grandson to Royden.

Raven glared at her a minute, then looked to Iver who confirmed with a nod.

Wolf shook his head. "You were the one responsible for arranging the marriage between me and Raven?"

"I am," Detta admitted.

Raven rushed out of her husband's arms to where Detta sat. "All this time you knew and you said nothing. You let us wonder, speculate, even worry that it might cause a problem one day."

"I knew it wouldn't—"

"It wouldn't?" Raven challenged. "You took a chance with your grandson's life. I could have been vindictive enough to kill him or he could have killed me."

"I knew that wouldn't happen," Detta said calmly.

"How could you know that and why did you do it in the first place?" Wolf asked, standing close to his wife, worried about her.

"Why don't I explain it all after you deliver the baby," Detta said, seeing Raven's face cringing with pain.

"AHHHH!" Raven cried bending over and holding her stomach.

"That's it you're going back to bed," Wolf said.

"NO!" Raven shouted. "I will not get in bed until she tells me everything."

"You're being stubborn," Wolf said.

"When isn't she?" Arran said with a laugh and pursed his lips when Purity glared at him, having run into the room along with Oria and Wren.

"Now! Tell me now!" Raven insisted.

"Tell her and be done with it," Wolf ordered.

"My grandson is a strong man and he needed a strong wife and one who would love him. I grew to admire you, Raven, through the years. You fight hard for those you love and, of course, a union between the two of you would bring solidarity between the clans as well as peace. But it was when I remembered your visit here to Learmonth those many years ago that made my decision easier." Detta smiled. "You climbed benches and tables, and your father had a difficult time keeping you in hand."

"That would be Raven, Arran said and received another glare from his wife but a little chuckle from his daughter.

"Wolf didn't though," Detta continued. "He was patient with you, took your hand and showed you how to climb, benches, tables, and whatever else you could find so you wouldn't fall. After that you followed him everywhere that day and was content to listen to all he taught you. I had never seen my grandson so patient with anyone."

"And I never saw Raven listen to anyone as she did to Wolf," Parlan said, recalling the day. "But he was introduced to me as a merchant's son and by a different name."

"I didn't let Burnell know who he was. I told him that the lad was the son of the merchant I traveled with. When I told my husband about it, he told me such a determined and stubborn lass would make Wolf a fine wife. I took a chance that he was right and arranged the marriage, making your king and my king think the other had proposed it and that it would benefit them. I knew Raven would never refuse if it meant having her brothers freed and returned home. I was quite impressed when she insisted on others being returned home as well and made provisions to protect her men."

Raven shook her head. "I barely remember that day, though I do recall being happy with what the lad had taught me."

"Isn't that the day we found you in the tree?" Royden asked.

Parlan laughed as he nodded. "When we arrived home, she hurried off to practice her climbing and wound up in a tree—far up in a tree."

"I took a chance," Detta said, looking to Wolf and Raven. "And I'm very glad I did. Your grandfather was right. Raven makes you a fine and loving wife."

Raven almost doubled over in pain and Wolf didn't wait this time, he lifted his wife gently in his arms.

"The pains come quick," Raven said.

"Which means the bairn may arrive sooner than thought," Wren said as Wolf walked past her to the bedchamber.

"Do you remember that day?" Raven asked, staring at his face, trying to recall the lad in him that had fascinated her all those years ago. "I do remember thinking how brilliant you were and how much you could teach me. But my da refused to ever take me back to Learmonth again since I had behaved so badly."

"I do remember, though your name had slipped from my memory. I thought you so brave for one so young and how quickly you learned what I explained to you. I thought you quite amazing for a little lass and I do recall telling my grandfather about you and what he said to me."

"What did he say?"

"He told me such a fearless, young lass would make a man a good wife. I believe he would be proud that that fearless lass was now my wife." He kissed her just as another pain hit her.

Raven cringed, trying not to cry out as she buried her face in the crook of her husband's neck.

"I hate seeing you in such pain," he said, his insides twisting with worry.

She labored to speak as the pain rolled off. "If you don't wish to see me in pain it would mean that we can no longer—" She laughed. "That's not going to happen."

"Thank the heavens," Wolf said, laughing himself and placed her on the bed.

"I believe this bairn is going to come faster than we thought," Wren said.

"I'm all for that," Raven called out.

"I can stay with you," Wolf said, sitting on the bed beside her and holding her hand.

"I appreciate that, but I assure you that I can do this."

"I have no doubt you can, wife, and I will await the birth of our son or daughter with great anticipation." He kissed her cheek and reluctantly left the room.

It wasn't more than an hour later that Oria came running into the common room, her face flushed and her eyes wide with excitement.

"You have a son, Wolf. Give us a few moments and—"

"Wait! Wait!" a shout came from the bedchamber.

Worry robbed Oria's excitement.

"What's wrong?" Wolf demanded.

"Let me find out. I'll be right back," Oria said and rushed off.

Wolf paced, staring down the passageway to the bedchamber door, fighting to remain where he was. It did no good. He had to find out if Raven and his son were all right. He halted abruptly when Oria rushed out of the room toward him.

Her face was aglow with excitement. "Another bairn. Raven is birthing another bairn."

"Twins?" Detta shouted.

"Aye, twins," Oria confirmed and rushed off again.

"You look like you're about to drop," Arran said with a grin. "You should sit and pray it's another son, since I don't even think God can help you if you have a daughter like Raven. Or maybe you can teach her to climb like you did Raven."

Wolf cringed at the thought and dropped down on the end of the bench.

"You do know we enjoy seeing you suffer, don't you?" Royden asked with a laugh.

"At least we got some kind of revenge on you," Arran said, his grin turning into a laugh.

Royden boomed with laughter. "A life lasting revenge with no chance of escape."

"A daughter! You have a daughter!" Oria shouted as she rushed into the room and Royden and Arran laughed harder.

***

Wolf shook his head. "You should be in bed. You birthed two bairns only a few hours ago."

"It was much easier than I thought once I got hold of the pain and battled it my way and pushed the two of them out as fast as I could," she said and grinned, it turning soft when she looked down at the twin bairns sleeping in separate cradles. "They are beautiful."

Wolf's arm went around his wife to ease her back against him and looked with pride on his son and daughter. "That they are. You did a good job, Raven, though your brothers will attend no more births of ours."

"They tormented you, didn't they?" She didn't wait for a response. "Now you know what I dealt with when young. Arran was the worse." She grinned. "But you will be happy to know that Purity has some news for him. She is already with child again."

Wolf laughed. "I hope it's another daughter. He already intends to keep Margaret locked away from all men."

"That's because he thinks of his endless escapades with women, but I think Margaret already fancies a lad. Do you see the way her eyes light up and how she smiles and chuckles when Tait is around? If she's anything like her aunt or her namesake, she knows full well the man she wants when she first meets him."

"I don't think I'll ever stop shaking my head," Wolf said. "Arran's daughter and Brynjar's son. He'll never allow it."

"Tait is Fyn's son and will grow into a fine man," Raven reminded.

"But would Arran see it that way?" His brow knitted. "Did you know you wanted me when we first met when you were barely five years?"

Raven turned to face him. "I've thought back on that day since reminded of it. I can't recall what you looked like. I can only recall how excited I was at what you taught me and I remember wishing I could see you again. Time faded that memory, but what didn't fade was what you taught me."

"How to climb," he said with a laugh.

"No. You taught me I could be me. You didn't tell me I couldn't climb or give me reasons why I shouldn't. You helped me to climb, showed me I could. You picked me up when I fell and told me to try again. And I did because I knew you'd be there to help me. I loved you that day for it and I love you now for letting me be me."

"I'll always be there to pick you up, Raven. I love you for who you are and I wouldn't have you any other way." He kissed her gently.

She took his hand and led him to the bed. "Your words warm my heart, but we have an important matter to discuss—names for our son and daughter."

Wolf pulled the blanket over her once she was in bed. "You have names in mind?"

"I've given it much thought," she said, turning on her side as he walked around the bed and she pulled the blanket back for him to join her.

"Tell me," he said, turning on his side to face her once in bed.

"I would like to name our son Noble. It is a good name, an honorable one, and a strong one."

"I have no objection to that," Wolf said. "That means I get to name our daughter."

"I have a name for her as well."

He smiled. "How did I know that? And what name would that be?"

"A name most fitting for her—Ylva."

Wolf stared at her a moment. "That's a woman's name meaning wolf in my language."

"She will carry her da's name with pride and strength," Raven said, then chuckled. "Wisdom as well, since she was wise enough to push her brother out first, making it easier for her to enter the world."

Wolf smiled and ran his finger along his wife's soft cheek. "I would be proud to have her carry my name."

Raven slipped into the crook of her husband's arm, resting her head on his chest. "I kept Brother Noble's brown cleric robe. Our daughter may need it someday."

"Raven!" he warned and she chuckled.

THE END

Printed in Great Britain
by Amazon